Praise for
SOPHIE NICHOLLS

'So as we raise our glasses (and cupcakes) to the successful launch of this already much-adored story, there is a certain something in the air, that little bit of sparkle you can't see, only feel. The sense of comfort a good book, favourite dress or a roomful of happy people can provide – **a moment of magic.**'

Yorkshire Times

'Trust us, **you're in for a treat**.'

Living North Magazine (Yorkshire)

'A light read about love, relationships and friendships as well as appreciation for fashion and handmade clothing . . . Nicholls' writing style is very easy to read, **the story is compelling and grabbed me from the start**.'

Prettily

'**This book is a wonderful read and I would definitely recommend it** . . . I can't wait for the sequels!'

Loubee Lou Blogs

'I immediately felt at home inside the pages. **It felt so magical and I adored the characters** too. The book is well written and charming.'

The Reading Shed Book Blog

Miss Mary's
BOOK of
DREAMS

Sophie Nicholls is an Amazon bestselling author. She lives in North Yorkshire in the north of England with her partner and young daughter. She likes swimming outdoors and eating dark chocolate.

Also by Sophie Nicholls

The Dress

Miss Mary's
BOOK of
DREAMS

SOPHIE NICHOLLS

ZAFFRE

First published in Great Britain in 2012 as *The Dream*

This paperback edition published in 2017 by

ZAFFRE PUBLISHING
80-81 Wimpole St, London W1G 9RE
www.zaffrebooks.co.uk

A CIP catalogue record for this book is available from the British Library.

ISBN: 978-1-785-76176-8

Also available as an ebook

1 3 5 7 9 10 8 6 4 2

Typeset by IDSUK (Data Connection) Ltd
Printed and bound by Clays Ltd, St Ives Plc

MIX
Paper from
responsible sources
FSC® C018072

Zaffre Publishing is an imprint of Bonnier Zaffre,
a Bonnier Publishing company
www.bonnierzaffre.co.uk
www.bonnierpublishing.co.uk

For Tom

Prologue

*A pair of leopard print shoes, size 37. A bracelet in the shape
of a snake. A handkerchief with embroidered initials.
A pair of red silk ballet shoes . . .*

When I first scribbled those words in my notebook a couple of
years ago, I thought that I was writing the end of a particular
story, the story of Mamma and me. I imagined that I was bringing the many different pieces together – tucking in the raw
edges, smoothing the seams and then fastening it all with a fancy
clasp, perhaps something made from crystals and emerald-
green feathers.

I'd forgotten that stories, like dresses, have a life all of their
own. They shape themselves to the sway of your hips, that soft
swell beneath your ribs, the curve of your collarbone, the rise
and fall of your breath.

Over time, their fabric becomes a little softer, fits itself to the
way that you walk, speaks in rustles or soft swishing sounds,
begins to make new meanings.

Sometimes, of course, a story finds a new wearer altogether.

'*You* are the storyteller now, *tesora*,' says Mamma, smiling
into the webcam in her kitchen on the other side of the ocean.
Her sunglasses are pushed up on to the top of her head and she's
silhouetted against the Californian sunshine that pours through
her floor-to-ceiling windows.

'You and only you, *carissima*, know how this next part of the
story goes.' And she sips from her little white cup of coffee where

I can see that her lipstick has already left its print like the wings of a scarlet butterfly.

But when I blow Mamma a kiss, click my own webcam closed and open up a new blank page on my laptop, I find myself faltering. As hard as I try, the words don't come. The screen hums. The pigeons clatter on the roof. The books creak and whisper on the shelves.

On some days, my fingers crackle with a familiar static. A restless wind sweeps into the courtyard, whipping up leaves and litter.

On other days, the air settles in ridges of grey and dusty yellow around my shoulders, pressing me close so that I can hardly breathe.

I once wrote that all you had to do to claim a story as your own was to raise your arms above your head, like this, and let the shape of it settle over your shoulders, just so.

But now I know that the form of things is always changing. There's never one true ending to anything.

Sometimes a waistband or a collar becomes too tight, your body straining against it, longing for more room. Sometimes a hem droops or a zip gets stuck or a button must be moved.

And in the same way, sometimes you outgrow a particular story. It no longer feels quite right. You follow sentences with your finger like seams, wondering where they might lead you. You find yourself saying a word over and over, under your breath, and it begins to take on a new meaning.

That's how it is. A story is never still.

And even though she's thousands of miles away, on the other side of the Atlantic, I can hear Mamma's words, soft and low, as if blown in on a mischievous wind, filling the spaces between my out-breaths.

Yes, you *are the storyteller of the family now, carina,* she's saying, *just like your great-grandmother before you . . .*

Mamma's grandmother, Maadar-Bozorg, is the only mother she has ever known. Although I've never met her, she has always been there, sitting at Mamma's shoulder as she filled me with her stories.

I remember, tesora, Mamma is saying now, *how people would sit in the cool of the courtyard at my great-aunts' house in Tehran, just to listen to Maadar-Bozorg's voice, how it teased you and tick-led you, the words running up and down your spine. My gift, for what it's worth, lies in the fabric – the feel of it against my skin, what it tells me when I rub it between my fingers. But* your *gift,* Ella-issima, *my darling, is Maadar's gift, the gift of the storyteller herself. You only have to stop for a moment, taste the words on the roof of your mouth, roll them around your tongue. They will tell you where to go next.*

And so I'm beginning to understand that it isn't my job exactly to shape this next part of the story, but simply to hold it gently in my hands for a while, to let it unfold for you. And then I'll pass it on, so that you can make it anew, stitching it with your own bright threads, spinning it into a new form, smoothing it over your own kitchen table.

I take a deep breath. I let my mind relax to its still point, let the words rise up in me from that place under my ribs and then flow down through my fingers as they move over the keyboard.

That's right, Mamma whispers. *What do you already know,* carina? *What do you feel, deep inside you?*

My fingers drift across the keys. Faintly, I hear them tapping, as if I'm somewhere far away, translating a half-heard music.

Can you hear it too?

1

To summon dream guides from the Other World: Find the place where oak, apple and birch trees grow together. Make an offering to the spirits there. That same night, look through a holed stone before falling asleep. If you know who you wish to see, call their name politely three times.
– Miss Mary's Book of Dreams

'Mummy. Mummy, I can't wear these boots with my mermaid costume. Mermaids don't wear *WELLINGTONS*.'

Ella turned to see her daughter, a whirl of wild, brown hair, glitter and turquoise nylon, in the centre of the shop floor. With one tiny hand, she was tugging at the spangled bodice of her dress. In her other hand, she waved a wand, topped with a pink plastic shell and trailing blue and green ribbons.

Behind her, Billy held up his hands in a gesture of helplessness, his face contorted into an expression that was half amusement, half exasperation.

'Tell him, Mummy.' Grace jabbed the wand at her bare feet. 'Mermaids *DON'T WEAR WELLINGTONS!*'

Ella sighed. Her head was throbbing from a combination of too much Pinot Grigio and a night of confused dreams. She took a slug from the coffee cup in her hand and frowned at Billy.

'Daddy, *OF COURSE* mermaids don't wear wellingtons. Especially mermaid *princesses*.' She balanced her cup on a pile of books and crossed to where Grace was poised on the brink of a full-on meltdown. 'You're absolutely right, darling.' She smoothed the curls from Grace's sticky forehead. 'Mermaids only have tails.

5

Poor things. Which is why they can't stomp around in all those puddles.' She glanced out of the window at the courtyard where the cobbles were gleaming with pooled water. 'Poor mermaids. Such beautiful puddles too, this morning.'

When she looked back, Grace had already hit the floor, her fingers catching in the handkerchief hem of her costume as she scrabbled to pull on her boots.

Billy applauded her silently.

'Socks?' he mouthed.

Ella shook her head.

'Come on then, Mademoiselle Mermaid.' Billy held out Grace's yellow raincoat with a mock flourish.

'Don't be silly, Daddy.' Grace was all smiles now, letting him slip her arms into the coat sleeves. 'I'm only a *pretend* mermaid, aren't I, Mummy?'

She flung her arms around Ella's neck, covering her face with moist kisses.

'Yes, darling.' Ella held Grace's face in her hands. 'For today, anyway.'

'Bye-bye, Mummy,' Grace sang. 'Love you.'

Ella put out her hand to slip the bolts on the shop door. She winced as a crackle of static, familiar shivers of green and silver, nibbled at her fingers.

'El?' Billy laid a hand on her arm. 'You sure you're OK?'

She shrugged. 'Of course. Just tired, that's all.' She found her coffee, raised it in a mock toast. 'Nothing this won't fix.'

'Write like the wind, then,' Billy said. 'Strictly no distractions.' He wagged a finger at her.

Ella watched them go. She stood in the window as they slithered hand in hand across the cobbles, Billy ducking under the archway that led out onto Grape Lane. The tall, slim man in jeans and a navy nylon parka. The little girl with blue-green streamers escaping from the bottom of her raincoat, stomping to make the soles of her wellingtons light up. Billy and Grace. Her family. The two people she loved most in the world.

She pulled the sleeves of her sweatshirt further down over her wrists, cradled the coffee cup to her chest. There it was again. That faint humming in the air. Unmistakable this time. A haze of silver around the doorway. Whispers in the corner of the room. The Signals. How often she found herself wishing that they would just leave her alone. It was always worse when she was tired. This so-called 'gift' that had been handed down to her through a long line of Jobrani women: Mamma, Maadar-Bozorg, the great-aunts back in Tehran, and so many women before them. Most of the time, she could control it, keep it at bay. But then it would come to her at the most inconvenient moments, usually when she was worn out, reaching the end of her tether. It was enough to drive you a bit bonkers.

When she'd first tried to explain to Billy how the Signals worked, she hadn't known how to put it into words. It wasn't like all that second-sight stuff – not exactly – because it involved *all* her senses. She saw colours and shapes but she could also taste the Signals, feel them on the backs of her hands, hear them crackle and whisper in the air. Around other people, they might shimmer and vibrate or spark in sudden warning.

'Synaesthesia,' Billy had pronounced. 'That's what it sounds like. Aren't all writers a bit like that?'

'Other people will never really understand, *carina*,' Mamma had always said. 'They will say there is a simple explanation. Or they'll think you're a bit, you know.' She tapped the side of her head. 'Cuckoo. Not quite right. Usually better not to tell them anything.'

Today, the courtyard outside the shop was empty and silent but she could already feel the air tremble around her shoulders, barely perceptibly, as if it was a second stretched skin. The marmalade cat, who usually came inside when it was raining, even allowing himself to be stroked by enthusiastic customers, was skulking in the overhang of the doorway, back arched, fur bristling.

Ella thought again of the dream she'd had last night. Mamma had appeared at the bedroom window, her fingertips tapping at the glass, and Ella had thrown off the duvet, tiptoed to the window and pushed up the sash.

Mamma's green eyes had burned into hers. She'd swung her legs over the windowsill, her bare feet spattered with mud, her dress clinging to her damply, her hair stuck to her face.

'Mamma, what are you doing here?' Ella had reached out and touched her mother's icy cheek. 'How did you get here?'

'I flew, *tesora*.' Mamma's voice was hoarse, hurried. 'I flew a long way. I came to tell you to pay attention, to listen to what the Signals have to tell you. To ask yourself what you already know, deep inside you.'

Mamma had raised her hand, the rings on her fingers flashing in the dark room. And then, just as suddenly, she'd disappeared, fading in front of Ella's eyes, leaving only the imprint of her wet feet on the rug and the open window, rattling in the wind.

Billy had switched on the bedside light, hauling himself up on the pillows, squinting at her. 'What're you doing out of bed, El? And close the window, will you? It's pouring out there.'

'I don't know, Billy. What *am* I doing? I had a dream and –'

She'd prodded at the damp footprints with her own bare toes. There was no explanation. Obviously, her exhausted brain must be confusing things.

Billy had rolled his eyes, grinned at her in that infuriating way of his. 'You and your dreams, El. Come back to bed. You can tell me all about it in the morning and then we'll work out what it means.'

There was nothing Billy loved more than a spot of amateur dream psychology. Ella found it irritating. Mamma, of course, had always encouraged him. It was no coincidence that the Popular Psychology section was one of the best stocked in their bookshop, Happily Ever After. The bookshop, of course, had once been Mamma's dress shop and there had been more than a little protest among Mamma's friends when Ella had taken over the lease. Mamma had already sold off most of her stock by then, readying herself for her move to San Diego with David. But it was one thing to close Mamma's shop down and quite another to dismantle the rails and display tables, screw oak bookcases to the walls, put up hand-drawn signs for reading groups and a children's book corner.

'What do they want me to do?' Ella had complained. 'Keep it as some kind of shrine to you?'

'Never mind them, *tesora*.' Mamma had winked, laying her hand on Ella's arm. 'Don't you remember? It's exactly what they all said when we arrived here. That I was a crazy person. That the shop would never survive. People didn't need vintage dresses.' She threw back her head and laughed. 'Give it a little time. You'll show them.'

And so now the shop was a different place entirely. It had shaped itself around its new owner, like one of Mamma's dresses.

The chandelier was still there, throwing wobbly rainbows across the polished wooden floor whenever the sun hit the windows. The shop doorbell still jangled in the same way. But now the walls of the shop were lined with books. There were books carefully arranged on the mahogany counter and, very often, more books spilling over into piles on the floor. Where once there had been little tables displaying shoes and hats and scarves, now there were leather armchairs, inviting any passer-by to curl up and lose themselves in the pages of a novel for an hour. And if any further encouragement might be needed, one corner of the shop had been fitted out with a gleaming stainless-steel cafe bar and a coffee machine.

Now, as Ella stood warming her hands on her second Americano, her body straining to catch the crackle in the air, she tried not to think about last night's dream. The clammy feel of it still clung to her, the fragrance of Mamma's damp skin, that strange look in her eyes.

'Get a grip, El,' she muttered to herself, turning purposefully away from the shop door, perching herself on one of the stools behind the counter, opening her laptop. She looked up at the big, pale moon-face of the grandmother clock in the corner, another addition to the space, a present from Billy after Grace was born. Half past eight. She had two hours, with a bit of luck, before the first customers started arriving. She needed to push on with this book. The manuscript was due just three months from now and yet it was all still a tangle of characters, ideas, the vaguest plot lines.

She opened up the document, took a deep breath, dived in . . .

It seemed only moments before the shop bell jangled her out of her reverie.

She looked up to see Laura, her friend from the Mother and Baby Book Group, wrestling a buggy through the door with one hand, steering Izzie, her protesting three-year-old, with the other.

Ella clicked Save, glanced at the clock. Ten o' clock. Bang on.

'Sorrysorrysorrysorrysorry . . .'

Laura threw back the hood of her parka. Ella could see now that she was biting back tears. She slid off the stool, wedged the door open wider with her foot. From under the buggy's rain hood came a long, high-pitched wail and Izzie started to join in, planting herself on the rug in defiance, her mouth opening and closing.

'So so sorry, El.' Laura's voice broke. 'I don't know what to do. We've been up most of the night.' She pointed at the buggy. 'I've got an appointment at the doctors with him in, um . . .' She looked at the clock. 'Oh, God. Like *now.* And Izzie just refuses to walk any further in the rain and –'

'It's OK.' Ella scooped the slick bundle that was Izzie up into her arms, balancing her expertly on one hip. 'Come on, Izzie. We'll have a lovely time, whilst Mummy takes Harry to his appointment, won't we?' She started to shoo Laura out of the door. 'Off you go. She'll be fine. Go on –'

'I'm so grateful.' Laura's face relaxed. 'And you were writing, weren't you? I'm so sorry. I owe you one. Big time.' She set off again, rattling across the cobbles, shouting over the renewed wailing, 'I'll text you.'

Ella closed the door behind her, held the little girl firmly on the edge of the counter, easing off her wet boots, keeping up a steady stream of soothing chatter. 'Now then, Izzie. What a treat. Just you and I, together. But let's see. What shall we do first? I don't think you like hot chocolate, do you?'

The little girl's face dissolved into dimples. She nodded vigorously and her fat, damp curls bounced on her shoulders.

Ella jumped her down from the counter and led her over to the Children's Corner. 'Oh? You do, do you? OK, well that's good to know. Because if you sit here . . . that's right, just like that . . .' She settled Izzie into one of the special fairy thrones that Billy had made, gilt carved frames, blue plush upholstery. 'And look at one of these nice books . . .' She opened up a copy of *The Queen's Knickers*. 'There we are. This is a very funny one. Yes. Exactly . . . Well, now, I'll go and make us a treat.'

And what could she do, Ella thought, as she spooned miniature marshmallows onto a mountain of whipped cream, trying to squash down the disappointment she always felt at being jerked so suddenly out of that other world, the one that she'd been making with words, just moments ago? She'd got in a good hour and a half, anyway. That was better than nothing. And Laura was a lovely woman, someone who'd become a dear friend over the last year or so. Ella knew that she'd do the same for her, if she could, but Laura was struggling. Anyone could see that. On her own with two very young children. Her husband just up and leaving like that, out of the blue. It wasn't easy at all.

She knew what Billy would say. 'You're too soft, El. They take advantage of you.' And sometimes that was probably true. The problem with the shop was that it was in such a central location, all too ideal for easy drop-offs. And the Children's Corner, Ella's pride and joy, was a natural draw. She'd designed it this way, of course, with the thrones and the strings of twinkling fairy lights and the dressing-up box and the blackboard table with its pots of coloured chalks and – everyone's favourite – the three iPads loaded with the latest children's titles. But she hadn't quite envisaged how popular it might be for parents looking for potential babysitting.

'I wouldn't care if the people who dropped their kids off here ever bought anything, the buggers,' Billy would grumble, picking his way through a knot of noisy children.

'Well, it gets people in, makes the shop look busy,' Ella would say. 'And it's lovely for Grace.' But she knew what he meant. Running a bookshop wasn't the easiest way to make money.

Now Izzie waved *The Queen's Knickers* at her, expectantly.

'OK, darling,' Ella said. 'I'll be right there.'

2

To dream of someone who is dear to you: Sleep with an item of the person's clothing under your pillow.
– Miss Mary's Book of Dreams

Fabia struck a match and moved between the tealights in their mercury glass holders, humming to herself softly under her breath as she lit each one.

She still hadn't got used to how suddenly dusk fell in California. Out on the shop's wooden porch, the strings of multicoloured bulbs had already flickered on and the cut-paper decorations fluttered pink and orange and yellow in the glow from the mock-Victorian gas lamps. There were nets of white fairy lights wrapped around the trunks of the palm trees all along Main Street. It gave Fabia that Christmas feeling.

Except that it wasn't Christmas yet. These were the weeks leading up to Halloween and, most notably for the traders in San Diego's Old Town, the Mexican Day of the Dead.

She wished she could share all of this with Ella. All Hallows' Eve, or 31st October, meant only one thing to Fabia – Ella's birthday. And it didn't seem right that she should be here, lighting candles, making her shop look festive for other people, whilst her daughter and granddaughter were on the other side of an ocean.

'Go,' David had said. 'Book yourself a ticket. Go and be with them.' But that didn't seem right either. David was working long hours at the university hospital. She wanted to be there when he came in from work. And who would take care of the shop?

'Close it,' David said, smiling. 'Take a couple of weeks off. When was the last time you took a holiday?'

Fabia tugged at the hem of the dress on the mannequin in the shop window, smoothing the silk so that it fell just so. Then she folded a piece of ribbon around the waist, pinning it expertly with a crystal brooch in the shape of a spider. The spider's eyes were made of little chips of red glass and its diamanté legs were hinged at each joint so that it could hook itself cleverly over the collar of a dress or a coat lapel. It was a lovely piece and she'd thought about saving it as a gift for Ella – except that she knew that it would probably languish at the bottom of her daughter's drawer. Ella would never remember to wear it. She smiled to think of Ella on her last visit, leaning into the wind at La Jolla Cove, her crazy brown hair whipping across her face, a beach towel knotted any-old-how around her shoulders. Despite herself, a sad little sigh forced its way between her lips.

She was proud of what she'd managed to build in the three or so years since she'd started up here. Fabia Moreno, San Diego-style was, in many ways, so much better than her shop in York had ever been. Certainly more lucrative, anyway. There seemed to be a larger appetite for what she could do here. Perhaps it was simply that the climate leant itself so much better to the wearing of dresses. The shop had been full of a steady stream of customers – a mix of locals and tourists – since its opening. They cooed over Fabia's carefully crafted confections, stroking the silks and embroidered cottons, and savouring the opportunity to have clothes made as one-offs or altered to fit.

'Darling,' they said.

'Charming.'

'So English.'

Fabia would smile. Life seemed full of such ironies. Here in the States, being different seemed an advantage. In England, she'd always felt uncomfortable, a foreigner, an incomer.

'Penny for them.' Rosita's face appeared at the shop window, her voice muffled by the glass.

Fabia threw the door wide. 'You wouldn't want to know.'

Rosita rubbed at her arms in her pink lambswool sweater. 'Try me,' she said. 'Getting chilly out there now.' She stomped her sheepskin boots.

'You have *no* idea.' Fabia pulled a face. 'Seriously. You Californians. You don't know what cold is. I was standing on the deck this morning in just my cotton robe. *In the middle of October*. In England, I'd be wearing two pairs of socks and a winter coat.'

Rosita grinned. 'Socks? I'd love to see that. Bet you've never worn socks in your entire life.' Her eyes sparkled with mischief. 'But how are things over there? In York? Made up your mind about visiting yet?'

'No.' Fabia shook her head. 'And it's not like me to be this indecisive but, well, I don't want to be in her way. You know how it is. Maybe Ella doesn't want her Mamma around for her birthday celebrations. I never really know what she wants, to be honest, even after all these years.'

Rosita rolled her eyes. 'Daughters, huh? I've always thought sons would be so much easier. That is, once they got past the throwing-themselves-out-of-trees-and-beating-one-another-up phase.' She shook her head. 'But then they wouldn't be half as much fun, either. And of course, sons grow up, get married, move away. You lose them in the end. But daughters will always need their mothers, don't you think?'

Rosita's daughter, Gabby, owned a beauty salon in LA. Just last month, Rosita had brought her into the shop where she'd cooed over 1920s embroidered kimonos and bought up silk scarves and beaded evening purses as gifts for her friends. Fabia had liked her immediately.

'But how come you never told me how beautiful this girl of yours is?' she'd said as Gabby flicked her glossy black curls and pulled a face.

'Oh, she'll do, I suppose,' Rosita had winked, beaming with pride.

'That's the thing, Rosita,' Fabia said now. 'I'm just not sure that Ella *does* need me anymore. I mean, in some ways, me coming out here was the best thing. Ella is different. She's changed. She's more confident. More independent. She has her own life now, completely separate from me. Perhaps I'm just a nuisance.'

'*Dio mio.*' Rosita pretended to cross herself. 'Are you kidding me? We'll never be free of our girls.' She held out a paper bag and grinned again. 'Anyway, I came over to give you this. Compliments of the season. It's the first one. Made it today. I wanted you to have it.'

Fabia opened the bag and drew out a small flat package wrapped in brown paper and pink and white twine, the trademark wrapping from Rosita's shop, the San Diego Tinsmith.

She tore the paper and the gift glinted in her palm. A bird, the breast and wings brightly painted in ruby and emerald with a tail made of long feathers of delicately punched tin. It twirled and flared from her fingers as she held it up to the light.

'It's exquisite. You're so clever.'

'It's a quetzal, the sacred bird of Guatemala, where my mother comes from. It's something new I'm trying this year.

I was looking through some old photos and I remembered that we had Christmas ornaments just like it when I was a kid.'

'Quetzal.' Fabia tested the word on her tongue. 'I like it.'

'Quetzalcoatl is the feathered serpent god, so the legend goes,' said Rosita. 'The Indian people, like my mother, think of the quetzal as having magical powers. It should never be caught or caged.' She smiled. 'I love the long, green tail feathers. Somehow, it reminds me of you.'

Fabia laughed. She nodded towards the framed poster behind the counter, her younger self in her favourite stage costume of emerald feathers and crystals. 'Thank you, Rosita. Thank you *so much*.'

She hung the bird from one of the fake cherry blossom branches that she'd arranged in a vase on the counter to display choice pieces of jewellery. It nestled among the diamanté necklaces and glass beads.

'There. He looks right at home.'

Rosita laughed. 'So. Any chance of a coffee?'

'Is that a serious question?' Fabia pulled back the curtain on the alcove at the back of the shop where she kept her little stove and poured fresh coffee beans into her grinder.

'Great.' Rosita nodded her approval. 'And I'll just have a little rummage through your rails here, if that's OK? Moises is taking me out for dinner tomorrow. I can't remember the last time we went out, just the two of us. I want to look nice.'

'In that case, *cara*, I've got just the thing for you.' Fabia pointed to a seventies wrap-dress in chartreuse silk jersey, hanging from one of the hooks on the wall. It was cinched in at the waist with a belt of the same fabric, finished with a large enamelled buckle in the shape of a panther, black and gold with jewelled amber eyes. She watched Rosita rub the buckle between her fingers.

'Perfect, don't you think?' Fabia reached up and slipped the dress from its hanger, laying it in Rosita's arms. 'It came in just this morning. I could have sold it three times over already. But the minute I saw it, I knew that it was yours. I've been keeping it for you. Now, what about shoes?'

3

To summon someone who is special to you: Wrap an acorn in a piece of their apparel, sleep with it for seven nights and then take it into the woods. Hide the parcel in the roots of a tree or dig a hole and bury it. Walk around the secret spot seven times sun wise, calling your beloved's name.
– Miss Mary's Book of Dreams

'I hope she enjoys it.' Ella laid the receipt in the man's palm, along with his change.

'Me too.' He pushed the coins into his trouser pocket, placing the paperback, which Ella had wrapped so carefully in the pale blue paper covered with tiny gold stars, at the bottom of his backpack. Wrapping was a kind of magic. She'd learned this from Mamma, of course. It made things special, transforming an ordinary item into something extraordinary. Later, this man's girlfriend would cut the ribbon and tear off the paper with anticipation. She would hold the book – a collection of contemporary reworkings of fairy tales – in her hands and it would seem not a last-minute panic purchase but a carefully considered gift.

'Thanks for your help, then.' The man turned to go, lingering for a moment at the small display of local interest titles by the door – maps, guidebooks, local history.

Ella glanced at the clock and then down at her laptop, now tucked safely under the counter. Five minutes to five.

She made herself wait, watching the man as he strode across the courtyard and out onto Grape Lane. If she closed up now, before anyone else could come in, she'd have another precious hour before Grace's bath time. Grace had been tired and crotchety after the morning's mermaid adventures and then a couple of hours spent playing with Izzie in the Children's Corner. Billy had gone to buy sausages from Braithwaites and then taken them both back to the flat for an early tea.

'I'll drop Izzie off with Laura,' he'd said. 'You see if you can grab a bit of writing time.'

Ella tried to think her way back into the scene she'd been writing that morning, before Laura's visit. She could already feel it slipping away from her. She felt the familiar mix of shame and frustration. Billy was only trying to help, she knew, but sometimes it just made her feel more pressured. He didn't understand that she couldn't always drop back into the writing like that, as easily as snapping her fingers. But she had to try. She had to push through this.

She came around the counter, ready to turn the sign to Closed, and that was when she saw the woman.

She was standing peering up at the shopfront. She looked uncertain, as if she were plucking up the courage to come in.

Ella's heart sank. It was always this way. The last-minute Saturday customers were what Ella dreaded. They always stayed longest, wanting to browse, killing time for a train, perhaps, or they were just a bit lonely.

The woman had seen her now. She looked startled. Ella opened the door wide, forcing her best smile.

'Were you closing? I'm so sorry. I –' The woman's voice was half snatched away by a sudden gust of wind.

'No, no. Come in. Please.' Ella hung on to the door, gesturing the woman through.

As the customer brushed past, Ella felt the air crackle between them, caught the faint scent of grass after rain, the woody fragrance of moss. The back of her neck prickled. Great. This was just what she needed. It had been a very long day indeed and now her imagination was playing tricks on her, picking up on Signals that weren't even there.

'Welcome to Happily Ever After,' Ella found herself saying. 'Can I help you at all? Or are you just looking?'

Her voice sounded too loud in the quiet of the shop.

'Oh . . . I'm definitely just . . . just looking.' The woman's face flushed and she fidgeted with the shoulder strap of her bag. Ella noticed her blue tweed coat, slightly too large for her tiny frame, and the toes of her sturdy brown walking boots, which were flecked with mud.

'Well, if there's anything I can help you with, just give me a shout.'

She smiled and the woman smiled back.

Ella turned and, to give the customer some space, she began to walk a line of shelves, running her finger along their spines, taking comfort, as she always did, in their solid shapes, the smell of the paper. She selected one – a slim volume scattered with engravings of wild plants and flowers – and began to leaf through it: *dog-eyed daisy, lady's slipper, brideswort, coltsfoot, mallow* . . .

The woman cleared her throat. 'Um, excuse me. There *is*, actually, something I'm looking for.'

Ella closed the book, retraced her steps. The woman had taken out a pair of reading glasses and was peering at her over the top of the lenses.

'Yes. One of those dream dictionaries. You know. A good one. Not one of those books that say, "Dream of your teeth falling

22

out and you'll meet a handsome stranger."' The woman blushed.
'I mean, not that there's anything wrong with that, of course. But
I'm looking for something with a bit more, um . . . substance.'

Ella felt her breath catch.

There it was again. That humming in the air. The shiver that
seemed to pass right through her. This was all getting a bit much.
She should have closed up when she had the chance. She was on
edge today. She really wasn't herself.

She laid the book in her hands aside and pointed to a large and
extravagantly carved bookcase up against the wall. 'This is our
Psychology section. Billy's . . . my husband's pet project. There's
Freud's *Interpretation of Dreams* and then Jung, of course, and
then all kinds of other things, some of it a bit obscure, to say
the least. But I'm sure you'll find something useful there.' She
gestured to one of the leather armchairs and plumped up a red
velvet cushion. 'And please. Feel free to make yourself at home.
Take as long as you need. I can make you a cup of coffee, whilst
you're at it?'

The woman looked flustered. 'Oh, it's late. I don't want to
impose.'

'You're not. Not in the slightest. I was just making another
cup for myself. Coffee and books go together, don't you think?
At least, that's always been the idea here at Happily Ever After.'
Ella pointed at the shining Gaggia machine and the shelf of
white cups. 'And I don't know about you, but I need something
to keep me going at this time of day. Now, let me guess. This is a
little game of mine. For you, I think, something milky, perhaps
with a hint of sweetness? A latte? With a splash of mocha syrup?'

The woman smiled and Ella noticed, for the first time, her
dimpled prettiness. She had one of those old-fashioned faces

that always look slightly in soft focus, milky-white skin, dusted with freckles, blue eyes that actually sparkled. Her faded brown hair was pulled into a chignon, wisps escaping around her face, and a pair of antique earrings set with tiny sparkling stones – opals, Ella thought – swung from her ears, catching the light.

'Well, yes,' she was saying. 'I am rather partial to a latte. But please don't go to any trouble.'

Ella watched as the woman dropped her bag to the floor and unbuttoned her coat. Her movements were small and nervous, as if she were used to doing things as quickly and quietly as possible, without taking up too much space.

'I'm Ella, by the way.' Ella held out her hand.

The woman's fingers were cool, her grasp limp in a way that usually made Ella recoil. But as their hands touched, she felt a surge of warmth infuse her palms and travel up her arms as far as her elbows. For a moment, she imagined that she heard the sighing of the wind and saw a flash of white branches against a blue sky.

She dug her fingernails into her palms. Ridiculous. She was being ridiculous.

'Bryony Darwin,' the woman was saying, 'and it's very nice to meet you.' She took a small square book from the shelf, its spine decorated in gilt-tooled lettering. Her fingers traced the letters as she read aloud. 'Miss Mary's Book of Dreams . . .'

'Ah. You've found Miss Mary. She's a particular favourite of my husband's. He's fascinated by her. Apparently, she lived somewhere up in the hills around here. A cure-wife, a cunning-woman, as they used to call them. In other words, a witch.' Ella searched the woman's face. 'If you believe that sort of thing, of course. She was imprisoned in the Tower here in York, so Billy tells me. But this isn't a dream dictionary. It's more like a book of instructions, a collection of Miss Mary's thoughts, a store of knowledge that she wanted to impart. Recipes, guidance on mending all kinds of things, from broken bones to marriages. Spells, I suppose you might call them. But part of the book is about dream prophecy, about using your dreams to tap into your intuition, to divine the future or heal the past. There are very few copies. Hence the awful price, I'm afraid.'

The woman smiled again. 'Intriguing,' she said, opening the book carefully at the first page.

Ella tapped the old coffee grounds from the filter into the sink and watched out of the corner of her eye as Bryony Darwin perched on the edge of the armchair, an expression of intense concentration on her face.

Who was she, this decidedly odd person? Ella rubbed at a teaspoon. It was irritating. She didn't like it, this pull she was feeling towards some random woman who'd quite literally blown in from nowhere at all, asking for books about dreams. Something about her brought back the texture of her own dream, the memory of Mamma's hair stuck to her cheeks, the smell of rain and wet earth, the rattling window.

She splashed milk into the chrome jug, held it under the steam. No, it was all a load of nonsense, a product of her over-sensitised imagination. What was it that her friend, Kate, had said in a stage whisper only a few days ago, leaning against the shop counter, gesturing just a bit too wildly with her coffee cup.

'You get some real weirdos in bookshops, don't you? They seem to attract, well, how can I put this, El? Misfits. Dropouts. Life's eccentrics?'

25

Ella had raised an eyebrow. She'd felt the sting of Kate's words. She knew, after all, what it was like to feel like a misfit herself.

'*Readers*, do you mean?' she'd thrown back, trying to keep her tone as light as possible. 'People who bother to read actual, real books? With difficult words in them?'

Kate had laughed. 'OK. Point taken,' she'd said. 'But you must know what I mean. How about What's-Her-Name in our book group, for example? Takes it all so, well, *seriously*.'

Ella had smiled. 'To some of us, Kate, reading is a very serious matter.'

Now, as she spooned frothy milk into a cup, Ella tried to let her mind go quiet, to relax it to that still, small point, to feel her way out of herself and towards the birdlike figure perched on the edge of the armchair. She didn't let herself do this very often. It was a skill that, over the years, she'd found best used only in very small doses.

But as she breathed deeply, staring into the bottom of the sink, she saw tendrils of softest green, the texture of moss, unfurling into flickering strands of white, patterning the air in the way that light filters through leaves.

She heard a sound as this odd little woman turned the page, like the rubbing together of dry branches. Her head bent closer over the book and a strand of her mousy brown hair fell over her cheek. She barely seemed to notice as Ella set the coffee cup down on the little reading table beside her then crossed to the door and turned the sign to Closed.

And now the shop was silent, except for the tick, tick of the grandmother clock and the sound of Bryony Darwin turning a page.

Ella opened her laptop and stared at the screen, but the words wouldn't come. They never did when there were customers. And this one, in particular, was very distracting. She tried not to sigh out loud. The cursor blinked at her, taunting.

Half an hour ticked round before the rain began again, flung against the shop windows in cold, hard handfuls. Bryony Darwin leapt up then, her coffee untouched, checking her watch, hastily buttoning her coat.

'I'm so sorry. I completely lost track of time. This is fascinating.' She fished in her bag for a bulky purse and drew out a fistful of notes. 'Thank you. Really. You've been so helpful.'

'A pleasure.' Ella smiled. 'And I hope we'll see you again some time.'

Ella watched as Bryony crossed the courtyard, the collar of her coat turned up against the rain, her boots treading firmly over the cobblestones. She stood for a little while after that, staring out of the rain-streaked window. Quite apart from the fact that she'd just sold the last copy of Miss Mary, one of the rarest, hardest to get hold of books in the shop, she had the sense that something important had happened, something that she couldn't quite put her finger on.

Who was this Bryony Darwin? Why was she looking for a book about dreams? What kind of person wore muddy hiking boots with a blue tweed coat and opal earrings?

She sank into the armchair where Bryony Darwin had been sitting just a moment ago and, as she ran her hands over the leather, she caught the ghost of that clean, green fragrance. But there was something else beneath it. Something that Ella couldn't quite hold in her mind.

'What do you feel, *tesora*?' Mamma would say. 'What do you know deep inside you?'

Ella closed her eyes, let her thoughts move to the rhythm of her breathing. Yes, there it was. Right there.

A blue-grey feeling, ragged around the edges, like the sky after a storm. And in it was such longing. And loneliness, perhaps. Something that pulled at your sleeves and wouldn't let go. Yes, thought Ella, Bryony Darwin was lonely. Perhaps even a little desperate. She was looking for answers. Well, wasn't everyone, in their own way?

She sat and watched as the rain stopped and the shop windows filled with orange light from the street lamp on Grape Lane.

She thought again of her dream, Mamma's voice still circling in her head: '*I flew, tesora. I flew a long way. I came to tell you to pay attention . . .*'

In the corners of the room, she felt the Signals stirring. Shivers of blue, tongues of silver. 'Ella,' they mocked. 'Ell-la. *Ell-LA.*'

'Oh, get lost,' Ella said, out loud, jumping to her feet, snatching up the cup of cold coffee and sloshing it into the sink. 'I'm too tired for your stupid games. And you're not even real, anyway. Leave me alone.'

4

To interpret signs: Watch for portents in the everyday things,
the movement of the wind through the trees, the patterns left
by small creatures on the woodland floor, a tree shedding
its leaves or coming into flower. A cunning-wife learns to
interpret these signs and uses them to her advantage.
– Miss Mary's Book of Dreams

Bryony didn't want it to happen. She was walking in the woods. The earth crumbled under her boots. She felt a new softness in the air and saw pieces of blue caught in the branches that were already beginning to lose their leaves. Bryony breathed in deeply, savouring it all – the scents of moss and damp soil, the sound of a bird somewhere above her head, singing its one small song over and over. But as she stepped into the clearing, there it was. She clutched at the collar of her coat.

'No,' she whispered. 'Please. No.'

The creature only smiled and shook his wings at her. They were gigantic wings, flashing silver, green, gold, from up there where he perched in the hawthorn tree.

'Leave me alone,' Bryony hissed. 'Go on. Shoo. I don't want anything else to do with you.'

She stamped her foot in its tightly laced boot and clapped her hands.

The creature put his head back and laughed. She heard the laughter echoing through the trees and bouncing off the water far below them.

'You think you can shoo me away, Bryony, like a little dog? Come, now. Shouldn't you know better?'

His voice was gentle, musical, like the sound of the wind through the birch trees.

Bryony turned her back. She rubbed at her face with her scratchy woollen gloves.

When I look again, she said to herself, you'll be gone. I'm imagining it all. It's like what Dr Murray said. It's all in my head. It's not real.

She felt the air tremble. A little eddy of leaves swirled around her and settled on the toe of her boot.

'Bryony, Bryony,' the creature's voice sang. 'You forget. Whatever you say to yourself, *I can hear you*. I can hear your thoughts, Bryony . . .'

She whirled round, her fists clenched.

'Leave me alone,' she said. 'There's no such thing as what you pretend to be. You're not real. I'm just making you up in my mind, that's all.'

The creature raised a bushy white eyebrow and gave a theatrical grimace. He thrust out his chest, which was like burnished silver, and rearranged his wings.

'But Bryony,' he said and his voice was patient, as if he were talking to a very small child. 'Why ever would you think that just because I'm only inside your mind, I'm not *real*?'

Bryony felt all the strength go out of her then. Her arms dropped to her sides and she fell to her knees on the damp red earth, pulling her coat around her. She screwed up her eyes and tried to concentrate on the ground in front of her, at the little patterns made by the twigs and leaves.

'Bryony,' the creature said again, or perhaps it was only the sound of the wind sighing through the lowest branches. '*Listen, Bryony. It's time.*'

The voice resonated somewhere in the back of her head and echoed through the woods.

But when she looked up again, the hawthorn tree was empty except for a wood pigeon, puffing out his pale chest, testing his wings.

She stood for a long time, straining after the last sounds, watching the wind moving across the surface of the lake and the sunlight turning the water black and then silver.

'*It's time, Bryony,*' the voice whispered again. '*It's time.*'

5

Threshold charm: On a Full Moon Friday, pull up a bay tree by its roots in one quick motion. Be sure to leave none of the plant in the ground. Bind the whole in strips of pure white linen and place it under your doormat for strong protection.
– Miss Mary's Book of Dreams

'But don't you think they're a bit too young for such frightening stories?' Kate thumbed through her copy of *Where The Wild Things Are* and shuddered. 'Perhaps I'm being a bit overprotective but, you know, personally I prefer this kind of thing.' She picked up a picture book with a clean white cover and an image of a pink stuffed rabbit in the centre, framed with a heart-shaped border of intertwining leaves. 'At least I know that this won't give Ava nightmares. I mean, isn't the world scary enough, anyway? I feel like I ought to be protecting her from frightening stories for as long as I can.'

Ella looked around the circle of women, their children playing at their feet or dozing in their laps. Kate's daughter, Ava, was determinedly dancing Grace's current favourite doll – a Disney Rapunzel with ridiculously long hair – over the ridges in the floorboards, chattering to herself. Grace was watching her intently. Ella could see that it was taking all of her self-control not to reach out and snatch the doll from Ava's hands.

'Well, they all look perfectly happy to me,' Florence said, setting her son, Alfie, down on his sturdy little legs, where he stood swaying his hips, as if to some imaginary music. 'And anyway, there's always the theory that it's good for children to be a little scared. In fact, I read somewhere that they're supposed to like it. It's how they learn. You know, that they're safe, what's OK and what's not, exploring the world, testing their boundaries. Alfie loves *The Wild Things*.'

'Yes, and isn't it also about anger?' Sarah fiddled nervously with the top button of her cardigan. 'I mean, I think I know what you're saying, Kate, but . . . well, in the story, Max learns how to express his frustration in a healthy way. You know, he gets to be King and do the wild rumpus. Lily just loves that part.'

'Really?' Kate frowned and Sarah blushed, as if embarrassed that she'd said so much. She looked down at the little girl dozing in her arms, her thumb half in her mouth.

Ella had started the Mother and Baby Book Group as a way of promoting the Children's Corner of the shop, but her real motive, if she was honest, had been to meet other mums.

There had been so many days over the three years since Grace's arrival in the world when she'd felt like standing in the courtyard and screaming. Motherhood wasn't coming easily to her. She found it fascinating and exhausting, wonderful and overwhelming. And on some days, when Grace cried or complained for hours on end and wouldn't be soothed or distracted in any of the usual ways, she found it frustrating and boring. She'd have a rising sense of panic that she'd made a terrible mistake, that she'd ruined her life, that she'd never feel normal again. But then Grace would look at her with those big, blue-grey eyes and Ella would immediately feel guilty. What was wrong with her? Why wasn't this sweet, curious little girl enough?

It had begun with Grace's birth. Not the home water birth she'd planned, in the blue rubber pool that Billy had practised inflating and filling in their tiny living room, but a tortuous three days and nights culminating in a labour theatre at York District Hospital. Forced to abandon the scented candles and carefully selected music that she'd prepared with so much happy anticipation, she'd lain for hours in a room with too-bright lights, hooked up to an oxytocin drip, only half covered by a sheet and mortified at the way that her body, so strong and buoyant throughout her pregnancy, had gradually been swallowed up by waves of pain. It couldn't have been further from what she'd imagined. The relaxation tapes that she'd listened to so diligently, visualising her cervix opening like crimson petals, hadn't prepared her for this.

When Grace's heartbeat had begun to flicker alarmingly on the monitor, she'd found herself sitting on the edge of the bed, hunched over a pillow, whilst an anaesthetist felt his way down her spine.

And what she remembered most clearly about Grace's arrival was not taking her baby into her arms and gazing into her eyes, as she'd imagined, but staring up at a white disc of lights above her head, whilst somewhere beyond the screen she could hear a baby's furious cries.

As the midwife, still wearing her mask, placed Grace next to her among the wires and tubes on the pristine bed and Grace wriggled herself forwards on her tiny forearms, searching noisily for a nipple, Ella had been deeply ashamed to discover that she felt nothing at all. A cold, blue numbness – the colour of the surgeon's scrubs – appeared to have invaded her body. When Billy reached for her hand, she arranged her face in what she guessed might be an appropriate smile for someone who had just become a mother and fished inside herself for some flicker of emotion.

It will wear off, she'd thought. I'm in shock. It's the drugs. It's the fact that I can't move anything from the waist down. But the numbness had lasted longer than that.

In those first weeks at home, as Billy lifted baby Grace from her Moses basket and into Ella's arms for every night feed, she'd look down into those blue-grey eyes and feel a gap opening inside her.

And when Mamma arrived from California, armed with a suitcase of knitted toys, antique quilts and aromatherapy remedies, the ease with which baby Grace had snuggled into her grandmother's arms had felt like a kind of betrayal. With each story that Mamma recounted of Ella's own babyhood, the black gap in Ella's belly where her happiness should have been had opened a little wider.

She would never be that competent. She would never be able to interpret her baby's tiny cries or hold her to her chest and know what it was that she wanted. It was as if Grace had a mysterious language all of her own that Ella couldn't decode.

'You'll work it out,' Mamma had said, guessing at a little of Ella's confusion, her cool hand smoothing Ella's forehead. 'It's normal to feel as if you don't know what to do. It will take time, *tesora*, for you to get to know one another. And you're exhausted. You've just had major surgery.'

But this only made Ella feel even more inadequate. How had Mamma learned to be a mother when she'd never known her real mother herself? And from where had she acquired such unshakable confidence, such certainty? Whenever Ella thought about the way that Fabia had managed all on her own, a young widow in a strange country, without even Maadar-Bozorg for support, she felt her own sense of failure more acutely.

She'd desperately wanted a baby, after all. In fact, she'd wanted three or four of them: a big, boisterous family. She'd decided that she wouldn't wait until her thirties like so many of the mothers she saw coming into the shop. She wanted to start whilst she and Billy were still young.

'What's the big hurry?' Billy had said. 'We've got plenty of time.' Ella knew that he worried about providing for them all. He was only just finishing his PhD, doing some teaching here and there, hoping for a permanent contract. But her book had been selling well, the shop was bringing in a small monthly income and the longing inside her was growing.

'Babies don't need much,' she'd said. So it was all her own fault. She only had herself to blame. And now it seemed that she wasn't cut out for either birth or motherhood, after all. She had no instinct for it. She found it all mystifying.

She began to Google for answers. How often should a newborn baby feed? Should she be woken if she slept for more than four hours? What temperature should the room be kept at? Her mind circled endlessly as she lay awake listening to Grace shifting in her Moses basket at the foot of the bed, her little caws and mews and grunts and rasping sighs. To Ella, she sounded more like a baby bird than a human baby.

She compared herself to the mothers of newborns on the forums that she found, late at night, in her frantic Google searches. She imagined them sitting at their computers in beautifully laundered lounging pyjamas, their living rooms carefully ordered around them, whilst she floundered in a tide of stale muslins and dropped dummies and milk-stained Babygros.

What was it that her old friend Katrina had said to her when Ella had announced the news of her pregnancy? 'Rather you than me, sweetie.' Her laughter had ricocheted down the phone from LA, where she was just starting filming on the sequel to the box-office hit *Reputation*. At least Katrina had the good sense to know that she was too ambitious, too caught up in the little details of her own busy and interesting life – yes, too *selfish*, even, was what she'd said – to ever become someone's mother. Whereas she, Ella, had been arrogant enough to think that she could do it all.

And the terrible truth, the thing that taunted her as she folded baby clothes, and that got in amongst the words she occasionally tried to pick out from her keyboard when Grace was sleeping, was that being the mother of a tiny baby was nowhere near enough. She envisaged the years stretching ahead of her – years of buggy-pushing and conversations with other mums, comparing details of children's developmental phases, sleep habits and bowel move-ments and the best place to pick up discount toys – and she had felt the tears pricking at the corners of her eyes.

So, in desperation, when Grace was nine months old, she'd printed out a sign and stuck it in the shop window: *Mother and Baby Book Group. Come and talk about your favourite books. Adult conversation and good coffee guaranteed.*

And they'd come. Every Monday morning for a couple of years now. Because Monday was the day when you had the whole week stretching out in front of you, when the week could feel like a mountain to be climbed.

They came and they kept coming. Some were women whom she'd met in the shop before, and some she'd never seen until that first morning. Women with clothes like hers, smeared with breakfast and toothpaste. Women with faces creased with sleeplessness, clutching their babies and a wild kind of hope. And for a while, she'd hoped for something too. Because these were women who seemed to get it. These were people who *understood* that being a mum wasn't everything.

But even now, sitting here in the middle of her own shop, surrounded by a group that she herself had pulled together, she couldn't quite shake the feeling that she was the imposter in a private members' club.

She found herself wondering how Florence, who had become her closest friend, always managed to look so attractive, in her slightly dishevelled but utterly seductive way. Even after a sleepless night with Alfie, she'd turn up with a silk scarf wound around her neck, just so, her eyes ringed with smudges of kohl, or a smear of lip gloss or a nice pair of earrings. And Sarah had somehow managed to run a half-marathon in aid of the local children's ward, just last month. And Kate always seemed to know exactly what to do in any situation involving small children. Whilst the only thing Ella knew about was stories and storytelling. And lately she didn't seem to be much of an authority on those either.

'Yes,' she heard herself saying now. 'What about all the stories we were told as children? All those fairy tales. Deep dark woods, wolves with big teeth. Or was that only *my* mum?' She laughed, perhaps a bit too loudly, and some of the women laughed with her. A few of them remembered Fabia, her reputation for flamboyance.

'Yes, that's exactly what I'm saying.' Florence was determined to press home her point. 'Kate, I don't mean to say that we should bombard our kids with horrible moral messages. You know, if you're not good, the bogeyman will come and get you or the woodcutter will chop off your feet. All that gruesome Brothers Grimm stuff.'

Next to her, Kate winced visibly and bent to stroke Ava's blonde head, but Florence was warming to her theme.

'Not *that* kind of scary stuff, perhaps. But I *do* think a bit of non-Disneyfied fear is *healthy*. You know, encouraging them to create these worlds in their imagination, where it's safe to experiment. Isn't this how we learn to control things, how we learn that bad things happen, yes, but we can also make the world bend to our will? I mean, you're the writer, El. What do you think? Perhaps you would never have written your novels if your mother hadn't told you all those scary stories?'

Ella poured more coffee into Kate's cup. The truth was, she thought, that recently she hadn't felt much like a writer at all. Her last book had been published almost three years ago, just after Grace was born and, since then, everything she'd written had been, in her opinion, a load of drivel.

'Oh, I don't know, Flo,' she said, carefully. 'I mean, yes, certainly my mum had a lot to do with me starting to write. And looking back, I can see that she always encouraged me to be my own person. I didn't appreciate that at the time, of course.' She caught Florence's eye and grinned. 'Back then, I just wanted her to be like other mums. Less . . . well, shall we say *eccentric*? But now I see that she was trying to show me that I could achieve anything, anything at all that I wanted.' She sighed. 'But do

I really *believe* that now? Do I actually *feel* that, deep down? I don't really know.'

She heard her own voice trail off. She glanced quickly at the faces around the circle. Alison, a new member of the group, shot her a sympathetic look. Some of the others looked down at their feet, studiously avoiding her gaze. But now that she'd started, she found that she couldn't stop. The words kept coming in a hot gush.

'Lately, I just *bore* myself. I mean, don't you sometimes feel as if whatever you do, it doesn't seem to be enough? You're always trying to do something *more*, something . . . well, *better*, and it never comes out right?'

Some of the women nodded or exchanged glances. Kate furrowed her brow and Sarah blushed. That's the problem, Ella thought. I've said something out loud that we're not supposed to say. We're not supposed to admit to each other that everything isn't just perfect and wonderful.

'Anyway,' she said, folding her hands carefully in her lap, forcing a smile. 'Which book shall we do next week? Any suggestions? Kate, I think it's your turn to choose?'

After the other women had gone, wrestling toddlers into hats and coats, buckling them into pushchairs, Florence helped her gather up the coffee cups and stack them in the sink.

'Darling, are you OK?' Her face was twisted in concern.

'Sorry, Flo. I think I'm just . . . just *tired*. As per bloody usual.' Ella pushed the hair out of her eyes with the back of her hand and squirted washing-up liquid over the cups. She felt Florence's fingers, warm and strong, squeezing her shoulder. 'Don't be nice to me, Flo. I might not –'

'Alfie! Do *not* jump on that chair with your shoes on. In fact, do *not* jump on Ella's chair *AT ALL*.' Florence bounded across the room and scooped up her son with one arm. 'God, he's getting far too heavy. I'm going to have to stop feeding him. Sorry, darling. Time for us to make our exit, I think.' She began stuffing books and toys into her already bulging shoulder bag. 'He's been an absolute terror all week. Not like this little cherub here.' She stroked Grace's cheek and Grace rewarded her with a picture-perfect smile.

Florence turned to Ella. 'Sweetheart, you take care,' she said, struggling with the zip on Alfie's coat. 'I'll call you, just as soon as Steve gets back from his London trip. We need a night out. We've not done that in so long. It's about time, don't you think?'

Ella nodded. She realised that she was biting her lip, trying to hold back tears.

She watched from the window as Florence negotiated the cobbles with Alfie's pushchair and then she turned back to the sink and dried each cup carefully, methodically, replacing it on the shelf. Grace stood next to her, stroking the backs of her legs.

'Mamma,' she said. 'Mamma, hug?' She lifted her arms for Ella to pick her up.

Ella wiped her hands on her jeans and bent.

'Ooof, you're getting too heavy for this, poppet.' She held Grace to her chest, breathing in her scent of biscuits and chamomile shampoo, then settled her on the rug with a collection of her favourite toy cars and a stack of books and opened up her laptop on the counter.

That was the worst of it, she thought. These days, Grace was what people called 'a good girl'. The first year of Grace's life had been a haze of sleeplessness, colic, teething and bad daytime TV. The second year, Ella had just about managed to get herself showered and dressed each morning. And for almost a year now, Grace had been settled into a routine of sorts. On the days that she didn't do her mornings at the nursery around the corner, she could happily entertain herself there on the rug in the middle of the shop floor for forty-minute stretches. She was bright and demanding, she still woke at least once in the night but, these days, she was asleep by eight in the evening and usually didn't try to get out of her little bed until six the next morning so that, in theory, Ella had a couple of writing hours to play with each day. So she had no real excuse anymore, had she?

'You're so hard on yourself, El,' Billy always said. 'You're being a mum, running a business. You've got hardly any time to think.'

But that was part of it, too. Billy's career had grown in the years since they'd married. He'd risen rapidly through the university ranks, publishing papers and then a couple of academic books, doing the conference circuit. He was on the editorial board of this, the committee for that. And yet he always made time for Ella and Grace. He got up early on Saturdays and got Grace out and about before the shop opened so that Ella could have some writing time. He took her to the park or to see his mum every Sunday so that Ella could have some time to herself. He did a lot of the cooking. He was, in fact, so bloody good. That was the problem. She didn't have anything to complain about. Not really. Not like Kate, whose partner never lifted a finger. Or Florence, whose husband was in management consultancy so that she only really saw him at weekends. Or Laura, who was on her own. Billy was kind and patient and supportive. It made her feel even more of a failure.

The cursor blinked at her from the bottom of a blank page. *Chapter Six*, she read, swallowing hard, feeling the edges of the black gap inside her begin to widen again.

With the last two books she'd written, the words had seemed to flow out of the ends of her fingers. She'd woken each morning, itching to get down to work. She'd scribbled notes on the backs of shopping lists, old invoices, restaurant serviettes. She'd stayed up well into the early hours, lulled by the rhythm of her hands on the keyboard, the blue-white hum of her laptop screen.

Now she breathed in deeply, trying to relax her mind, to feel her way outwards into the words. She imagined putting out slender antennae that would tremble in the air, catching the slightest signal. Or a net – yes, that was better – a net of silver that she could spread just beneath the surface of things to catch the sentences as they unfurled.

But already her mind was jumping, clicking, whirring. She was thinking about Bryony Darwin in her bulky coat and sensible boots. The way that she'd clasped that square red leather-bound book to her chest as if it were a life raft. How tendrils of feeling had seemed to unfurl all around her with the fragrance of mingled earth and rain.

And then the sadness that Bryony had left behind her, the feelings that had lingered in the room for days after. Those ribbons of blue-grey longing.

Ella didn't want to admit it but she knew that it hadn't all been just her imagination. She couldn't shake the feeling that her dream – the one where Mamma had arrived on her window-sill in the middle of the night – and Bryony's sudden arrival at the shop were somehow connected. But how?

'*Brrrrm-brrrrm*,' said Grace, wheeling a fire engine over the rug and up to the counter. '*Peep peep*, Mamma.'

'Yes,' she heard herself saying, as if from far away. '*Peep peep*. Time's up.'

6

To banish unwanted dreams or nightmares: Write the dream on a piece of paper and burn the paper in a candle flame. Every bit of paper must be reduced to ashes. Throw the ashes immediately out of an open window or door. The ringing of a bell of pure silver will also encourage any dream spirits to fly away.
– Miss Mary's Book of Dreams

Bryony opened the front door and then immediately shut it again.

She gripped the hall table, steadying herself, closing her eyes and then opening them as if this might make what she'd just seen on her doorstep disappear.

'Come on, Bryony. Aren't you going to let me in?'

That clipped voice with its cultured vowels. The glossy, blonde hair. The perfectly white teeth.

Bryony sighed. First the creature in the woods. Now this. Why couldn't they all just leave her alone?

She opened the door again, just a crack this time, and peered out.

'Ah, there you are.' The pointed toe of a boot appeared, shoved between the door and its frame. The leather was black and expensive and polished to a perfect sheen. The boot ended in a long leg in glossy black tights and the hem of a black tailored coat. Bryony curled her fists and forced herself to look directly into the familiar cold, green gaze.

'No need to be coy, Bryony. I'm allowed to come and check on my little sis from time to time, surely?'

'I'm fine. Thank you.' Bryony heard her own voice. It was a tiny croak of a voice, barely a squeak, the voice of something you'd step over in the street, some poor little defenceless thing. She hated how Selena always made her feel this way. She cleared her throat. 'Actually, this isn't a good time, Selena. I'm very busy . . .'

Selena put back her head and laughed. Except that it wasn't a laugh. It was more of a crackle in her throat, like the sound of paper thrown on a fire.

'*Busy* Bryony? Doing *what* exactly? Looking in on your little rental properties? Gosh, that must be tough.'

Bryony felt her cheeks burning. She looked down at Selena's foot, still firmly wedged halfway across her doormat. She wondered if a well-aimed kick would be enough.

'Bry? Are you all right? I thought I heard the door.' Ed squeezed himself into the tiny hallway behind her.

'It's nothing. I mean, no one.' Bryony turned to him, relaxing her grip on the door handle and Selena seized her chance, launching herself through the gap.

'Selena Darwin,' she said, holding out her hand. 'Bryony's sister. *Elder* sister, to be exact. I was just passing. Thought I'd call in. Such a long time since we had a catch-up. But I don't believe we've met before?' Her gaze flickered briefly over Ed's face and Bryony saw her lips twitch with amusement. 'Bryony, you dark horse. Aren't you going to introduce us?'

'Ed. Ed Baldwin. Bryony's fiancé.' Ed laid his hand proprietorially on Bryony's shoulder. 'And I've, erm . . . Well, I've never heard Bryony mention a sister.'

Selena laughed again. 'Really?'

Bryony shot Ed a look. He was staring at Selena, like a rabbit caught in the headlights. Bryony tried to intercept his gaze. If she could just make him look at her again then maybe he wouldn't say it. No. It was too late.

'Well then, Bry. Aren't we going to offer your sister a cup of tea?' He smiled at Selena. 'You'll have to forgive her, Selena. She's sometimes a bit *distracted*. Since . . . Well, you know . . .'

And then he winked. A bubble of rage burst in Bryony's throat. How dare he talk about her as if she wasn't there, as if she were a five-year-old? Not that you'd treat a five-year-old in that way, either.

She pushed past him into the kitchen and began banging mugs onto a tray. Behind her, she heard Ed ushering Selena into the living room. She caught the rise and fall of Selena's voice and Ed's loud guffaw in reply. No doubt he'd be utterly charmed by her, she thought, sloshing milk into her best jug. Peas in a pod, those two, her mother would have said. Funny how she'd never thought of that before.

She pushed through the living room doorway, balancing the heavy tray. Ed had Selena by the elbow and they were standing together looking out at the tiny courtyard garden. He'd bore the pants off anyone, given half the chance, about his stupid pots of beans and tomatoes.

'Tea,' she said, shoving the tray onto the coffee table on top of a drift of Ed's old newspapers.

'Oh, lovely,' said Selena in that silly, tinkly voice that Bryony knew she only ever used on men. 'Now, Ed, I hope you won't be offended, but the thing is . . .' She looked down, blushing prettily, every inch of her mimicking perfectly the damsel in distress.

'I really need to talk to Bryony about something, well . . . a bit *personal*. Delicate, you know. I hope you won't mind.'

'Not at all. Not *at all*,' said Ed, winking again, eager to show that he understood exactly, as if, thought Bryony, he was one of those men she read about in magazines, the kind who was used to making space for Bryony and Bryony's friends and their little private confidences. 'I'll leave you girls to it, then.' He snatched up a mug and a biscuit from the tray, tiptoeing dramatically across the room and closing the door softly behind him.

Selena stood perfectly still for a moment in the middle of the rug, waiting until she heard Ed's footsteps creaking up the stairs.

'My God,' she hissed. 'You *do* know how to pick 'em, don't you, Bryony? Or should I say, *Bry*?' She pulled a face. 'He's quite something.'

She put down her mug and wiped her fingers with distaste as if she were wiping them free of Ed's handshake.

Bryony sat down heavily on the sofa. She was determined not to rise to Selena's bait.

'How's Letty?' she said. 'She must be, what, fourteen now?'

'Yes,' said Selena. 'She's fine. What can I say? A teenager. A pain in the bum. Stop changing the subject.'

Bryony swallowed. She thought of her sweet-faced niece. The last time she'd seen Letty, she'd had her hair in plaits and one of her front teeth had been missing. The image made her eyes prickle with tears.

'I miss her,' she said now, to Selena. 'I really miss her. Did she get my birthday card? The little present I sent?'

Selena frowned. 'Yes, yes.' She waved her hand dismissively. 'She did. Now tell me about this Ed person.'

Bryony drew herself up straighter in the chair. She could feel her body braced against Selena's onslaught now. She glanced down at the ring on her left hand. Its tiny diamonds glittered. When she looked up again, Selena was watching her, that horrible half-smile fixed to her face.

'Not that it's actually any of your business,' she said. 'But he's been very good to me. Since my . . . you know, my breakdown. He works . . . well, he used to work at St Jude's, you see. That's where I met him. He's a volunteer. Well, he used to be. Before we got together. They have this scheme. He used to come and read to me. Bring me books and . . . Well, we just got talking. He understands, you see.'

'I bet he does.' Selena shuddered. 'And he seems to have done rather well out of it, wouldn't you say? Tell me, did he even have anywhere to live before he met you?' She made a mock shudder. 'Actually, don't tell me,' she said. 'I don't even want to know.'

She settled herself in the only armchair, plucking a needle-point cushion from the pile and staring at it quizzically. 'And is this the sort of thing you do then, these days?'

'That,' said Bryony, 'and lots of other things. I have a nice life. A nice, quiet, peaceful life.' She forced herself to look into those cold, green eyes again. 'And I need it to stay that way, Selena.'

'Yes, of course,' said Selena, smiling. 'You've got the place looking very *nice* indeed, I must say.'

Bryony watched her eyes moving over the duck-egg blue paint-work and the pale blue velvet sofa, an infuriating smile quivering at the corners of her mouth. How she hated that about Selena. The way in which, with just one look, she could make everything that Bryony loved most seem suddenly silly and frivolous.

'Of course, I'd *like* to say,' Selena continued, brushing biscuit crumbs from her skirt, 'that I can't quite believe that you've let him move in here. But I can. Because you always were a complete pushover when it comes to men.' She threw up her hands in mock despair. 'I mean, why, Bryony? Why would you risk all this? Your house, your security?' She shook her head. 'From where I'm sitting . . . I mean, in my precarious situation, it's difficult to get my head round it. But I'm sorry.' She rubbed at her forehead with her manicured fingers. 'I'm not here to interfere. Quite the opposite. I just need one *teeny* favour . . .'

Bryony's stomach lurched. 'No,' she said. 'Whatever it is, Selena, I won't do it.' She heard her voice rise. She felt it get higher and faster, begin to get away from her, to flap against the walls like a cornered thing. 'Last time, that was *exactly* what you said: "Just this one thing, Bryony. Just this one little thing . . ." And look where your one little thing got me. Dad didn't speak to me for two years straight. So just don't expect anything else of me. I've had it up to here. Don't you see? I'm finished with all that now.'

In her mind, she saw her five-year-old self, gripping the edge of the drawing-room fireplace, stamping her feet, her fists curled in frustration, whilst Selena watched and smiled her irritating smile.

'So you still have your little problem, then?' she said now, slowly. 'I'd hoped things might have changed . . .'

'My little problem is none of your business. It's not what you think. There are reasons for it. Actual chemical reasons. I take tablets. They help me to control it. You don't know everything, you know.'

'Oh, rubbish.' Selena put her mug down noisily on the table and Bryony moved quickly to slip a coaster underneath it. 'What utter bollocks, Bryony. *Chemical*, for goodness' sake. I've never heard anything more ridiculous in all my life.'

'It's *not* nonsense,' said Bryony. 'It's been a huge help to me. I realise now that it's all in my head. When I'm stressed or scared, I make things up. Not consciously, of course. But I pay too much attention to certain thoughts. The tablets and . . . and well, *therapy*, if you must know . . . they've stopped all that. I feel so much better.'

Selena frowned. 'That would explain it then.'

'What?'

'Why you've ended up with *him*.' She jabbed a thumb in the direction of the stairs. 'You never did have much get-up-and-go, Bryony. But now you've got some *therapist* filling your head with mumbo-jumbo, now that you're popping pills for God's sake, any backbone you ever had has probably got up and left for good.'

Bryony realised that she was holding her breath. She breathed out slowly and tried to make her voice as calm and quiet as possible. She could feel the old anger licking up her spine. She mustn't let it get the better of her. Selena would only laugh harder.

'No, Selena,' she said. 'You can't just come here like this, you know – just turn up on my doorstep after all this time – and talk to me like that. I'm perfectly happy as I am, thank you very much. I *know* where I am, what's real and what isn't. And I *know* what I need. I know it much better than you ever could.'

Selena smiled again, indulgently. 'So are you saying that you don't still see things that aren't . . . um, how shall I put it? That aren't exactly *there*, in the traditional sense? You know. The angels in the trees, the faces in the teacups?'

Bryony looked down and saw that her hands were trembling very slightly in her lap. She hoped Selena wouldn't notice. She'd always had that way of reaching right into her head, finding that one place in her thoughts where things were still wobbly and unformed and then pressing hard. She thought of what she'd just seen – the creature in the woods.

'I'm not saying that I've got the hang of it all yet,' she said. 'I'm still working on that.'

'With this therapist?' That infuriating smile was pulling at the corners of Selena's mouth. Bryony curled her fist.

'Yes. With my therapist. Who happens to be very respected in her field, actually. And Ed, of course. He helps me too.'

'I see,' said Selena. 'Well, it sounds as if they've got it all worked out for you. All very convenient. So I only have one question for you, Bryony. How do you know that they're *right*?'

Bryony looked down again at her hands lying in her lap. Suddenly, they didn't feel like her hands anymore. She kneaded a fold of her skirt between her fingers. The truth was that she didn't know. Not for sure, anyway. She still had all kinds of questions. But as soon as she started thinking about them, a familiar wave of blackness swept over her and she felt as if she were falling down a tunnel inside herself, down and down, her hands and feet scrabbling for a hold.

'Shut up, Selena,' she said, quietly. 'It works. For *me*. I prefer it this way.'

'Really?' Selena raised a perfectly groomed eyebrow. 'Does it really work for you?'

'Yes,' said Bryony, sticking out her chin. 'It does. It has to.'

For a moment, she saw something pass over Selena's face. An expression she'd never seen there before. It looked something like sadness.

'Well, you know what I think,' said Selena. 'And you know what Mum would have said, if she was still here.'

Bryony felt the anger force its way up into her throat again, hot and red. Her fingernails cut into her palms.

'Actually, no. I don't. I don't think you have a clue what Mum would have said. And I don't know how you've got the nerve, Selena, to pretend that you understand. And I'll tell you something else. If Mum *was* still here, she'd understand exactly that I have to do this my own way. She never liked your stupid little games either.'

'Is that so?' Selena's eyes glinted.

Bryony breathed hard. She suppressed the urge to punch the sofa in frustration.

There were footsteps on the stairs and Ed's head appeared around the door.

'Can I get you girls anything?' he said. 'How are we getting on?'

Bryony felt his eyes searching her face. She stared at a patch on the wall just above his shoulder.

'Selena was just leaving,' she said.

Selena sprung to her feet, slipping her arms into the soft, wide sleeves of her coat. 'Thank you for the tea, *Bry*.' She lingered over the abbreviation, her mouth twitching again, then flashed a final smile at Ed. 'And it's so very nice to have met you. No, don't worry. I can see myself out.'

*

Ella and Grace were word-hunting. It was one of Ella's favourite games. The rules were very simple. You selected a book from one of the shelves, opened it, letting the pages fall wherever they would, and then you picked the first word that you happened to notice. You weren't allowed to choose. You just had to go with the word that your eye chanced on first.

Of course, Grace couldn't read yet. She was just learning to make out and sound the shapes of letters. But this only added to her excitement. She loved to race up and down the shelves, taking out books, letting the pages flutter in her hands until they settled, then pointing to a word that Ella would help her to sound: *pumpkin, race, eventually.*

They collected all the words on the blackboard table in the Children's Corner. Ella wrote them out in coloured chalks. So far, today they had:

yellow
elephant
chocolate
nervous
already
bathrobe
plump
twentieth
lunch
reported
shy
portable
150 g
Anna
bonfire

Sometimes, Ella would rearrange the words to make a kind of poem, or – and this was usually Grace's favourite – they would use all the words to make up a story.

Occasionally, customers liked to join in, calling out a word from a book or suggesting a twist in the plot.

Billy had once suggested that Ella should advertise word-hunting evenings. 'People love that stuff,' he said.

Ella frowned. 'I like that it's just for us – for Grace and me,' she said. 'Do you remember, Billy, when we used to come back here after school? And I used to get so embarrassed because you were always asking Mamma to tell you stories. And then you'd mess about and act them out and try to make me laugh?'

Billy grinned. 'I had to try to impress you *somehow*,' he said.

Now Grace did the same. In fact, some of the contents of the dressing-up box in the Children's Corner contained remnants of those earlier times that Mamma had left behind in her move – a hat with a veil, a tasselled shawl, a jewelled Venetian mask, a length of velvet ribbon.

'P,' Grace shouted now from the Cookery section. 'I've found a P, Mamma. What does this word say?'

Ella leaned over her shoulder. Grace held a book of southern Indian recipes, her finger stabbing at the page. 'Pineapple,' said Ella, smiling as Grace began to chant the word. 'Look. There's a picture of it here. You tried some once. You didn't like it.'

'Pine-apple,' Grace said. 'Papple, pineapple.'

The Story of the Yellow Elephant

'Once upon a time there was . . .'
'A yellow elephant.'
'And he liked to eat chocolate.'

'It was his favourite food. But one day his Mummy said, "No, you can't eat chocolate for your breakfast," and so the yellow elephant felt really, really sad . . .'

'And a little bit nervous.'

'What does *nervous* mean?'

'A bit worried . . . But it was all right because he had already hidden a piece of chocolate secretly in the pocket of his bathrobe.'

'Naughty elephant!'

'Yes, very naughty. And so, when his Mummy wasn't looking –'

'He ATE IT ALL UP!!!!'

'Yes, how did you guess? And this made him very plump.'

'Plump? What's *plump*?'

'Hm. A little bit round and squishy?'

'Like a little bit fat?'

'Sort of.'

'OK.'

'And his Mummy said: "That is the twentieth time I've told you not to eat chocolate for breakfast."'

'"And you are very naughty and you forgot to clean your teeth too."'

'Yes.'

'And so . . . um, what's the next word?'

'Lunch.'

'So you can't have any lunch because you are too fat. I mean, plump, Mr Yellow Elephant.'

'Gosh, is that a bit mean? He's going to be very hungry.'

'Well, maybe only a bit of lunch, then.'

'OK, so he had just a small amount of lunch. What did he eat?'

'A banana. Because they're yellow and they're good for you.'

'OK. Good idea. So he ate a banana for his lunch and then, when he'd finished, he went for a walk down the road and he came across an enormous hole. It was so huge and wide and deep that it was even a bit dangerous for a very plump, yellow elephant like himself. He was worried that, if he fell in, he'd never get out again.'

'HA!'

'And so he reported it to the police.'

'And did they put him in prison?'

'No, he hadn't done anything wrong, except maybe eating the chocolate when his Mummy said not to.'

'What did the police do, then?'

'Um, they went to try to fill up the hole so that no one would fall down it and hurt themselves. But they couldn't find anything big enough to fill it up.'

'Not even e-n*ooooo*rmous rocks? Not even trees?'

'No. And so what happened next?'

'Um. They all went home.'

'OK. They all went home and it started to rain and the hole filled up with rainwater. It was like the biggest, deepest puddle you've ever seen.'

'Were there mermaids in it?'

'Yes, of course. There were mermaids. Quite a few of them. And one of the mermaids was very *shy*. She was too shy to come and sit on the pavement at the edge of the puddle with all her friends, but it was very cold in the puddle and so she started to cry.'

'And the elephant comes and rescues her!'

'Right. So the elephant, because he had very, very big ears, could hear the mermaid crying, even though he was inside sheltering from the rain, and so he came to help. He saw the poor, cold mermaid and he put down his head and dangled the end of his trunk, which was like a kind of lifebelt, into the water. "Come on, little mermaid. Climb on my trunk," he said. "But I'm too shy," said the mermaid. "I don't want anyone to see my tail." So the elephant wrapped his trunk once, twice, three times around the little mermaid. And because mermaids are small and very, um, *portable*, he lifted her up and put her on his back and she was so light . . . no more than *150 g –*'

'Grams?'

'Yes, it's a way of measuring weight.'

'Oh.'

'She was so light that the yellow elephant could walk around with her for days and no one could even see she was there. She was called Anna. And they became the best of friends.'

'Yes. Friends. So what words are left, Mummy?'

'Bonfire and pineapple.'

'And everyone had a bonfire party and ate pineapple, which is very good for you – better than chocolate –'

'Yes.'

'And they ALL LIVED HAPPILY EVER AFTER.'

7

To influence another's thoughts: Whilst preparing a meal,
simply hold your desired outcome in your mind. Allow your
thoughts to mingle with the steam. Have the object of the
spell eat the food immediately.
– Miss Mary's Book of Dreams

All morning, Bryony argued with herself. Or rather, she felt the familiar conversation circling in her head.

'You know you're curious, Bryony.'

'No, I'm not. I'm really not.'

'You are. You know you are. Selena's right, you know. It's time you stopped letting people tell you what to do. Dr Murray, Ed, all of them.'

'I can't trust Selena.'

'Maybe not. But you can trust yourself.'

'I can't. I was ill. Very ill. I don't *ever* want to feel like that again.'

'You won't. You were just exhausted, confused. That's never going to happen again.'

'But what if it does?'

Round and round the voices went, closing in on her, getting louder and more urgent until, by lunchtime, there was a tight band of pressure above her eyes and she wanted to scream.

This was exactly what she didn't want to happen. The only thing that Bryony wanted these days was a bit of peace.

A family history of mental illness, that's what her official medical notes read. Depression, possibly clinical. But Dr Murray, her therapist, had explained that this kind of thing is more

59

common than most people realise. The pressure that Bryony had been under over the years, the unresolved grief around her mother's early death, burn-out from work, a bad relationship, all of this had left her utterly exhausted and led to her breakdown. Severe stress could cause the human mind to buckle. Lack of sleep and anxiety could lead to terrifying hallucinations. Seeing things, hearing voices. What she'd needed at the time, Dr Murray said, was not medication but rest, proper rest, a bit of TLC, someone to help her make sense of things, a notebook in which to write down her thoughts, the kindness of friends, good food, long walks in the fresh air, simple pleasures.

It had a been almost a year now, since her discharge, almost a year that she'd been visiting Dr Murray in her book-lined room with the box of tissues and the vase of flowers on the table. She'd been making steady progress. Feeling stronger all the time. Wasn't it OK, then, to begin to expand her life a little? Wasn't it OK that she felt drawn to the bookshop in the courtyard off Grape Lane, that she wanted to find out more about this whole phenomenon of dreaming and visions, to begin to understand more about what she remembered from her childhood? The candles, the cards her mother had kept hidden in her bedside drawer and had even let her play with when her father wasn't around? The funny words, the whispered prayers? The minute she'd set foot in the shop, she'd had the most peculiar feeling that she'd find the answers there.

But it wasn't just that, either. There was something about that young woman, Ella. She seemed so lost, somehow. In some strange way, she reminded Bryony of herself. Bryony couldn't explain it, not exactly, anyway. It was like a gentle tugging sensation, something that had caught hold and wouldn't let go.

She placed an onion and three cloves of garlic on the wooden board, stripping them of their papery skin, focusing on chopping them as finely as she could. She threw the pearlescent pieces into the frying pan, watching them turn gradually translucent under the tip of her spoon. Then she grated potato, letting it sizzle, before cracking the eggs and dropping them into the pan, nudging them gently as they began to bubble. Gradually, the rhythm of her own movements calmed her.

She threw in a handful of basil leaves, savouring the fragrance on the tips of her fingers, and black pepper, turning the big glass grinder, one, two, three, four, five times. The steam rose up from the pan and she let herself breathe it in.

She set down the white plates on the scrubbed pine table, taking pleasure in their symmetry and in the knives with the bone handles that had belonged to her mother. On a whim, she added a miniature cut-glass vase with a single rose from the garden, the rain still clinging to the creamy petals.

'Very fancy.' Ed was already forking the food into his mouth. 'What's the occasion?'

'Oh, you know. Nothing in particular.'

He looked at her then, one of his long, hard looks. 'Feeling, all right, Bry?' he said.

She nodded.

'You're not overtaxing yourself?'

She shook her head.

But when the plates were cleared away and he'd gone out to his shed across the courtyard to tinker with whatever it was he tinkered with in there, she stood at the sink, her hands loose inside the flaccid, pink rubber gloves. An orange scum floated on the surface of the cooling water. She could hear the clock ticking on the wall behind her, the hands creeping steadily round towards two o'clock.

She felt a wave of something beginning to build in her stomach again. Hot and red, pulsing and then pulling. It wasn't fear. It felt more like desperation.

She ripped off the gloves and flung them dripping onto the draining board. She crouched and slipped the book from the back of the kitchen cupboard where she'd hidden it behind a stack of saucepans, somewhere Ed would never look. Because it really wouldn't do for Ed to find out about this. He was just like Father had always been about this kind of thing. *Superstition. Complete nonsense. Is it really helpful for you to be filling your head with this kind of stuff, Bryony? Don't you think you have enough trouble working out what's real and not real, Bryony?*

But the red leather cover felt cool and smooth in her hands. She carried it up to the bathroom and locked the door.

Sitting on the cold lino, her back wedged against the side of the bath, she balanced the book on her knees and glanced down at her hands. On impulse, she slipped Ed's ring from her finger. It stuck beneath the knuckle and she had to give it a sharp tug. She must have put on weight, then, in the last few weeks. That would keep them all happy.

She set the ring carefully on the floor beside her. It had never felt quite right.

'I'm sorry it's so small,' Ed had said, when she'd opened the box. 'I'll buy you a better one, when I'm a bit more flush.' But she didn't want a better one, whatever that was supposed to mean. She wasn't even sure now if she wanted *this* one.

These past few weeks, she'd felt different, somehow, in a way that she couldn't describe. As if she'd been sleep-walking through her life and now she was just waking up. Her work with Dr Murray, the decision to flush those stupid tablets down the loo – and Ed most definitely mustn't find out about that – it was all helping her to get some perspective.

And she would never have admitted it to Selena but, of course, she'd been right the other day. What she'd said about Ed. Now that Bryony could see him more clearly – really get a good look at him – she wasn't sure if she even *liked* him. He'd just been there, at St Jude's, smiling and bringing her cups of tea, plumping her pillows, taking charge of things.

'Will you be OK, Bry, when you go home? Will you be able to manage on your own?' he'd said.

And she hadn't been able to answer. The truth was, at the time, it had seemed an almost impossible feat to decide what to have for breakfast.

That's when Ed had offered to stay with her for a while.

'We could continue our little arrangement,' was how he'd put it. And so, almost without her agreeing to it, he'd moved in, driving her home from St Jude's that spring day, his own small bag in the back of the car.

Three months later, he'd presented her with the ring. But Bryony wasn't even sure what the *arrangement*, so to speak, was anymore.

He pottered about, mainly in the shed. He'd given up the voluntary work at St Jude's. He told Bryony he'd retired early, had a bit of a pension, some savings. He'd been a lorry driver, up and down between Scotland and France. Didn't have any family. Bryony had no idea where he'd been living when she first met him.

Now she slipped the ring into her pocket. She was getting that breathless feeling, as if there were hands pushing down on her chest. This was always what happened whenever she tried to think about what she should do about Ed.

She went back to the book, began to turn the pages. The slightly musty smell of the paper, speckled in places from damp and age, wafted up to her. As she read, she felt her mind beginning to quieten again:

A question that is often asked of me is 'What is magic?' Indeed, it is the question that I have often asked myself. I am a simple woman. I live on my own in the house that belonged to my mother and her mother before her and I practise the skills and knowledge passed down to me by the same lineage. Whether this should rightfully be called 'magic' or whether it is simple common sense – the Old Ways, the ways of women for generations and the way of anyone who opens her mind to the bountiful nature around us – I cannot tell, and I think it is not for me to say. These are questions debated by great men – of the Church and of philosophy. I am not wise or learned in books and the ways of men. I have never travelled and I do not possess the wit to join these conversations.

I only know how to recognise those herbs that may ease a sore heart or heal an ailing limb, or how to read in the moon's face the courses best suited to help a body that is lost or taxed to its limits.

I know how to guide a woman who is with child and how to soothe a sickening infant. And when the time comes, I know what words to say that a person needs to hear in order to snatch life from the jaws of death or recover his strength of mind when all seems hopeless.

*If this is magic, let people say that this is so. For me,
it is the knowledge that is there for all to learn when they
open their eyes and hearts to the Great Mysteries with
which God has surrounded us . . .*

When Bryony looked up, the late afternoon sun was slanting
through the bathroom window, making patterns on the tiles
through the frosted glass and glinting off the chrome taps.
She glanced at her watch and realised that almost an hour had
passed. She stood up stiffly, rubbing her legs.

The house beneath her was silent. In the hallway, she
put the book into her bag and scribbled a hasty note to Ed:
Gone for a walk. Needed some fresh air. If she didn't tell him
something, he'd only come looking for her. He could make a
terrible fuss.

She snatched her coat from the hook, pulled on her boots,
checked in her pocket for her keys and closed the door softly
behind her.

Outside, the pavement was slippery with wet leaves. She went
slowly at first, careful of her footing, but as she reached the end
of the street and passed through the iron gates into the park, she
put her head back and gulped mouthfuls of the cold air.

Out here, she was free. There were the trees bending their
branches down to cradle her in their arms. There was the sky, so
much wider and bigger than her, opening to receive her.

And now, if she let herself think of who she really might be,
just for a moment, it felt not like some fixed thing but something more like weather, some force that was both inside her and
outside her at the same time, something that was always moving, always changing, like the leaves falling from the trees or the
shadows shortening and lengthening again.

And how, Bryony thought, could any of this not be real? Right now, she could taste it on her lips and feel it pressing just under the surface of her skin.

She passed the boarded-up cafe and thought, not for the first time, how much she would love to bring it back to life. Its sad, blank windows seemed to plead with her to throw them open to the air. The trees that drooped their branches over its broad, brick terrace seemed to call out to her in a low wail. Bryony imagined how the empty terrace might once have looked, filled with children clutching ice-cream cones and loud with the clatter of cups and tin trays. She'd seen photos in the Castle Museum, when the cafe had been full of life – families grouped around the wooden tables, people queuing up the slope to the little hatch, above which a painted sign read: *Cream Teas 2/.* But now it was as if the cafe was sleeping, ivy growing up its walls and beginning to twine itself around the windows.

She walked along the path past the dovecote, watching the flurry of white feathers as a little girl threw fistfuls of bread onto the murky green water. People had once swum here. She'd seen that too in the photos. Little boys wading with their trousers rolled up and groups of bathing beauties in knitted costumes, arranging themselves along the walls in the sun. It must have been lovely, Bryony thought, on a hot summer's day when the water was clear and silvery. She imagined it slipping over her skin like silk.

It was only as she came out of the park, following the path by the river in the direction of Lendal Bridge, that she realised where her feet were taking her.

*

Ella moved her fingers over the laptop trackpad, flicking from one photo to another. Lately, she'd developed an appetite for property websites. She found herself clicking through photo tours of houses she'd never be able to afford. Town houses with huge, high-ceilinged rooms and tall, shuttered windows, pale plaster walls and elaborate cornicing. Farmhouses with beamed kitchens and inglenook fireplaces and gardens giving onto misty, blue hills.

Every so often, she'd flick back to the two or three lines of black Palatino font at the top of her empty document or glance up to see Grace playing on the floor by herself and she'd feel her stomach tighten and the familiar panic rise up into her throat. Why couldn't she just get a grip?

The shop bell jangled. Bryony Darwin stood in a pool of sun-light, stamping the wet from her boots and fiddling nervously with the strap of her bag.

'How lovely to see you again!' Ella came forward, smiling what she hoped was a welcoming smile. She felt a sudden inexplicable urge to kiss Bryony on both cheeks, just as Mamma would do, to press Bryony's cheek against her own, breathing in that scent of moss and damp leaves, but she sensed that Bryony wouldn't want it. Her Signals were fainter today, trembling at the edges, those green tendrils dampened, her wool coat steaming a little in the warmth of the shop. 'Coffee?' Ella said. 'Or perhaps hot chocolate? I was just going to make one for Grace here.'

Grace held out her Rapunzel doll in a chubby fist. Bryony, glad of the distraction, crouched down and smiled, making exaggerated admiring sounds. 'Oh, she's very beautiful. How lovely.'

'Yes,' said Grace. 'And her hair is really, really long. Look. And I can comb it, like this, with this special comb . . .'

'I don't approve, of course. Have you seen the size of Rapunzel's waist?' Ella sloshed milk into a chrome jug and flipped the switch on the coffee machine. 'So how are you today? How are you getting on with Miss Mary?'

She saw Bryony's cheeks colour. 'Well, that's just it,' she said. 'I absolutely *love* her.' Ella could see her trying to cover her enthusiasm. 'And . . . well, I was wondering if you knew anything else about her. I'm sort of intrigued.' She pulled the book out of her bag and stroked the cover. 'It doesn't say much here. It's more or less just as she wrote it. There's an editor's note, talking about how she chose to leave it mostly in Mary's original form, just modernising spellings and so on, for ease of reading, but nothing very much about who Mary was . . . where she lived, well . . . her *story*, I suppose. And I remembered that you said that your husband might know more. I just wanted . . . well, I suppose, if I'm honest, I *really* want to know what happened to her.' She shrugged apologetically. 'For reasons I can't even explain to myself.'

Ella spooned foam into the mugs of chocolate and added chocolate curls. 'Ah, so she's already got you hooked. She seems to do that to people. My husband, for example.'

She set the mugs on one of the little tables and arranged herself in an armchair, Grace wedged between her knees. 'Well, I think I can tell you a little. She was quite a character, Miss Mary. That much I *do* know. Please. Do have a seat.'

Bryony was hovering, fidgeting with her bag again. It was making Ella feel on edge.

'All I really know', Ella began, when Bryony had perched on the edge of a chair, 'is what Billy has told me. My husband's a lecturer at the university and he has a sort of special interest in social history, from a political angle, mostly. He went to a conference a few years ago about religion in the thirteenth century – magic, superstition, that kind of thing – and he came back all excited about this particular paper, which mentioned Mary. Because she's so local, I suppose. She lived somewhere up on the Moors . . . north of Pickering, I think. A bit of a bleak spot. An isolated cottage. There's a book somewhere in the History section. I'll look it out for you.'

'And was she . . . Well, did people accuse her of witchcraft? That's what I've guessed, reading between the lines.'

'Witchcraft', said Grace. 'Is that a word?'

'Yes, darling.' Ella held the mug so that Grace could dip into the foam with her spoon. 'Yes, she was a cure-wife, as they were called back then. She knew about herbs and she delivered babies and she knew how to reset broken bones. Here. Could you?' She handed the mug to Bryony. 'Grace, Bryony's going to help you with your hot chocolate whilst Mummy just goes and finds something.'

Grace leaned herself obligingly against Bryony's knee. 'Are we going to play word-hunting?' she said.

'No, darling. Not right now.'

Bryony looked worried. 'What do I . . . ?'

'Oh, just let her stir it a bit. She tends to spill more than she drinks. Don't worry. I can see you're a natural. She loves you already.'

On the other side of the room, Ella dropped to her hands and knees and crawled along the length of a shelf.

'Yes. Thought so. Here it is, hiding in this corner.' She jumped up again, dusting off the knees of her jeans. '*The History of Witches and Goddess-Worshippers in North Yorkshire* by J. L. Cruikshank,' she read. 'Sounds like a nice bit of light reading, doesn't it?'

She opened the book and ran her finger down the contents page. 'Here we go. Page 116 . . . Mary Cookson. Shall I read it?'

Bryony nodded, spooning chocolatey foam between Grace's half-parted lips.

'In the seventeenth century, Mary Cookson, a woman of about twenty-eight years, lived out on the Moors in a stone cottage, concocting healing ointments and tonics out of herbs she carefully gathered and stored. One dark winter's night, a man rode on horseback to Mary's door and pleaded with her to treat his father, a farmer who'd fallen and suffered a severe leg wound. Mary gathered up her herbs and went with him. She spent all night crouching over the sick man, cleaning the wound, applying compresses and holding her special tisanes to his lips. Later, when the farmer had fully healed from his injury, the rumours of Mary's witchcraft began to spread. People began to walk many miles to consult her and it was said that she had brought about so many healings and miracles that she must have access to a strong magic. But in the autumn of that same year, a woman died after giving birth to a stillborn baby, as a result of severe haemorrhaging. Mary had supplied ointments and medicine but she hadn't managed to save her life. The woman's husband accused Mary of black magic . . .'

'That's so unfair!' The words seemed to surprise Bryony as they burst out of her.

'Yes,' Ella nodded. 'That's the way it went, back then. You just couldn't win. Save someone's life and you were a witch. Someone died in your care and you were a witch, too. Anyway, it says here that she was brought to York and imprisoned before her trial. It seems that the only visitor was a sympathetic doctor, a man of science, who thought all the rumours were a load of nonsense. He listened to her story and wrote it down. Apparently, they have it in the museum archives, and that's how we know about her. Here. Have a read.'

Grace waved her spoon at Bryony. 'More?' she said.

Bryony smiled. 'Of course, sweetheart.' She guided Grace's chubby fist towards the mug and smiled at Ella. 'Why don't you read it to me? If that's all right?'

'OK. Here we go. This is what Dr Wythenshawe wrote: *At first, I was merely curious about this crone, and thought it might be useful to gather information about her so that I might teach others the evils of her ways. But she was such a small, pitiful thing, sitting there on the foul-smelling straw. There was something about her face, the pale cheeks and the mass of dark hair, which reminded me – God forgive me – of my eldest daughter.*

'I began to see that Mary – Miss Mary Cookson, as she first introduced herself to me with a little curtsey – had been much maligned by those whom she'd treated only with kindness. And the local doctor, a man about whom I can testify from my own bitter experience as being a drunk and a scoundrel, had only encouraged

71

this ill-treatment, for he feared the loss of his income to Mary's skills with herbs and healing plants.

'I began to feel, as she sat there, quiet and unprotesting in her chains, that she had a heart that beat as good and fierce and godly in her breast as my own. It is my great regret that I could not save her from her fate, a fate I now firmly believe to have been thoroughly undeserved. I write her tale here in the hope that others will read of it and that other good wives and curewives in the future may be prevented from her suffering.'

'Oh, that's just awful,' Bryony said, quietly. 'And then they . . .' She dropped her voice to a whisper. 'They *hung* her?'

Ella nodded. 'I think so. Yes.'

She saw that Bryony's eyes were brimming with tears.

She thought of Clifford's Tower, standing on its mound at the edge of the city, the place they'd have used as a lock-up, back then. She imagined the cold, dank cell and Mary's wrists and ankles rubbed red and sore by iron chains. She imagined how she must have longed for the cold, clean air of the Moors again, those wild places where sheep grazed and where you could walk for days, seeing no one, talking only to the wind.

'Poor Mary,' Bryony said.

'Who's Mary?' Grace said, instinctively snuggling closer, hoping for more chocolate.

'I've been thinking,' said Bryony. 'You mentioned that your husband might know where Mary once lived. I'd like to see the place, get a sense of what it was like up there for her. Do you think it's still there?'

Ella shrugged. 'I've no idea.'

She felt the intensity of Bryony's gaze.

'You know,' Bryony was saying. 'It's funny. I can't explain why exactly, but I'm just so curious about her. And I don't suppose . . . I mean, it's probably a mad idea, but I don't suppose you'd fancy coming with me? To try and find the cottage? Or, at least, where it used to be?'

Ella felt the heat creep up her neck and into her face.

'Oh, I'm sorry,' she said, 'I don't know if I could. I mean, I'm so busy with this place. It's hard to get away, you know . . . with Grace and –'

Bryony waved her hand. 'No, no. Of course. Silly of me. And you've been more than kind already. I'll probably head up there myself. And report back. If that's OK?'

Ella nodded. She was sure that her face must be bright red by now. Wasn't she being a bit mean?

'Yes. And you must come and tell us how you got on. I'm sure Billy would love to hear about it. You'll have to come back when he's around. Saturday lunchtime is usually a good time to catch him.'

As Bryony crossed the courtyard and slipped out of sight, Ella felt the strange humming that had filled the air around her slowly begin to subside. It was bizarre, this physical reaction. She couldn't make sense of it.

'Mamma.' Grace was pulling at her hand.

'Yes, darling?'

'She's nice. I like that lady.'

Ella smiled and smoothed Grace's hair. 'Yes, she's very nice, isn't she? Very kind.'

8

To invoke dream prophecies: Sew rose petals inside a conjure
bag made of leaves or silk and wear it around the neck at
night. In the morning, you must burn the bag outside to
release any troublesome dream spirits.
– Miss Mary's Book of Dreams

Fabia is falling and falling. She looks down between her bare feet and sees a blur of green and brown as the earth rushes up to meet her.

She looks up and sees that the air above her is thick with birds, huge birds with red beaks and long green tail feathers, their emerald wings beating furiously, circling and swooping against the clouds.

She hears a voice, Ella's voice, from far away.

'Mamma,' she cries. 'Mamma. Where are you?'

Just before she hits the ground, she wakes up with a start. She lies for a long time, her eyes closed, watching the dream still moving over the translucent screen of her eyelids.

*

Fabia dropped a sugar lump into her cup and watched it dissolve. 'I think I'm going to stop drinking coffee,' she said.

Over the rim of his mug, David's eyebrows shot up. Fabia could see him making a valiant attempt to stifle a laugh.

She smiled. 'I know, I know. But I'm having these terrible dreams.' She shuddered and pulled her robe more tightly around herself.

Through the sliding glass doors, a warm October breeze played across the decking. She breathed deeply, the scent of salt and pine trees. The air seemed to tug at her, plucking at her sleeves, making her feel restless. She wondered if she'd ever get used to the weather here in California, where, it sometimes seemed to her, there were no seasons at all, just expanses of blue sky that went on forever.

She thought of York and the way that the wind would be buffeting around the corners of the minster, sweeping in and out of the courtyard on Grape Lane, whirling litter and wet leaves in spirals. All the years she'd lived there, she'd hated the way that the cold seemed to reach right inside her clothes, making her bones feel as if they might snap at any moment. But now she found herself remembering wistfully the patterns made by the frost on the shop windows and the snow in the courtyard that muffled all sound so that it had sometimes felt as if she and Ella were floating, suspended in time, like tiny figures inside one of those glass snow globes.

She wondered if Grace would already be wearing the little red coat with the horn buttons and the yellow mittens with the fake fur trim that she'd parcelled up and posted off just a week ago. In her mind's eye, she imagined Grace, buttoned into the scarlet wool, kicking through drifts of leaves in the Museum Gardens, her cheeks flushed the colour of windfall apples. She must ask Ella to email her a picture.

Then she thought of Maadar-Bozorg, standing at her apartment window in Tehran, drawing her winter shawl around her shoulders, watching the dusk fall thickly and silently and the city spreading itself below her on the other side of the glass.

That familiar feeling uncurled itself from the pit of her stomach, cold and gelid.

'What kind of dreams?' David was watching her from across the table, his copy of the *New York Times* set aside and neatly folded by his plate.

'Oh, you know. Just silly things, really.' She pressed her lips together and tried to keep the quiver out of her voice.

David's hand was warm and firm on hers. 'Fabia, you're missing them all. It's completely normal. You need to get yourself a plane ticket. I've told you. It's that simple. Just do it.'

'I can't believe how silly I'm being.' Shivers of blue and silver, as if the air above David's shoulder had begun to tremble like water. She gripped the edge of the table and pushed her chair back. 'I'm sorry. I don't know what's the matter with me.'

David smiled. 'Nothing that a nasty British Airways breakfast won't sort. Trust me.'

'But what about you? What will you do if I go?'

'Me?' The corners of David's eyes crinkled in that way that she'd always loved. 'Oh, no doubt I'll survive.' He grinned. 'Might even get to watch some decent football and eat pizza until I explode.' He patted his stomach and winked.

*

'*Hola, chica!*'

Fabia elbowed open the door of Rosita's shop, two takeaway cups of hot chocolate and a paper bag of churros balanced precariously between her hands.

Rosita seized them with enthusiasm and set them down on the counter. The aroma of chocolate, nutmeg and chilli filled the shop.

'From José. He wants to know why he hasn't seen you in days.'

The owner of the corner cafe took great pleasure in supplying his 'two favourite ladies' with a steady supply of the house speciality chocolate, fragrantly spiced. Today, he'd thrown in the churros, homemade twists of pastry glazed with burnt sugar. Rosita sank her teeth into one and sighed.

'Heaven,' she said, between mouthfuls, flakes of pastry dropping from her fingers. 'Forgot to have breakfast again.'

Fabia smiled. 'I guessed as much. Your lights were still on when I left yesterday.' She looked around the shop, admiring Rosita's work. Every conceivable surface was hung with her creations. Garlands of coloured tin twinkled from the old beams. Rosita's labours of love, the six-foot-tall mirrors framed in intricate tin lattices of branches, leaves, flowers and birds, leaned against the walls. The shelves spilled boxes of decorations – skulls with feathered eyelashes, owls with roses twined around their necks, birds of paradise perched on crescent moons – all cut and punched in tin and enamelled or glazed in vibrant colours.

This was Rosita's busiest time. She'd once told Fabia that she made seventy per cent of her profits during the holiday season. She'd been arriving at the shop before sunrise for weeks now. Every morning, when Fabia was opening up, Rosita's canary-yellow pickup would be parked on the kerb outside and when she was closing, at six o'clock, she'd see Rosita's lights still blazing from the back workshops where she turned the stacked sheets of metal into her fantastic creations.

There were dark shadows under her friend's eyes and, Fabia thought as she examined her now, she looked much too thin under her linen apron.

'Rosita, I think you're more than ready now,' she said. 'Everything looks incredible.'

Rosita shook her head and took a large gulp of chocolate, her upper lip curling as the chilli hit the back of her throat. 'Not quite. Still some candle-holders and pocket mirrors to finish. Those always sell like crazy. I want to make sure I have enough.'

Fabia knew there was no use in protesting. She and Rosita were too much alike. And if Rosita had made up her mind that this was how it was, there'd be no convincing her otherwise.

'So what I'm desperate to know,' Fabia said, tapping the side of her nose, 'is how your dinner went with Moises? And how was the dress?'

'Oh, darling.' Rosita's cheeks dimpled. 'It was absolute *perrrr-fection.*' She set her chocolate down on the counter and did a little shimmy right there on the spot. 'I felt a million dollars. The dress was amazing. I came down the stairs and Moises . . . Well, I swear his jaw just hit the floor. He hasn't seen me look like that in years. I put my hair up like this.' She demonstrated, twisting her black curls into a high French pleat, pulling a few strands around her face, fluttering her eyelashes. 'And I wore the gold heels and the amber earrings. He was a pussycat, darling. I could have asked him for . . . for *the moon.*' She picked up a decoration in the shape of a crescent moon trailing strands of tiny stars and dandled it from her fingers. 'I swear he would have brought it to me right there, on a plate, in the middle of the restaurant so I could gobble it all up.'

Fabia smiled. 'A good evening, then?'

Rosita laughed. 'More than good, darling. It was just what we both needed. It was –' She seemed to be searching among the coloured leaves and petals festooned from the ceiling for the right words. 'It was *magic.*'

Fabia heard the familiar whispers from the corners of the room and felt them flicker up her spine in blue and yellow. That dress with the panther-clasp belt. She'd known it would be just right. And she'd taken particularly special care with her embroidery of the words, unpicking the hem and hiding the phrases carefully inside, using her magnifying glass to make the stitches as tiny as possible, each word no bigger than the pips of a juicy Californian lemon, then hand-rolling and stitching the difficult silk jersey back into place so that Rosita's sharp craftswoman's eyes would not detect a thing.

In the darkness, love reinvents itself, moves on velvet paws, stretches itself beyond the shadows . . .

She didn't know where those words had come from. She never really knew. She'd come to accept that this was how it was, each time she let her mind go quiet, contract to the tip of her needle. The words would form themselves easily behind her eyelids and then all she had to do was translate them into careful stitches, selecting the colours of the embroidery silk, letting her fingers move of their own accord: *Love moves on velvet paws, stretches itself beyond the shadows, knows when to wait patiently, growing bigger with the waxing moon and when to leap, leap into the light . . .*

Over the last couple of years, she'd grown to love Rosita like a sister. And she liked Moises too. She wanted them to be happy.

She'd watched them nurse Moises's mother through cancer at the beginning of the year, and she suspected that they'd had some money worries too. Of course, Rosita would be far too proud to ever share that with her. And then there was Gabby, about whom she always seemed anxious. 'It's such a cut-throat world that she moves in,' Rosita had once said, 'and she's so sweet, my girl, such an innocent. I worry that someone will take advantage of her.'

Now Fabia hugged her friend, feeling the slenderness of her shoulders through her sweater.

'I'm so pleased,' she said. 'And I have something to tell you too. I've decided to go. In time for Ella's birthday. I managed to speak to Billy yesterday, whilst Ella was out. He was very enthusiastic about it. Says he's sure she'd love to see me, that he'll throw a special party, surprise her.'

'Ah,' Rosita smiled again. 'This is *good*, darling. *Very* good. I wholeheartedly approve. She needs you. Even if you think she doesn't. And don't worry,' she said. 'I'll keep an eye on David for you, keep him out of mischief.' She winked.

They both knew that the chances of calm, sensible David indulging in mischief were about the same as those of Moises forgoing his Wednesday night poker game at the sports bar with the boys. No, what worried Fabia was that David would work too hard whilst she was gone.

'Well, if you wouldn't mind dropping by every now and then, just to remind him to, you know, *eat*.'

'Consider it done. I'll invite him over. I think he likes my tortillas, no? Don't you worry, my darling. Just have a nice time.'

Fabia took her friend's hands in hers, turning them over, examining the black smudges and red indentations on each fingertip from her long hours working the tin.

'And you,' she said. 'You take care of yourself. I'll leave you the key to the shop. Try everything on. Borrow anything you want. And set another date with Moises. *Bewitch* him.'

*

'Your ring, Bry.' Ed set his watering can down on the bench and took her hand in his. 'You've lost it!'

Bryony felt the heat in her cheeks. She pushed her hand into her skirt pocket. Thank goodness. It was still there.

'Here it is.' She held it up with a little flourish and it winked in the pale light. 'Silly me. I took it off when I was washing up. Didn't want to lose it down the plughole. I must have forgotten about it.'

Ed's face relaxed. 'Right. S'pose it's a good job I noticed.' He picked up the watering can. 'I've got the bulbs in, anyway. Lots of tulips. They'll be lovely, come spring. I was just thinking about a cup of tea. Wondering where you'd got to . . .'

'I went for one of my walks. You didn't see my note?' Bryony hoped her face didn't give her away. She'd always been a terrible liar.

Ed shook his head. 'I was cracking on. Out here. Trying to get things nice for you. You've been doing a lot of that recently, Bry.'

'A lot of what?'

'Walking.'

'Yes, well, it's good for me. Stops me thinking too much –'

'Thinking? About what?'

Ed's eyes narrowed. He had very blue eyes. Some would say they were cold. In a weird way, they reminded Bryony of Selena's.

'Oh, you know. Stuff. All the stuff that it isn't really that helpful for me to think about. I'll go and put the kettle on, then.'

'Right-o.'

She set out mugs, began to warm the teapot.

Outside, Ed began to sweep the yard. The sound of the brush against the stones went straight through her.

It was funny, thought Bryony, how she'd lived with this person for a year, slept next to him every night and yet she realised that she really didn't have a clue who he was. It was as if she was looking at him for the first time. The thought made the gap inside her open up again. She swallowed, poured water, fetched the milk from the fridge.

It was all right. She was going to be all right.

She took a breath, took it down deep into her stomach, in the way that Dr Murray had suggested she might find helpful. An image of the shop swam into her mind. The rows of bookcases. The little girl, Grace, playing in the corner, her pink cheeks and bobbing curls.

Yes, she thought. It would be OK.

Miss Mary's words, the ones she'd read just that morning, drifted back to her:

I am a simple woman . . .

I live on my own . . .

The Old Ways, the ways of women for generations . . .

If this is magic, let people say that this is so . . .

9

To divine the future: During the waxing moon, set a glass outside at night and let it infuse with moonlight. On the very next night, dress your bed with clean white sheets and sprinkle them with the moon water. As you fall asleep, hold your subject or question in mind and let the dream work begin.
– Miss Mary's Book of Dreams

'What's with this witchcraft obsession all of a sudden?' Billy grinned. Ella was sitting on the floor in the middle of Happily Ever After's History section, surrounded by stacks of books.

He picked up a thick paperback, pretending to stagger under its weight. 'The History of Witches and Goddess-Worshippers in North Yorkshire,' he read. 'Hm. A little light reading, huh? And here was me thinking you despised this kind of stuff.' He stopped to peer at the title of another. 'A Book of Instruction for the Modern Witch. Really? I thought you'd rather be seen dead than –'

'It's not an obsession.' Ella frowned. 'It's for that customer. You know, the one I told you about? The one who bought our last Miss Mary? Well, she comes in every week now. She can't get enough of all this history stuff and witchy stuff. And she wanted me to go on some kind of field trip with her. Up to the Moors. See if she could find the spot where Mary used to live.'

Billy raised an eyebrow.

'Yes, I know. A bit weird. I think she's quite lonely.'

'Sounds like fun, actually.'

'Really?' Ella pulled a face. 'She's lovely. Absolutely lovely. But I think she might also be slightly nuts.'

Billy laughed. 'Well, that would make two of you, then. But, seriously, El. When do you ever go anywhere anymore? Apart from this place? It might do you good.'

Ella shook her head. 'No way. Not my idea of fun at all. But I must admit, it's been making me think.' She picked up a book from the pile and shook it at him. 'I mean, do you *know* how many women were wrongfully hung or burned as witches, just because they healed people with herbs or saved women from dying in childbirth or delivered a stillborn baby? It's outrageous.'

Billy was looking at her, his head on one side, with that annoying amused expression. She decided to ignore him.

'I was thinking, actually, that I could write about it. There's a book in all this somewhere. But anyway, *you* can talk. What was it last month? Socio-political movements of the eighteenth century? Bonnie Prince Charlie?' She scrambled to her feet, poked a finger under his ribs. 'Obsessed, are you?'

Billy grabbed at her. 'The only obsession I have is an Ella obsession. Come here. I haven't seen you properly all week.'

He smoothed her hair from her face and kissed her.

Ella felt Billy's hands on her waist and quickly breathed in, tensing her stomach muscles. These days, she could hardly bear for him to touch her. She still hadn't managed to shift the baby weight and the idea of his fingers sinking into the soft roll of fat above her jeans made her flinch. She felt the tears pricking at her eyes again, that empty feeling welling in her stomach. She knew she was her own worst enemy. Why did it all have to be so difficult?

From behind the shelf, Grace came dancing in her new red patent shoes. She held a large square picture book by its corner. 'Will you read this to me?' she said, fixing Billy with her most adoring expression. 'Daddy? You are the best Daddy in the whole wide world.'

'Competition,' said Ella, grateful for the interruption, taking the book from Grace and handing it to him. 'I'd better leave you two to it and go and make something for us all to eat.'

Ella crossed the courtyard and unlocked the door to their flat. She made her way up the narrow stairs, dragging her feet like lead weights. What the hell was wrong with her? She had a beautiful daughter and a husband she adored. She was so damn lucky. Other women – Laura, for instance – would kill for a husband like Billy. Someone who loved her. Someone she could love. So why couldn't she shift this dark feeling that, on days like this one, threatened to swallow her up completely?

She knew the kinds of things that she *ought* to be doing. She should be making more of an effort, getting her hair cut, having a bloody makeover, or at least taking Flo on a shopping trip, buying some new tops or something. You were supposed to do that kind of thing, weren't you, to keep things interesting, to keep the spark going? Every women's magazine she'd ever picked up told her so. But what if you'd never been into that kind of thing in the first place? What if, in fact, you'd spent your whole life actively resisting getting dressed up? It was all so confusing and every time she tried to think about it, she just wanted to lie down in a dark room. She'd lost herself somewhere – clearly that much was true – but all the advice about finding herself again didn't make any sense at all.

And she'd spent the last few weeks increasingly distracted, this unsettled feeling inside her growing more urgent, insistent. Now she found herself thinking more and more about Miss Mary and Bryony. Weird things. Things that didn't make sense.

Again and again, her mind circled back to Mamma, Mamma and her box under the bed, her reluctance to talk about the signals and what she'd always called 'the gift'. Her insistence that such things shouldn't be dabbled in too deeply, that what she called 'everyday magic' – the ordinary magic that is all around us, if we only stop to notice – was all that anyone should require.

Bryony's pinched face swam into her mind, those big, grey eyes that always seemed half terrified, that way she had of holding herself as if she were afraid of something.

She sighed and emptied a tin of chopped tomatoes into a pan, adding a handful of oregano from the pot on the windowsill, watching the sauce begin to bubble.

And then there was her book. Such a knot of ideas. Sometimes she thought she would be better abandoning it completely. Starting again. But something – the smallest beginning of an idea – was forming itself at the back of her mind. If she could just let it, if she could stop herself from prodding at it or examining it in any way, she knew that it was just about to surface.

She took the wooden spoon and stirred carefully.

And here were Billy's feet on the stairs and Grace's small high voice floating up behind him.

'Selena. Sel-ena ... Silly, silly-lena ...' she chanted. 'Is she coming to play, Daddy?'

Ella felt her stomach contract as if someone had punched her there, hard. Selena. Billy's colleague at work. She'd never met her. Billy's department was one of the largest in the university. There were at least forty lecturers and researchers. But Billy talked about Selena from time to time. Recently, perhaps, a little too much. *Selena said this, Selena thinks that . . .* They were working on something together. Some big funding proposal. But why was Grace now chanting her name?

And here was the stupid dream again: *'Ella, El-la. I came to tell you to pay attention . . .'* Shivers of silver, flashes of green.

She heard Billy's laughter drifting up the stairs. 'No, sweetheart. Selena's not coming to play. Grown-ups don't do that. Well, at least . . .' His voice trailed off and he laughed again, softly to himself. 'Selena is someone I work with, Grace. She called because she just wanted to ask me something. Something about work.'

On a Saturday? Ella thought. *Really? Was that necessary?* Her throat felt tight. She swallowed hard and jabbed at the tomatoes in the pan. And why was he going to such lengths to explain all this to their three-year-old? Was this all, in fact, for Ella's benefit?

'Hello, gorgeous.' Billy was kissing her now as she stood at the stove, his hand encircling her waist. 'Mmmm. Something smells good.'

She moved backwards, banging her hip on the edge of the countertop.

'What's the matter, El? Are you OK?' Billy's face was screwed up in that face he pulled when he was worried. Ella felt a flush begin at the base of her throat.

'Fine. I'm fine,' she said, going back to her stirring, squishing a tomato extra hard under the wooden spoon. Was he worried about her or was he worried that he'd just been caught out? She could feel her heart banging in her chest, tears pricking at the corners of her eyes.

It was ridiculous. Why did she always have to be so damn insecure? She peered at her reflection in the stainless-steel flash-back, and then quickly looked away again.

*

'Bryony. It's me . . .'

A voice, like the crackle of dried leaves.

Bryony leant against the kitchen wall, swallowing hard.

'How did you get this number?'

'*You* gave it to me. Remember? When I came to see you in the hospital . . .'

Bryony held the phone away from her ear and let her mind slip backwards. Could that be true? That time was all such a blur – white sheets, soft white pillows, faces that came and went above her bed in a kind of haze. She had the vaguest memory of Selena perched on the edge of her bed, picking pieces of lint from her pristine black sweater, but the image dissolved as soon as she reached for it, got swallowed up in a haze of white. She heard again the rattle of a trolley, the squeak of rubber-soled footsteps in the corridor outside her room and the cold chink of metal on metal.

She breathed hard.

'So I do still need to ask you for this little favour, Bryony,' Selena was saying. 'Just this one time more and then I promise I'll never bother you again. I'll disappear. Pouf! Just like that . . .' Selena made a little laughing sound, but underneath it Bryony could hear the pressure building, her voice forming ridges of scarlet, vivid edges, her barely suppressed frustration.

'I already told you. I won't go there again. It's too . . . too *humiliating*, Selena. You'll have to talk to him yourself this time. I can't keep doing it for you.'

'Oh, but sweetie.' Selena's voice took on a wheedling tone now. 'You know he won't listen to me. He thinks I'm just a hard-faced cow. That I'm always trying to get something out of him. Whereas you . . . He *likes* you. You make him feel . . . well, *guilty*. You remind him of Mother. That's what it is. Whereas me, I just remind him of himself.'

Bryony let out a long breath. *Sweetie*, she thought. Since when had Selena ever called her *sweetie*?

She heard her own voice, the words a staccato. 'What about Simon? What's happened to *him*? I thought you said he was loaded? Why can't *he* help you?'

There was a pause. Then Selena's voice with the hard edges again. 'Oh, you know how it is, Bryony. All men are useless in the end. The truth is, he's buggered off. Left us. Left me in a bit of a spot, actually . . .'

Bryony bristled. She heard Selena's words from a few days before: *You do know how to pick 'em, Bryony.* Her throat tightened.

'Well, you can't expect me to feel sorry for you, Selena. And anyway, you're not telling me that there isn't someone else waiting in the wings? You usually have someone lined up.'

Selena laughed. She likes that, thought Bryony. She's actually flattered.

'Well, as a matter of fact, there *is* someone,' she said. 'Someone at work. Gorgeous man. Very sexy. Come to think of it, you'd like him a lot. He's into your kind of stuff. Social history, folklore. God, even the weird *witchy* stuff. You know, *magic*.' She laughed again. 'But he hasn't got a penny to his name. He's just a poor, old lecturer like me.'

Somewhere at the back of Bryony's mind, there was a tiny click like a catch. Lecturer. Social history . . .

'And is he married too, then, this man?' Bryony couldn't keep the disapproval out of her voice. 'Because, you know, maybe that was the issue with Simon, don't you think? His wife? His three young children? Have you ever thought that perhaps you need to find someone a bit more . . . well, *available*?'

'Oh. My. God. Bryony's giving me advice *on men*.' Selena's voice was knife-edged. 'For goodness' sake, Bryony. You were always so, so –' But then she checked herself. Her voice dropped an octave. 'Look, it's not really me that I'm worried about, anyway. It's Letty. She's heartbroken. She won't leave her room. She was very . . . Well, let's just say that she'd got very *attached* to Simon. And the bloody landlord's put the rent up again. I told him, it's not on. The gutter needs fixing and the boiler's not reliable anymore. But he's not having it. And I don't want to uproot Letty again. She's got exams, all sorts of stuff going on. School trips and music lessons and so on. And that's all more expense, of course . . .'

Something inside Bryony softened, as it always did at any mention of her niece.

'I think you should take her to see Daddy, Selena. Letty, I mean. I think you should tell him everything. After all, she *is* his only grandchild. Surely there's been enough water under the bridge by now. I think he'll want to help you. I really do . . .'

Selena was laughing at her again. The sound grated in Bryony's ear. '*Really*? You really think so? For God's sake, Bryony, you can be so . . . so damn *naive* at times. Do you honestly think he's going to want to meet . . .' She lowered her voice to a whisper. 'The teenage offspring of his wayward daughter and his *business partner*, his oldest, most trusted friend? After all this time? Do you think he'd even believe me, all these years on? Can you imagine the fallout? All the repercussions of that?'

'But you don't have to tell him that part –'

'Oh, don't be ridiculous. I mean, it's bloody obvious, isn't it? She looks *exactly* like her father. The red hair's a bit of a give-away, don't you think? Daddy would cotton on, the minute he clapped eyes on her. And then he'd insist on having it all out with *him*. You know damn well that he would. And once that cowardly little shit got a whiff of it, my life wouldn't be worth living, would it? And Letty's too. He'd want to be . . . *involved*, wouldn't he? I'd never be rid of him.'

'Well, would that be such a bad thing? At least you'd have money, security. I mean, I've been thinking, Selena. Doesn't Letty at least have the right to know who her dad is? And the right to his financial support, too? Perhaps for *her* sake –'

'Oh, *please* don't start lecturing me, Bryony. We haven't all got the luxury of a nice little private income, you know.'

Bryony pressed her lips together. She was suddenly acutely aware of her own breathing. She felt the air moving in and out of her mouth, very hard and fast. Was it her fault that Selena had spent the inheritance left by their mother's death on back-packing around the world, buying herself into a string of dodgy business deals with handsome and usually married older men that had never amounted to anything, whilst she, boring, sensible little Bryony, had stayed in York and invested wisely in a couple of small rental properties? Selena had laughed at her at the time.

And then, when it looked as if Selena was finally settling down a little – into an expensive PhD in the history of women's health in the nineteenth century, generously funded by one of her unsuitable men – she'd announced that she was pregnant. It turned out that Selena had been having an affair with their father's business partner, someone he'd known since his Oxford days, a family friend.

Bryony, as far as she knew, was the only person in the world who had this bit of information. She'd pressed Selena to come clean to their father, but Selena wasn't having any of it. Bryony never could understand exactly why. Perhaps Selena thought he would finally cut her off for good; although Bryony thought it more likely that he'd turn on the man in question.

Anyway, once the pregnancy news was out, Selena's latest boyfriend hadn't stuck around for long. Perhaps he'd guessed that the baby wasn't his. Perhaps he was just running scared. Since that time, Selena had lurched from one ill-fated relationship to another, dragging Letty along with her. You had to hand it to her. In the midst of all this chaos, she'd managed to carve out a successful academic career. She was sharp, determined and absolutely ruthless when she put her mind to something. Bloody-minded, was what their father called it. For a time, he'd supported her, turning up at her graduation ceremony glowing with pride, offering holidays at his villa in southern Spain with his own new wife and daughter; but when it became evident that Selena wasn't going to play by his rules, he'd become frustrated, first withdrawing his emotional support and then his money. And all the time, he'd remained oblivious of Letty's existence. Selena had always kept her fiercely hidden.

Bryony had watched the whole thing from the sidelines, with a mixture of envy and distress.

'Tell him,' she'd said, when Selena had yet again managed to hide his granddaughter from him. 'She's his granddaughter. It's all part of the dynasty, isn't it? Shoring up the great Darwin empire, for goodness' sake. He'd be over the moon. Just tell him.'

She couldn't understand it. She'd have given anything to bask in her father's attention even for just one afternoon. But Selena and her father were just too alike to ever get along peaceably.

'Stubborn as mules, those two,' is what her mother had always said. 'And not at all sensible, either of them. She may have got the brains and the looks, Bryony, dear, but you got all the common sense.'

And that was probably true. Selena was certainly a disaster when it came to money. She spent far more than she earned. Academic salaries weren't high, Bryony knew, but Selena always had to have three holidays a year, the best clothes, the best . . . well, everything.

'It's just how I am,' she'd once said. 'I can't help it.'

Bryony wondered if it was really Selena's fault. She'd been so thoroughly spoiled by their father as a child. She'd never had to learn the value of money.

Now Bryony swallowed. 'I'm going to end this conversation now, Selena. I think we've both said enough.'

'OK. But just think about it, will you? Come on, Bryony.' Selena's tone was wheedling. 'And, as you said, just then, it's for Letty's sake, not mine. It'll just help me to tide us over. I've got a promotion due. It's going to happen, I just know it . . .'

After the line went dead, Bryony stood for a long time, staring at the phone in her hand. But she wasn't seeing the phone or the kitchen floor with its black and white chequered lino. What she saw instead was a small girl in a green and white school uniform, sitting on the bottom step of the staircase in her father's house. The girl's face was wet with tears and she was sitting on her hands so that they'd stop trembling.

Above her, Selena hung over the banister, her face contorted. 'You're such a scaredy-cat, Bryony.'

10

To direct the future: On full moon nights, undress and open
all your windows. Take the moon's silver full onto your body.
When you fall asleep after bathing in moonlight, what you
dream of will always come true. Full moon bathing has great
power. You must rest for three days after this dreaming.
– Miss Mary's Book of Dreams

Zohreh Jobrani woke to a sharp cracking sound at the bedroom
window. She fumbled for the light switch, expecting to see the
pane shattered by a hurled stone, until she remembered that she
wasn't at the village house in the mountains but in her fourteenth-
floor apartment in Tehran.

She reached for the glass of water on her bedside table and
took a gulp, letting the air-conditioned liquid slide down her
throat. Her nightdress clung to her and her lips burned on the
cold rim of the glass. She waited for her heartbeat to slow itself
to the soft hum of dawn in the city far below.

She'd had the bird dream again.

Zohreh Jobrani had dreamed this same dream only three
times before. The first time had been on the night that her
granddaughter, Farah Jobrani, was born; the second time had
been in the early hours of that terrible day when Farah's mother
had taken her own life; and the third and last time had been
twenty or more years ago now, just before she'd woken to the
phone's shrill ring and heard a distraught Farah – or Fabia as
she'd begun to call herself by then – sobbing down the line all
the way from England, the terrible news that her husband, Enzo,

was dead. Birth and death. The dream – and the bird - seemed to weave them together.

Now she sat up, clutching the duvet to her chest with one hand and twisting the thick plait of her hair around the other.

Zohreh Jobrani's thick grey hair was her last defiance in the face of old age. She stubbornly refused to give in to the idea that long hair was somehow aging and that women in their seventies should wear their hair cropped close to their scalps. Instead, every morning and evening she took the silver-backed brush, which her mother had given her for her sixteenth birthday, and swept it through her hair, exactly one hundred times. In the mornings, she wound it into a neat chignon at the nape of her neck, and in the evenings, after she'd brushed it out with those hundred vigorous strokes, she smoothed it into a single plait that hung straight down her back as far as the waist of her rose-coloured silk pyjamas.

Now a stray strand of this hair snagged on the amethyst in her signet ring and she winced. What news could the dream be bringing with it this time, this dream that flew through the dark on its red and green wings? What did the bird want with her as its beak opened and she looked straight into its open throat, heard it cry out with its voice that was almost human, before finally hurling itself against the window and falling away again into the night?

In the corner of the room, she felt the familiar Signals shaping themselves, whispering from the shadows: *Zohreh, Zohreh* . . . They were strong tonight, and insistent. As she switched off the light again and lay down, they seemed to creep between her pillows, taunting her with a soft hiss: *So what will you do, Zohreh? What will you do? What's to do, to do, to do, to do . . .?*

She lay for a long time watching the slither of sky above the heavy bedroom blinds brighten to white and then silver. By the time the city was fully awake beneath her, she'd already made up her mind.

She'd been putting it off for months, after all. And now Farah needed her. That much was clear. She could feel it all the way through her body, in the crooks of her elbows and the backs of her knees and that quivering feeling in her stomach.

She was old. Her hands lying on the cotton sheet were speckled with brown age spots and, as she shifted on the mattress, she felt her hips click and creak. She wanted to see Farah at least one more time before they put her in the ground. And if that terrible girl wouldn't come here to Tehran – that girl, with all her talk of visas and counter-terrorism laws – then she, Zohreh Jobrani, would have to go to *her*.

'Maadar,' she'd said in their last phone call, 'I want to come. I really do. But you have no idea, the problems I had getting this visa to the States. I'm worried that if I go back to Iran, they won't let me leave again.'

Zohreh was a little ashamed now when she thought of her reply. 'Why don't you marry this nice man of yours? This David,' she'd said. 'After all, you love him, don't you? Wouldn't that make things easier?'

Why had she said that? She, Zohreh, had managed, her entire life, not to marry anyone. She'd gone out of her way to avoid it. And each of her sisters had done the same. They'd remained resolutely single, running the family dressmaking business, keeping the village house, belonging only to themselves in this country where so many women were treated like little more than decorative objects, right until the last. Why should she be telling Farah to do something different?

She must really be getting old. Old and tired. Perhaps she was finally losing her marbles. Well, then, she would just have to go there. It was easier to talk face to face. She'd be able to see for herself. Assess the situation. Farah had sounded odd. There was a break in her voice that hadn't been there before.

She was needed. And it was good to feel needed, after all this time.

She checked her small gold wristwatch and took her address book from the bedside drawer, flicking through it impatiently until she found what she was looking for. Propped up on her pillows, she punched a number into the phone, frowning at a chip in her French-polished nails.

'Yes,' she said and she heard her voice sound out in the small room, brisk, practised, professional, without a hint of the concern that she felt fluttering in her chest. 'Dr Zohreh Jobrani. Yes. Standard class . . . Just as soon as you have availability . . .'

The Story of the Simurgh

Zohreh is standing in the courtyard, looking in through the open French doors at the large salon where her grandmother is working.

She watches as her grandmother takes a long feather and tucks it into the hem of the blue cotton *kameez* that she's sewing. The feather is golden yellow, the same bright colour as the yolks of the hens' eggs that Mahdokht cooked for her breakfast this morning. It flashes briefly in the dim room. She watches from the doorway as her Maadar takes another feather, holds it in the air for a moment, whispers something in Farsi and then sews this feather too into the hem.

'What are you doing, child?' Maadar never looks up from her work but she knows that Zohreh is there.

'Watching, Maadar,' she says, running her foot in its new sandal up and down the back of her calf.

Her grandmother frowns. 'Come. Come closer.' She beckons with her thimbled finger.

'What are you making, Maadar? Why are you sewing in feathers?'

Her grandmother ties off her thread and drapes the half-finished garment over the back of the chair. She crosses to the bookshelf and takes down a large square book.

As she opens it, the spine makes a cracking sound and a single green feather falls to the floor. Maadar bends to pick it up.

'Look,' she says, using the feather as a pointer. 'This is the *Shahname*, the Great Book . . .' She turns the pages carefully. 'And here is the story of the Simurgh, a magical bird with special powers . . .'

Zohreh is mesmerised by the picture, which spreads over the entire page. The bird is gigantic. It has the head of a dog and the claws of a lion and its wings are covered with feathers in many dazzling colours: red and green and black and gold.

'The Simurgh,' says her grandmother, 'carries messages between the Earth and the Sky. Whenever she's hungry, she simply puts back her head like this . . .' Maadar tips her head towards the ceiling and breathes in deeply. 'And she draws the wind through the many tiny holes in her beak, like this . . .'

'She eats the air?'

'She does.' Her grandmother nods. 'She's a very clever bird . . . And tender-hearted, too. That's how she comes to take the Boy Prince Zal into her nest at the top of the mountains and raise him as her own fledgling . . . You want to hear the story?'

Zohreh nods. She sits down on the floor at the foot of her grandmother's chair and tries not to stare at the old woman's bony toes in their plaited leather sandals.

'According to the Great Book,' her grandmother begins, patting the heavy volume that now lies open on her lap, 'the son of Saam, Prince Zal, was born with hair and eyelashes as white as snow and eyes as colourless as diamonds. Today we might call him *albino*. You know this word?' She fixes Zohreh with a questioning look.

Zohreh nods. 'I think so, Maadar.'

'Good. Now, where was I? Ah, yes. So in those times, people thought that when a child was born with such pale looks, there must be some kind of evil at work, a curse, or the work of bad fairies or some such nonsense . . .' She waves her hand in the air dismissively and makes a soft t*sk*-ing sound with her tongue. 'And so when Saam saw his baby son, he was very afraid and he took the poor child from his distraught mother and rode with him many kilometres out from the city and into the mountains, where he left him to die.

'But the child's tiny cries were heard by the Simurgh, who lived among the highest peaks. With her keen eyes, she saw the tiny baby lying bundled in a cleft in the rocks and she swooped down on her mighty wings and took him in her mouth and carried him off to her nest, where she warmed him and fed him on honey and insects and the fragrant petals of flowers until he was old enough to hunt for himself.

'She also taught him everything she knew, all the wisdom she'd learned from her hundreds of years of dwelling on the mountain-top, from where she could sweep her eyes over the horizon from east to west and see everything. And Prince Zal grew to become knowledgeable and loving just like the Simurgh herself.

'But then the summer came when Prince Zal was a fully grown man and began to long to rejoin the World of Men. He was curious to know what it would be like to live among his own kind. The Simurgh was both saddened by this and also very afraid. She knew that great unhappiness might lie ahead of her beloved adopted son. But she also knew that she must let him go. So when the day came for him to fly on her back and descend into the world from which he had come, she made him a gift of three golden feathers.

'"If you ever need my help," she said, "you must burn these feathers and, wherever I am, I will see their golden smoke and fly to you."

'And so Prince Zal returned to his own world, where he was welcomed by his true mother, who had long ago abandoned hope of ever seeing him again. When he appeared in her door-way, she recognised him immediately and was overjoyed that, not only was he alive, but he was also such a fine, strong and handsome young man, with a wisdom beyond his years. It wasn't long before many of the families of the nobility began to come forwards to offer their daughters in marriage.

'But it was the beautiful and gentle Rudaba who enchanted Zal. She had golden skin and golden hair and there was some-thing about her kindness that reminded him of his second sky mother. They were married in a simple ceremony and Rudaba was soon with child but, when it came time for their son to be born, her labour was long and terrible. From the birth chamber, she cried out in such agonising pain that Zal was certain that he would lose her.

'So he took the feathers from the place where he carried them, inside the lining of his embroidered coat, close to his heart, in a special pocket he'd had made. He laid them on a golden dish and lit them and soon the smoke from the feathers was curling up around his shoulders, fragrant with snow and honey from his old mountain home.

'And then, at the window of the birth chamber, the Simurgh appeared, her wings outspread and shimmering with a thousand colours. She perched on the windowsill and spoke to Zal in her calm clear voice, whilst all the time Rudaba writhed in pain on the bed.

'The Simurgh ordered him to fetch fresh water and showed him how to clean a knife and how to make an incision in Rudaba's swollen belly and take out his child as easily as taking a stone from a ripe fruit . . .'

Zohreh shudders. 'How terrible.'

Her grandmother looks at her and smiles. 'In fact, how wonderful. For otherwise Rudaba and her little baby boy would have died.'

'It was a boy?'

'Yes, and they named him Rostam. And he grew up to be a great hero. But that is another story. Now, where was I? Oh, yes. They say that, when Zal lifted his son in his arms, the first thing that the baby saw was the Simurgh, perched on the windowsill, her beautiful wings outspread, and the baby's eyes widened to see the many colours of her feathers all shining there in the moonlight – green and red and blue and black and gold . . .'

'And what happened to the Simurgh, Maadar?'

'Oh, no one knows for sure, my dear. But sometimes, I'm certain that I hear her, drawing the wind through her beak, like this . . .' Her grandmother tosses back her head again and some of her long white hair comes loose and tumbles over her shoulders.

'And that's why you're sewing the feathers into this *kameez*? Just like Prince Zal carried them, for protection?'

'Maybe, child. Maybe . . .' Her grandmother presses a finger to her lips. 'But this must be our secret. Yes? Just yours and mine? You must never tell anyone else . . .'

And Zohreh never had. But she had always loved the story of the Simurgh, carrying it close, just as Zal had carried his feathers against his heart.

Who was she, Zohreh had often wondered, the wearer of that blue *kameez*, and did she ever discover that the feathers were there?

Years later, when Farah had sent her a copy of her first programme from Paris – with that photograph of herself in the racy costume made of nothing but emerald-green crystals and feathers and inscribed with her new name – the first thing Zohreh had thought of was the Simurgh with her iridescent wings.

And when Farah had phoned to tell her about Grace's birth and how Ella had laboured so hard to bring her into the world, Zohreh had thought again of Prince Zal, Rudaba and Rostam and the kind-hearted bird watching over them from the windowsill, its wings outspread.

'She will be a very great person, this little girl,' she told Farah. 'It is an auspicious way to enter this world. Be sure to tell Ella that.'

*

Fabia Moreno looked at the person behind the desk. She raised an eyebrow, arranged her lips into a smile and watched as this girl, who must be no more than eighteen and had chewing gum wadded in the corner of her cheek, clicked her little mouse thing – clickety-click – and ran her fingers through her long, lank hair and squinted again at her screen.

'Sorry, ma'am. I just can't get you on a flight this week,' she was saying. 'And definitely not by Wednesday. I can put you on standby . . .'

Fabia sighed. It was an inward sigh, a sigh that no one else in the cramped travel agents' office would have heard. In fact, anyone who cared to pay attention would have seen that Fabia's lipsticked smile only became a little more polished and her perfectly groomed eyebrows rose a little higher.

But inside her, a tremor of disappointment travelled up her spine. It was a cold, blue-grey, the colour of her disappointment, but even as she stood there it began to change, to sharpen at the edges into irritation.

'Check again,' she said, her smile tightening.

'I'm sorry, ma'am?' The girl pushed her hair out of her eyes and stared at Fabia.

'Check again. Would you, please?'

Fabia ran her tongue over her teeth, gripping the edge of the desk. But even as she sat there, among the fake potted palms and the piles of glossy brochures, she knew that she wasn't actually annoyed at this silly young girl with her chewing-gum habit. She was annoyed at herself. Now that she'd finally made up her mind, it seemed that it was all too late. She'd wavered for too long.

And then somewhere among the many things that began to jump and circle in her mind, a single thought broke away from the rest, forming itself into a perfect shape. A certain kind of shape, to be exact. The oval shape that was sewn into the lining of the pocket in the coat that she happened to be wearing right now. Her lucky charm, the polished bit of metal, a little like a lopsided moon, with the funny engraved lines across its surface. The charm that she'd carried with her everywhere, in her pocket or her purse, for more than twenty years, from the day that she'd found it in the garden at Maadar-Bozorg's village house. She felt for the edge of it now through the thin cotton of her coat, tracing it with her thumbnail.

And then she looked again at the girl behind the desk.

'I hope I didn't sound rude,' she said. 'It's just that it's terribly important. Are you absolutely sure there's nothing at all? I don't suppose you would check just one more time?'

The girl barely managed to hide her impatience. 'Sure, but this screen updates every thirty seconds. I don't see how –' And then her finger paused on the mouse. She looked up at Fabia and shook her head in disbelief. 'Well, I've never seen *that* happen before. Must be your lucky day. A seat has just this minute come available.'

Fabia smiled and reached in her handbag for her purse.

11

Betrothal dream: Bathe in the light of the waxing moon in a bath strewn with rose petals. Then dress by candlelight in a nightdress of pure white cotton and place a sprig of rosemary under your pillow. In the morning, the first man you see will be the man that you are going to marry.
– Miss Mary's Book of Dreams

Ella arranged carrot sticks around the dollop on Grace's plate.

'C'mon, Grace,' she said. 'You *love* hummus.'

Grace shook her head, holding her arms stiffly at her sides. 'I don't, Mummy. I don't like it. Yuck.' She screwed up her face.

Ella sighed. 'Well, it's funny how, right up until this very moment, it's always been your favourite.' She handed Grace a breadstick. 'C'mon,' she coaxed, 'and then you can have some pudding.'

'Pudding?' Grace's eyes lit up. She pushed her plate away. 'I want pudding, Mummy. Strawberry ice cream?'

Ella shook her head. 'Definitely not.' She scooped hummus into her own mouth and chewed exaggeratedly, holding Grace's gaze. 'Not until you've eaten this.'

Grace's eyes filled with tears. 'Daddy. I want my daddy,' she said.

Ella tried to stifle her exasperation. She sneaked a glance at the notebook lying open on the counter.

Woods, clearing, moon . . . she'd written. Well, it was a start.

Grace's hummus-spattered hand reached for Ella's face. 'Sorry, Mummy. If I eat one breadstick and all my avocado, can I have ice cream?'

'We'll see.' Ella pointed to Grace's plate. 'C'mon then.'

Feeling of needing to find something. Feeling lost. Searching for a way out, she scribbled.

'Mamma –' Grace was waving her breadstick. 'This one's got funny bits on it.'

Ella closed the notebook. It was hopeless.

'Grace,' she said. 'What would you like to do this afternoon? We don't have to go to the shop. Daddy's doing his seminar thing there. We've got the afternoon off.'

'Um, park?' said Grace, hopefully.

Ella smiled. 'Eat up your hummus, OK? And then we'll go to the park.'

Ella crossed to the sink. From the kitchen window, she could see the group of people – students, mainly, plus a few of Billy's colleagues – milling about in the courtyard below. The window was open and the sound of their voices drifted up to her. One voice in particular caught her attention. It was loud and cultured – what Billy's mum would call posh – and it was coming from the striking-looking woman in the black wool dress, her blonde hair pulled back from her face so that Ella could admire the angle of her cheekbones.

Jason, one of the lecturers in Billy's department, turned to her, nodding. 'Well, exactly, Selena. You're bang on, there –'

The woman turned her head, and her blonde hair blazed around her shoulders. Ella felt as if someone had stabbed her in the heart.

So *this* was Selena? Billy's colleague. The one who had called him the other night? The one he always seemed to be talking about, these days.

My God. She was stunning.

Even from up here, Ella could appreciate her slim outline. She was tall and elegant, with glossy, groomed hair that reached down past her shoulders.

The shop door jangled as Billy propped it open. He stepped out into the courtyard and Ella instinctively drew back a little from the window.

'Afternoon, everyone. Thanks for coming. We're ready for you now.'

He turned then and smiled in Selena's direction. Ella saw him run his hand through his hair in that way he did when he was thinking about something. Her stomach lurched. She held on to the side of the sink. Look up, Billy, she willed him. Look up and see me.

But then she saw Billy's hand move to the small of Selena's back, steering her inside the shop. Selena was laughing, saying something that Ella couldn't quite catch.

'Mamma.' Behind her, Grace banged her fork on the edge of the table. 'I've eaten four pieces. Ice cream, now?'

*

Fabia turned off the lights and took her handbag from under the counter. She stood for a moment in the centre of the shop, looking at the dim shapes of the dresses hanging on the rails, the shoes arranged in pairs on the little tables as if waiting for someone to ask them for the next dance, the velvet busts wearing their hats and headpieces at jaunty angles. She remembered how the teenage Ella had once confessed that she'd liked to lie in bed in the flat above their shop in York and think of the dresses and shoes and gloves and hats in the darkness below taking on a life of their own; how the satin prom skirts would whisper together in a corner and the little veiled and feathered hats would turn snootily away from their neighbours, the cloches and boaters and wool berets; how the sequinned evening shoes would click their heels together and the silk scarves would shake out their careful folds and flutter up to the ceiling like a flock of butterflies.

Fabia smiled. Her San Diego shop would never feel the same as the little place in York, with its three small rooms above, where she and Ella had started out. But over the last few years, she'd filled this new shop with treasures, things she'd shipped over, things she'd found in private sales and markets and, of course, her own special vintage-inspired creations. She'd pinned silk kimonos from the ceiling, their sleeves outspread like the wings of exotic birds, folded lace handkerchiefs into fan shapes and dangled sparkling necklaces and earrings from specially painted branches. There was her sign above the door and a stack of her trademark bags in white card trimmed with simple black ribbon under the counter. This shop didn't have a traditional window as such but wide sills that she could fill with flowers and candles, and the mild Californian weather meant that she could use the porch space to advertise, creating little arrangements of shoes and gloves and hats on a table draped with a silk piano shawl.

This past year, thanks to her connections with Katrina Cushworth, now the star of *Reputation* and other box office hits, she'd dressed several actresses for red-carpet events in LA.

Yes, Katrina had done well for herself, as Fabia had always thought she might. That girl had been given such an awful start in life but, after Jean Cushworth had fallen ill, Fabia had been able to take Katrina under her wing a little. And it turned out that Katrina's father was very well connected, getting her all sorts of auditions before she was even out of drama school. It all made perfect sense now. Katrina, the actress, the consummate performer. But she was happy, with a very nice husband, very good-looking. And she'd never forgotten Fabia.

David had grinned to see Fabia described by the *San Diego Sun,* when they photographed her behind her counter in one of her own polka dot tea dresses, as 'a sought-after stylist and designer to the stars'.

'You see? What goes around come around,' he'd said.

But would she miss any of this whilst she was away? The truth was, she didn't know. She felt – how did Americans say it? – *in two minds* about it.

America, as she'd always hoped, was a place where you could leave the past behind. Whilst York creaked under centuries of history, San Diego still felt mostly new, even in the Old Quarter among the Victorian street lights and Colonial-style buildings. And yet, on evenings like this one, when she stood on the shop's porch or on the deck of her beautiful house in La Jolla with its perfect view of the ocean, Fabia could still feel the pull of the past. At night, she felt the shape of the ocean in the dark, shifting and rolling, whispering her name, just as the River Ouse had once flowed through her dreams, urging her on, stretching itself beneath her. Had it really been less than a decade ago that she'd heard the river's voice reaching down inside her – *run, Fabia, run, run* – away from York and David? It felt like another lifetime. Back then, she'd thought that she'd known what she was running from. Those words, the cruel words that had always seemed to follow her everywhere: *stranger, foreigner, who do you think you are?*

But now she lived in a place where almost everyone was a kind of stranger. It wasn't just the tourists passing through the Old Town and the business people crowding the hotels, but the Mexicans making the journey every day across the border from Tijuana, some of them living illegally in the shadows, some of them, like Rosita, now settled here comfortably, opening restaurants and stores full of handicrafts and souvenirs and fine jewellery. David's colleagues at the hospital were from India and China and Poland and even Iran, as well as from far across the great expanse that was America. Yes, this was a place where anyone could reinvent themselves.

And yet still, in her dreams, she felt the dark water rising again, floating her forwards into the lure of a different future. Perhaps, after all, she wasn't running from anything. Perhaps she was simply not meant to settle down. Maybe a part of her would always be that girl in Tehran, begging Maadar-Bozorg for a pair of red ballet shoes, feeling this same rhythm tugging at her elbows and prodding her between the shoulder blades: *Run, Fabia. Don't look back. Keep moving . . .*

Tonight she could feel the darkness closing in again and the far-off sound of that old music. Was it simply that the Day of the Dead was drawing closer, that time when people here believed that the membrane between the worlds of the living and the lost ones grew thinner, when restless ghosts slipped through the gaps?

Outside, she watched the strings of lights blink on, twining around the trunks of the palm trees and twinkling between the buildings. On the corner of the street, two small boys played with firecrackers, sending sparks jumping across the pavement.

She scooped up the paper bag of gifts she'd bought to take back to England with her and tucked it under her arm. There were tin skulls decorated with roses from Rosita's shop and papier mâché skeletons with long thigh bones and lopsided grins from the touristy general store. Grace would enjoy those – and Billy too. There were Mexican earrings in silver and turquoise for Billy's mum and coral bracelets for old friends. And then finally there was a book of Amerindian creation myths for Ella, with exquisite woodcut illustrations.

Fabia closed the door and turned the key in the lock. A movement in the shadows made her jump, her hand flying to her throat. A familiar figure leaned on the porch railing, his blond hair gleaming in the carnival lights.

'David! You scared me half to death!'

David grinned. 'Sorry. But I wanted to surprise you. Come on. I'm taking you out for a celebratory dinner.'

'Celebratory?'

'Yep. We're celebrating the fact that in just a little while, now, you'll be with Ella and Grace – and Billy, of course – and having a wonderful time.'

Fabia smiled.

'But won't you miss me?' She pretended to look hurt.

'Of course. Which is why I'm determined to make the most of you, whilst I've still got you all to myself.' He looked at her in that way that he had, a smile playing around the corners of his mouth. 'I mean, I'm not even entirely sure that you'll come back.'

A scribble of green, a shimmer of yellow. David's Signals darted around them in the dark. Sometimes it was as if he knew exactly what she was thinking. Fabia knotted the arms of her little cashmere cardigan defensively around her shoulders.

'What do you mean? Don't be silly, David.'

'Oh, c'mon. Isn't it time you admitted it? You miss York like crazy.' He was covering. His voice was playful but she could detect the serious note.

'I do not.'

'Yes, you do.'

'I do not. Well, I miss Ella and Grace. That's true, but –'

'But you do miss the *place* too, if you're really honest. The old shop, your old life, the one you'd built for you and Ella, before I came along to complicate it all.' He grinned again.

She smiled back. 'David, don't be silly. You know that's not true. Not at all.' But even as she said the words, she realised that he was at least partly right. 'Of course, I'll come back.'

'Will you?'

She couldn't see his face properly in the darkness but she could hear the concern in his voice.

He was holding her at arms' length now under the street lamp. 'Stay there a minute. I want to get a good look at you. So that I can remember.'

'Remember what?'

'Tonight.' He held up an imaginary camera. '*Click*. There. Captured for all time.'

He turned away, opening the passenger door of his silver Corvette, parked illegally at the kerb. 'Your carriage awaits,' he said, making a little mock bow and then, as he tucked her into the seat, 'So is there any place in particular you'd like to go?'

'Eduardo's,' she said, without hesitation.

He put back his head and laughed.

'Good job I've made a reservation for us then, isn't it?'

The road to La Jolla curved white under the light of an almost full moon. Fabia let the scent of salt and pine and the end of summer blow through her. Later they sipped ice-cold margaritas on Eduardo's terrace and talked their way through platters of shellfish and fresh green salads, watching the ocean glittering beneath them.

'Fancy a stroll?' David's face was boyish with eagerness. They walked down through the town to the cove and took off their shoes and walked barefoot over the damp sand.

'Fabia, can I ask you something? I've wanted to say this for so long. Never really managed to pluck up the courage. But now that you're going, well, something tells me that I'm a fool not to have said it before.'

She hadn't seen it coming. A blur of black and silver, the rasp of the pine trees, the sound of the ocean calling her again: *Fabia, Fabia, it's time* . . .

She watched David fumble in the folds of the jacket he was carrying slung over his arm.

He stopped and took her hand. 'It's just that, Fabia, I've always wanted you to be happy. That's all I want. To make you happy, I mean. Because that's what you deserve. I haven't ever wanted to . . . well, *press* you, I suppose. I haven't ever really been sure how you felt about it all. But I'd hate you to go without knowing . . . *really* knowing how important you are to me.'

Fabia reached up to touch the side of his face. His cheek was smooth and pale in the moonlight.

'David, I know. And you *do* make me happy –'

That was when he dropped onto one knee in the sand and looked up at her, holding a small red box on his open palm. 'Fabia, you don't have to answer now. You can take your time. But I want to ask you if you'd possibly . . . that is, if you'd consider at all at some point . . . well, marrying me?'

*

Ella shifted her position on the imitation velvet upholstery and watched as, on the other side of the room, Laura beckoned the barman to lean in closer.

Friday night and the place was heaving. Laura was already tipsy after her first glass of wine and Ella felt nervy and irritable.

'You promised,' she hissed at Florence. 'You bloody promised.'

Florence shrugged. But it was true. She'd been insistent.

'I'm organising a night out,' she'd said. 'You, me and Laura and I'm not taking "no" for an answer. Don't worry. It'll all be very sedate. That new place, Cafe What's-It. And I promise I'll get you home before you turn into a pumpkin.'

'Carriage,' Ella had said. 'It's the carriage that . . . Look, can't we just get a couple of bottles of wine or something, round at your place?'

'No.' Florence had almost shouted down the phone. 'Steve's actually going to be at home for an entire week. We are DEFINITELY going out.'

Now Laura was weaving towards them with three more glasses of wine.

'Oops,' she said, giggling and launching herself in the direction of their booth.

Florence rescued two of the glasses from her hands. 'The wine! Don't waste the wine, Laura!'

Ella took a sip of her Sauvignon. She shot another look at Florence and pulled at the strap of her top. She'd borrowed it – from Florence, of course – and it was slightly too loose at the front, made of some slippery, silky stuff that kept sliding off her shoulder.

The bar was full of women. They were beautiful, she thought. Beautiful and young. This one, just coming in through the glass double doors, looked like something out of a magazine: long, bare legs in one of those short all-in-one things. What were they called? A playsuit? Hair and make-up perfect. A group of more young girls at the bar smiled and waved her over.

I don't belong here, thought Ella. I never did. Not even when I was that age.

She looked up at the cluster of enormous, red Japanese-style lanterns suspended from the vaulted ceiling. Then she looked down at the mirrored floor, edged with tiny blue-white lights. It all made her feel slightly dizzy.

Next to her, Laura nudged her arm and said something that was impossible to make out over the music. Florence thrust a menu in a blue leatherette case into her hands and jabbed at it with a glittery gold fingernail.

But Ella had already looked. It wasn't real food. *Nibbles*, the menu announced. *Sharing plates.*

What she really fancied was a proper meal. One of Billy's curries. A big bowl of pasta with lemon and basil and parmesan.

For possibly the fiftieth time this evening she looked at her phone, checked that she had reception. What was wrong with her? She knew that Grace would be more than fine. She'd left her racing a wind-up mermaid and a penguin around the bath, Billy adjudicating, beer in hand. They probably wouldn't even notice she was gone.

As she looked up again she met the eye of a man leaning by the bar. He smiled. She smiled back. And then she caught herself. It was the customer from last weekend. The one buying the present for his girlfriend. But there was no sign of a woman with him. He was surrounded by guys, all clinking beer glasses and toasting something. And now this man was raising his glass in her direction. She couldn't see properly from here. The lights were making her eyes go blurry. But it looked a bit like he was winking at her. What did you do in this kind of situation? Had she given him the wrong idea?

She clutched wildly at Florence's arm. 'I've got to get out of here,' she mouthed.

Florence screwed up her face. 'What? Can't hear you?'

There was a flurry of activity from outside, the bouncers parting to allow someone up the steps, and then a woman swept through the glass doors. Ella swallowed hard. Her heart thudded in her throat. It couldn't be, could it?

Blonde hair swept back from her face. Chiselled profile. Long legs in skinny grey jeans, and black suede boots. The group of guys, including her customer, turned and looked.

But it wasn't. It wasn't her. Ella was furious with herself. Why was she seeing Selena everywhere, imagining her everywhere, thinking about how she might bump into her every time she set foot outside the shop door?

It was getting ridiculous. She'd only ever seen her once, from an upstairs window. She needed to just calm down.

Oh, God. The customer guy was coming over to them now. His eyes locked on hers. She swallowed. She could feel her heart banging above the music.

He reached the edge of their table.

'Hi,' he said, smiling at her, nodding at Florence and Laura. 'I just wanted to come over and thank you. For the book. My girlfriend loved it. Really loved it. You got me major brownie points, I can tell you.'

Ella swallowed again. 'Oh, that's brilliant. I'm so glad. Did she have a nice birthday?'

'Yeah, great. *Really* great, in fact.' He paused. He seemed to be about to say something else and then thought better of it. 'Anyway, I hope you ladies have a lovely evening.'

He made a little bow and turned on his heels.

'He seems very nice,' Laura said into her wine glass.

'He *so* fancies you, El,' Florence snorted. 'Bloody hell. *And* he's gorgeous.'

Ella felt her stomach contract. She punched Laura in the arm. 'Don't be an idiot,' she said. 'I must be about ten years older than him.'

'So?' Florence raised an eyebrow.

Laura studied the menu again. 'I'm starving,' she said. 'I've got to eat something before I pass out or just make a total fool of myself. I'll go and order for us. By the way, what do you think of the barman?'

Ella tried not to meet Florence's eye. They both worried about Laura. She seemed to have this internal heat-seeking device that could home in on a completely unsuitable man in five seconds flat.

'I think, my love,' said Laura, reaching over Ella and patting Laura's arm, 'that he's a professional bloody flirt. I think that there might be slightly more suitable candidates here that you could choose.'

'Like where?' said Laura. 'Because I don't see any.'

They all surveyed the room.

Ella looked through Laura's eyes at the cluster of young guys by the bar, the booth of suited office workers who immediately turned their heads in their direction.

'Oh, God. Don't make eye contact,' Florence said.

Over in the corner was a glossy, white grand piano around which a hen party – women with pink feather boas and rhine-stoned T-shirts – were gathered. One of them started to dance a slow, drunken dance, holding her glass above her head. Two of the suited men got up and made their way over to her.

Florence rolled her eyes. 'OK. Point taken.'

'How about him? Dark hair, leather jacket, over by the door?' Ella stopped herself from pointing. They watched as the man crossed the floor to where a lovely young woman in a skimpy silver top was waiting for him.

'Oh, God. She's *SO MUCH YOUNGER* than him.' Laura shook her head. 'You see? You see what I mean? It's impossible to meet anyone in a bar. They're all either complete tossers or already with someone. Not exactly *daddy* material.' She took another gulp of wine. 'I may as well just get drunk. I mean, what's the point?'

Ella heard herself making soothing noises. But it was true. There was a thought that had been growing in the back of her mind, a horrible thought, all dark and jagged, and now with the wine, it was getting bigger all the time that she sat here. What if Billy left her, like Laura's husband had done? Would she ever find anyone else? In a couple of years' time she'd be thirty, like Laura. And Laura was right. Who was interested in a perman-ently exhausted woman in her thirties with young children, bills to pay and everything getting a bit, well, droopy?

It wasn't right. It was completely bloody unfair, of course. But it was how it was, how things worked.

'What about internet dating?' Florence's voice was artificially bright.

Laura pulled a face. 'You wouldn't know,' she said. 'You haven't had to do it. They all lie about their age. They're all looking for sixteen-to-twenty-five-year-olds. It's . . . a *nightmare*.'

Ella's phone flashed. She pounced on it, eagerly. A text. From Billy.

All fine here. G in bed no problem. Don't worry. Hope you're having fun. Love you xxx

'Everything OK?' Laura looked concerned.

'Yes. More than.' Ella was immediately flooded with guilt. She was being ridiculous. Ridiculous and selfish.

She turned to her friend. 'You know, Laura, you are so lovely. Beautiful and funny and . . . and clever and *kind*. And you're a great mum. And one day soon someone's going to come along who really bloody values that. Someone who actually deserves you.'

Florence raised her glass. 'I'll drink to that,' she said.

12

To remove obstacles: At the crossing of three roads, take a small handful of dirt and put it in your pocket. Leave at once and do not look back.
– Miss Mary's Book of Dreams

'Best 'shrooming ever.' Billy set the carrier bag carefully on the kitchen table. 'We found absolutely *loads* this year.'

'Chanterelles!' Ella turned one admiringly on her palm. 'Look, Grace. What's this that Daddy's brought home?'

She held her hand out for Grace to see – the creamy dome, the fluted undersides, the frilled edges. If it wasn't for the crumbs of soil clinging to the stem, she thought, you'd think that it was something from under the sea. You could imagine its rubbery shape opening and closing like a mouth.

Grace prodded at it with a fingertip and then shrugged and turned back to her toy cars.

'She's unimpressed by my treasure,' said Billy, pretending to look hurt. 'Seriously, El. The woods are full of them this year. I've never seen anything like it. A real bumper crop.'

Ella hung over the carrier bag and breathed. There was the scent of loam, tangled tree roots, secrets.

'One *risotto extraordinario* coming up, then,' she said, taking out their biggest pan, setting it on the stove.

As she boiled water and chopped onions and celery, Billy sat at the kitchen table, sipping at a glass of red wine.

'It was quite an afternoon,' he said. 'Selena knows just about everything it's possible to know about mushrooms. Like a

121

walking mushroom-pickers' field guide, she was. Told me that her grandmother used to cook up chanterelles to make some kind of poultice, that she claimed they had antibiotic properties. I thought of you and your new interest.' He winked at her over the rim of his wine glass.

'Selena?' Ella tried to keep the surprise out of her voice.

'Yeah, she loves that kind of thing.' Billy swirled the wine around his glass.

'I didn't realise she was going to be there. I wouldn't have thought it was her scene. She looks . . . well, more sophisticated.'

Billy raised an eyebrow. 'I didn't know you'd ever met her?'

Ella felt her face flush.

'Yes, I – um . . .' She nodded over to the window. 'The other day. When you had your symposium thingy in the shop. I was standing at the sink. I saw her waiting.'

Billy smiled. 'Right. Well, yes, I suppose she does come across a bit like that, doesn't she? And believe me, at work she takes no prisoners. But she has a much softer side as well. She's much gentler, once you get to know her better.'

'Really?' Ella felt that contraction in her chest again, as if someone had taken her heart and squeezed it. She turned back to the stove and continued to stir.

She thought of Selena LaSalle, her long, blonde hair blowing around her face, the way that her pert little bottom would have looked, encased in denim – designer, probably – as she strode through the woods ahead of Billy.

She took a mouthful of wine from her glass, rolling the velvety texture of grape skins around on her tongue, then threw a ladleful of stock into the pan, listening for the fizz against the hot metal, moving the wooden spoon in circles. Usually, she loved Sundays like this one, winter rubbing itself against the darkening windows and the three of them held close inside the kitchen's glow. But now it was as if something alien had crept in, sidling between the lazy heat of the stove and the wine tilting ruby-red in Billy's hand. A false note. A glimpse of something half seen. Those words: *sophisticated, softer, gentler* . . . What was he doing, getting to know Selena better? She hated herself for the envy she felt spreading under her ribs. People were wrong about envy, she thought. It wasn't green. At least, this feeling wasn't. It was a dirty yellow colour.

As they sat and ate, Billy splashing more wine into her glass and mumbling appreciative noises through each mouthful, she felt that something had changed. The little flashes of instinct she'd been having. Maybe they weren't just a product of her over-active imagination, after all. Maybe she really couldn't ignore them any longer. This was how things started, wasn't it? Affairs. Infidelities. One person too preoccupied or self-absorbed, look-ing the other way; the other finding novelty in someone else, in *getting to know them.*

'You know, Billy, I wouldn't have minded going 'shrooming with you. I'd have quite liked it, in fact.' She held a spoonful of the rice and mushroom mixture on her tongue and felt a wave of sadness flow through her.

'Really? You would? Sorry, El. I never thought. Actually, I didn't realise it was going to be so good this year. So many people. I thought it would just be a few old blokes and me. Usually is.'

Ella concentrated on chewing. Inside her mouth, there was a quiver of excitement that she could feel distinctively as Billy's. It was as if his eagerness had rubbed off on his fingers as he gently pulled the mushrooms from the ground. There was a faint tang of old leaves and then a slightly metallic taste that she remembered from way back in her childhood, when she used to stand outside and catch raindrops on her tongue. And something beneath that, too. Small, dry granules. If she had a word for it, it would be something like *longing*.

She saw, in her mind's eye, a mushroom growing in the dark earth, speeded up as if on one of those time-lapse films, its pale mouth reaching hungrily for the light.

She saw Billy taking a mushroom from Selena's perfectly manicured hand, a flicker of thinly disguised desire passing between their fingers.

'Is it OK?' she said. 'This risotto, I mean. I think it tastes a bit overdone.'

'Delicious.' Billy laid down his fork with a satisfied sigh, smiling at Grace who was determinedly spooning rice between her lips and scattering it onto the table. 'Delicious, Gracie, no? Mummy's excelled herself, I'd say. I think I'll help myself to a bit more, if that's OK?'

'Of course.' Ella waved her fork. 'It won't keep.'

What was wrong with her? It was crazy. The food cloyed in her mouth. It was as if she could separate out all the layers that had gone into growing those chanterelles – earth, rainstorms, sunlight. And then something else. Billy's *feelings*?

She remembered how Mamma always talked to the plants on her windowsill, whispered conversations of encouragement: *Grow, little plant, grow. Reach for the sun. Drink it all up, that's right.* Her pots of basil and chives grew glossy and fragrant, their thick leaves lasting months, and she always claimed it was because of the words they soaked up with their daily watering.

But this? This was something else. She'd never heard of anyone being able to taste *emotions* before.

'Oh, Billy,' she snapped. 'Look at the mess you've made now. You've dropped it all over the top of the cooker.' She sprang up from the table and scrubbed angrily at the sticky globules. 'Why can't you at least *try* not to be so clumsy all the time?'

Later, when Billy had tucked Grace up in bed and lay sprawled across the sofa with the Sunday papers, Ella stood alone in front of the open fridge.

First, she dug a spoon into a jar of peanut butter and lifted it to her mouth. Nothing. Next, she chewed on a slither of her favourite Manchego cheese. Clean grass dotted with tiny yellow flowers, a little breeze, scented with spring. She let the flavours separate on her tongue: the oak wood barrel where the curds had been kept, the creamy milk, still warm from the cow, the faintest whiff of an enamelled milk pail. But no emotion. Nothing.

She wrapped up the cheese and thrust it back in the cheese box. What a total idiot she was. As if such a thing was actually possible, anyway.

But she lay that night, listening to the rhythm of Billy's breathing, going over and over things in her mind. It was true that she'd been neglectful recently, so wrapped up in her own struggle with herself that she hadn't really noticed how Billy was feeling. Could she really blame him if he'd begun to look for some attention elsewhere? There'd been that late-night meeting last week. He'd come home a little worse for wear, saying he'd gone to the pub with the lads, had one pint too many. What if all the time he'd been with Take-No-Prisoners Selena? And what about the conference in Rome that was coming up in a couple of months' time? Hadn't he said that Selena was co-presenting something with him? That meant that they'd be staying in the same hotel for four days and three nights. Probably booked on the same flights. Was she right to be worried about that?

The next morning, she was up at six, making porridge in the microwave, hesitantly lifting the spoon to her lips and tasting, with relief, the hot, fresh taste of the oats.

'Morning, early bird.' Billy put his arms around her as she stood at the sink, rinsing her bowl. 'Sleep OK?'

'Not really.' Her skin under his fingers prickled with irritation.

'Is there something on your mind, El?'

She turned to look at him then, into his calm blue-grey eyes that were so like Grace's. She nearly asked him. She wanted to come right out with it: *Are you having an affair?* But the words seemed too ridiculous to say out loud, too painfully needy. Just give it a bit longer, she thought. Chances are, it's nothing at all. Something will happen, he'll do something or say something and then I'll know for sure that it was all just my imagination.

'Nothing,' she said, gently pushing his arms away. 'Just tired. And I'm late opening up. Got a big delivery arriving today.'

Billy frowned. 'I've been thinking. Do you want to go out one evening this week? Just the two of us?'

'You mean, like a date night?'

Billy grinned. 'I s'pose it would be, yes. But I think you need a break. I'd like to take you somewhere nice. And we could get my mum to babysit. In fact, we haven't done that in ages, have we, El?'

She shook her head. She could feel that black feeling opening up inside her again. She tried to swallow it down.

'Yes. OK. I mean, I guess –'

'You don't seem very keen.'

Billy was watching her, that worried look on his face.

'No, it's just. I'm being silly. I . . . God, just ignore me, OK? I'm ridiculous at the moment.' She forced a laugh. How could she say that everything felt all wrong? That she was worried that he was just being extra thoughtful because he felt guilty? That she was too tired? That she didn't have anything to wear? 'Yes. OK.' She arranged her face into a smile. 'But what day, then?'

'I'll call my mum, sort something out.' Billy grinned, bent to kiss Grace on the top of the head, took his work bag from the peg on the back of the kitchen door. 'Right. Good. That's settled. Date night.'

*

'I hated it.' Kate flung the paperback onto the table in front of her. 'Absolutely hated it. What is it with this Christa woman? She was so damn passive, so *irritating*. I just wanted to take her by the shoulders, tell her to get a grip, take control of her god-damn life.'

Beside her, Ella felt Florence bristle. She and Kate usually clashed over the books. But it was Laura who spoke first.

'I think that's a bit harsh. I mean, she'd doing her best. It's really hard for her. She's all on her own with all those children in the middle of nowhere, this man has been an absolute pig to her, quite frankly . . . So what's she supposed to do? Just suddenly go out and grab herself a pair of high heels and some high-powered job? How? It's not actually that easy. Who'd look after the baby?'

At the sound of Laura's voice, Harry woke up and started to cry. Laura coloured. 'Shush, now,' she said, bouncing him up and down in her arms. 'Shush.'

'Well, look, I didn't mean –' Kate shrugged.

'No, I agree,' Florence cut in. 'I think the story works *precisely* because we see how difficult it is for Christa. How trapped she is. It speaks to so many women's lives. It's – complicated.'

'And what about Emma?' Sarah thumbed through her copy, looking for the right page. 'You know, I really love that bit where – does anyone remember the bit I mean? – where Emma is looking out of the window and she sees Christa, pushing her buggy down the street, and she thinks that she should go and say "hello" but she feels like she can't. I thought that was so well done. Such beautiful writing. How we can feel like it's just too much distance to cross between our own life and someone else's. How we're all having the same experiences and yet we're afraid to share that and so we end up feeling completely isolated.'

Ella found herself nodding. She glanced over at Grace and Alfie, who were playing happily in the Children's Corner. They each had police helmets on. Grace's had slipped endearingly over one eye.

'But I suppose I hated the way that Christa just lets this woman walk all over her.' Kate shook her head. 'She basically swoops in and steals her husband, her life . . . everything. And Christa doesn't actually *do* anything. So I found it hard to feel much sympathy for her. I wanted her to at least *fight* for it.'

'But that's just it,' said Florence. 'She's so ground down by it all. She's so completely knackered. She does what she can but –' Her hand mimed something fluttering off into the distance. 'It's already gone.'

'Well, yes,' said Sarah, in her usual thoughtful way. 'I really wanted to *hate* Samantha. I mean, obviously, she's the villain. She's supposed to be a real bitch. But I couldn't hate her, in the end. Because she's just as needy and insecure as the other women. I thought that was what was so clever about the writing.'

'Yes, the person we should really get angry with is the husband,' said Florence. 'But he's just weak and vain. Not a very interesting character at all.'

Ella stood up. Everyone seemed to look in her direction. 'Sorry. Just going to put some more coffee on.'

She felt Florence's eyes follow her as she went over to the cafe area, scooped coffee beans from the tin. She tried to shake off the effect of the words on her mood. The conversation was too close to the bone for her this morning. And for once, she found herself agreeing with Kate. She hadn't liked the book much either, but she hadn't quite been able to put her finger on why.

She turned. Florence's steady gaze met hers. What *was* this? Did Florence know something?

She hit the button on the coffee grinder. Its familiar buzz calmed her nerves.

*

'You look fantastic, El.' Billy poured wine into her glass. 'Really fantastic.'

'Thanks.' Despite herself, she felt that familiar flush starting at the base of her neck. 'You don't look so bad yourself.'

It was true. She was aware, as they'd got older, that women looked at Billy in a certain way.

'He's the kind of man that grows into his looks,' Mamma had always said. And, sure enough, that tall, skinny boy with the long legs and bony wrists had become a stronger, more athletic-looking man. His hair was still thick and black, although he kept it cut much shorter now. But it was his eyes that you noticed first. Blue and full of mischief. They were twinkling at her now as she reached for her glass.

'It's weird, this, isn't it?' She looked around the room, a proper grown-up restaurant, with dimmed lighting and tealights on the tables and some kind of jazz on the speakers. Not a family in sight, just couples like them. 'It feels like something – or should I say *someone's* – missing.'

Billy nodded. 'But we should have done this ages ago. We should make a regular thing of it, you and me. Mum was only too happy to help out.'

Ella thought of how much she missed Mamma. Billy's mum was lovely, of course, but it didn't feel quite the same, somehow, leaving Grace with her other granny for the evening. She'd Skyped Mamma just a couple of hours ago. The connection had been a bit crackly, dropping in and out, and she'd seemed particularly far away.

'Mum, what can I wear?' she'd said. 'Nothing fits me anymore. Nothing. I don't have stuff for a fancy restaurant.'

Mamma had laughed. 'I never thought I'd hear this,' she'd said. 'Not ever.'

'What? Me seeking fashion advice?'

'Exactly. But the thing is, *tesora*, you've just got to be yourself. That's what Billy wants, after all. *You* are the woman he fell in love with.'

Ella hadn't said anything about her fears, about Selena and all the worries that were creeping in.

'So, jeans, then?' she'd said.

Mamma had looked doubtful. 'Well, do you have nice ones? That you can wear with a little heel, perhaps?'

'See? Exactly. That's what I'm saying.'

'OK. Well, maybe . . . No, you'll get annoyed with me –'

'Go on.'

'Well, up in the wardrobe, there are still a few of Eustacia's dresses . . .'

Ella had smiled. The wonderful Eustacia. The woman whose family had once gifted Mamma an entire wardrobe of beautiful vintage clothes, each carefully catalogued. That all seemed like a lifetime ago.

'You mean the swirly patterned one, don't you?'

It was perhaps the only dress that Ella had ever lusted after. She remembered sneaking up to the bedroom and holding it against herself in the mirror.

'Yes. The Missoni. It's so . . . well, *you*. And it's different. Unique, in fact. And actually, you won't want to hear this, *tesora*, but it's actually very on trend. There's a very bohemian vibe around at the moment. Folksy. Lots of embroidery and colour. You could wear it with ankle boots. Those nice black ones with the wedge. You'll look adorable. *And* sexy.'

And, of course, Mamma had been right.

When Ella fished the dress from the back of the wardrobe and put it on, it was perfect. The colours were interesting but not garish in any way. The bold swirls of the silk chiffon skimmed her body in all the right places so that it was flattering and hung just so. It didn't feel too tight; she didn't have to keep pulling at it. She'd pinned her hair up in a kind of chignon thing, the way she'd seen Florence do sometimes, and in the bottom of a drawer, next to one of Grace's old dummies and a Lego princess figure, she'd found a pair of earrings with jade beads that Mamma had once given her.

When she'd walked into the kitchen, all dressed and ready to go, Grace had clapped her hands excitedly and Billy had wolf-whistled.

'You look bea-*uuu*-tiful, Mamma,' Grace had said. And Billy's mum had smiled.

So now here they were, she and Billy, looking at one another over a flickering flame and a blue glass vase containing a single gerbera. But Ella couldn't think of anything to say. Except how the bathroom light needed fixing and should she order some new cups for the cafe corner – a few of them were chipped – and Grace had a new teacher at playgroup and a customer had ordered twelve copies of an obscure poetry collection for Christmas presents. My God. Her life was so thrilling.

'So,' Billy said. 'Tell me more about this Miss Mary hunt. Your customer. The one who wants to track down her cottage. Shall we do it? Shall we go?' He actually looked eager. 'It might be something good for us all to do together as a family? What do you think?'

Something was nagging at the back of Ella's mind, a thought like an aching tooth. She wanted to run her tongue over it. Instead, she nodded. 'OK. That's a good idea. I'll suggest it. Next time she comes in.'

In the shower earlier, she'd thought that perhaps she could ask him about Selena, probe him, very casually, without alerting him to her concerns. But now she could feel the wine already making her head foggy.

And what was she supposed to say, anyway? *Billy do you still fancy me? Do you find me the slightest bit interesting anymore?* How embarrassing would that be?

Instead, she leaned back in her chair and tried to let the music flow over her.

Later, she lay next to him in their bed, the covers drawn up to her chin.

He rolled over and placed a hand on her stomach, nuzzled his nose into her neck. His breath smelled of wine. His hair tickled her ear.

She breathed in, tensing her stomach muscles.

'Relax,' he said. 'Just relax.'

'Billy.' Her voice was barely a whisper in the darkness. 'I'm *soooo* tired. And Grace will be up in less than five hours.'

'OK, OK. Sorry.' He rolled over and, within seconds, he was snoring.

13

To overpower an enemy: On a waxing moon, pluck a single hair
from the person's head and bury it under a hawthorn hedge.
– Miss Mary's Book of Dreams

Ella reached into the pocket of Billy's jacket, pushing her hand to the bottom. She drew out a balled-up tissue and the key to the office cycle lock-up.

Her heart beat loudly in her throat. She could hear the sound of Grace's laughter in the next room, her voice raised in delighted protest. 'Stop it, Daddy. Stop it.'

Billy was sprawled with her on the living room rug, playing Snakes and Ladders. He was probably cheating. It was only a matter of time before Grace came to find her.

She tried the other pocket. Her fingers closed over a thin slip of paper. Her heart missed a beat. But when she drew it out, it was only a receipt from the university library canteen. One coffee, one sandwich.

Even though she was standing alone in the cupboard under the stairs, Ella felt her face burn. How could it have come to this? This suspicious scrabbling in Billy's pockets? The surreptitious checking of his phone, which he was always leaving on the kitchen table or on the floor by the bed? Hardly the behaviour of a man with something to hide. But then there had been a couple of texts recently. From this Selena person. She had memorised each of them:

Lovely to see you today. We shld have a drink some time. x

Sorry you couldn't make it. We missed you. x

And the most recent, sent at 10.31 a.m. last Monday, which was right after the weekend of their date night:

Like the new haircut. xxx

Ella had felt sick when she'd read that one. So it hadn't all been just her imagination. That was definitely flirting. No two ways about it. There had been no reply from Billy. At least, not one that she could see. But who's to say that he hadn't replied in person? Their offices were just down the hall from one another.

And the worst thing about it was that, when she'd checked Billy's phone yesterday, the texts had disappeared. All of them. And why would he delete them if they were completely innocent?

She knew that she was probably being stupid. Her imagination was running away with her. The most likely explanation was that he'd got rid of them because he didn't want Ella to be hurt by them or because he was embarrassed. Perhaps this woman was being inappropriate. Perhaps he'd told her to stop. Over the years that they'd been together, women had occasionally got the wrong idea. There'd been that woman who started to come into the shop, asking for Billy. She'd been mortified when she'd discovered that Ella was Billy's wife. Billy was kind to people. He listened. He was interested in what they had to say. But she'd never seen him flirt. Not once. And he always told her everything. They didn't have secrets from one another, did they?

This was Billy, after all. Kind, generous, reliable, totally sensible Billy. The one person she'd always trusted above all others, even Mamma. Mamma got emotional sometimes. She didn't always see things clearly. But Billy – Billy was usually right about things.

However hard she tried, though, she couldn't stop thinking about it. *Like the new haircut. xxx*

She thought of last Sunday, how she'd spread the old sheet in the living room and cut Billy's hair. She'd always done it for him, ever since they'd first moved in together, when Billy was still doing his PhD and they were just getting the shop going, when they'd been so hard up that they didn't have seven pounds for the barber's. And then the habit had just stuck. Once a month, on a Sunday night, when Grace was in bed, she'd unfold the sheet, spread it on the floor, bring a chair from the kitchen and Billy would sit patiently while she snipped. A few times, she'd suggested that they didn't have to do it anymore, that he could try the Turkish place on Monkgate.

He'd just grinned. 'Don't spoil my fun, El. No one would ever do it as well as you,' he'd said, taking the scissors from her hand, kissing her full on the mouth.

Now, thinking about how Billy's hair felt in her fingers, her eyes blurred with tears. Seeing this Selena woman – and what kind of name was that, anyway? – talking about his hair like that made this precious thing, *their* thing, the thing they'd shared together for so long, feel cheap, silly.

Like the new haircut. xxx It was a come-on, an invitation. But maybe she was laughing at her, too? Ella couldn't imagine that a woman like Selena would ever be caught giving a man a haircut. Maybe she was poking fun at Billy's ridiculous wife who still cut his hair.

And maybe it *was* ridiculous.

Ella sighed. She'd tell him that she didn't have time to do it anymore, that it would look better if he had a proper job made of it.

She slipped the jacket back onto its peg. What exactly had she been looking for, anyway?

'Mamma, I need you!' Grace's voice cut in. 'Daddy's winning. Again. It's not fair, Mamma. He's got the dice and he won't give it to me.'

*

'Bottoms up.' Florence handed Ella a glass, chinking her own against it with a flourish. 'Here's to us.'

Ella smiled. 'Why do I always feel like a naughty schoolgirl when I'm with you?'

Florence took a slurp of Sauvignon and wagged her finger disapprovingly in Ella's direction. 'Precisely because you never *were* a naughty schoolgirl,' she said. 'Unlike me, of course.'

It was true, Ella thought. At school, Florence had been one of those effortlessly cool girls. She'd arrived after Ella, right before they were all about to start A-levels. She'd been an outsider too but, unlike Ella, she'd never seemed to care about not fitting in. Back then, at the beginning of Sixth Form, Katrina and Billy had been Ella's only real friends. After all the stuff that had gone on with her mum, Katrina had been a changed person, kinder, less full of herself. It had been almost sad, in some ways, how she'd lost some of the attitude. Her Mum's overdose, her parents eventually splitting up, it had all been a bit of a scandal, wiped that daft smile off her face, as Billy had put it. But she'd been a much nicer friend to Ella as a result.

And then Florence had arrived. Florence Barrault, all the way from Paris, with her French accent and her French way of dressing. Half the Sixth Form had fallen for her, boys and girls. She'd quickly acquired a following, her own in-crowd. They went clubbing in Leeds and hung about on the riverbank, and Florence started a band – Never the Never – in her dad's garage and they got gigs in Manchester and even Camden. Ella wouldn't have dared to speak to her in those days. She would never have risked Florence's scathing sarcasm, for a start.

She could never have guessed, back then, that she and Flo would have ended up all these years later as such close friends.

They'd met at an antenatal class, each of them slightly appalled to find themselves there, glancing at each other, looking away. In the second week of the course, the teacher – a large woman in a voluminous cotton kaftan – had asked the roomful of cross-legged women to relax and close their eyes as she began to read a poem that she'd written herself, dedicated to 'the unborn child'.

'Dear Little One,' she'd begun, in a high sing-song reading-a-poem voice and, in an effort to stifle a giggle, Ella had sneaked a glimpse through her eyelashes at the other mums-to-be, to see Florence sitting bolt upright, her mouth twitching, her chest silently heaving. She'd caught Ella's eye and they'd both had to look away before they embarrassed themselves. But that was the moment that she and Flo became friends.

Since that time, they'd mapped out new motherhood together. The night feeds, Alfie's colic, Grace's projectile vomiting – all of it they'd discussed in minute detail, in one another's living rooms or sometimes over the phone, a baby clamped to one hip. They'd compared notes on everything from baby monitors to breast pumps and complained to one another about leaky milk and sleep deprivation. Florence was the only person besides Billy to whom Ella had confided her feelings of failure after her C-section and her worries about being a completely inadequate mum.

Now Florence pushed aside a pile of ironing and flung herself onto the sofa. 'So, come on,' she said, wincing and removing a handful of Alfie's Lego bricks from behind the cushions. 'Out with it. What's up?'

Despite the wine, which was going straight to her head, Ella felt the gap opening itself again in the pit of her stomach. She held out her glass for a top-up. 'I don't think I've had quite enough of this yet.'

Florence obliged, upending the bottle. 'Come on. Tell Aunty Flo. You'll feel better. You know you will.'

'OK.' Ella took a deep breath. She felt the black empty feeling rise up into her throat so that the words came out in a painful gasp. 'OK. I'll just say it. I think Billy's having an affair . . .'

The words – those sordid little words that she'd hardly dared to say even to herself inside her own mind – now hung in the room between them. To Ella, they looked like splashes of red and green, running down Florence's white-painted walls and pooling stickily on the rug at their feet.

For a long moment, Ella watched Florence's face register shock, then disbelief. Finally, she began to laugh.

'*Billy*? Oh my God, El, darling. It just can't be true. What makes you think –? I mean . . .'

'I know, I know. Billy. Wonderful, devoted, bloody perfect, God-I'm-so-lucky-to-be-married-to-him Billy, right? No one would believe it, would they?' Ella took another slurp of wine. 'Not even you, Flo.' She twisted the stem of the wine glass between her fingers. 'But the truth is, you know, I've not exactly been a barrel of laughs, lately. I mean, living with me is never exactly easy and then, just recently . . . To be honest, I've been struggling a bit. I haven't been there for him at all. You know, to listen to his stuff, ask him about his day, all the things I used to do before Grace came along. And we haven't . . .' She felt her face flush in that way that always betrayed her at the moments when it most mattered. 'Well, we haven't had sex in . . . in *ages*. I can't even remember the last time.'

Florence grinned. 'I'm terribly shocked, darling.' She pulled her most sarcastic face. 'God, I can't even remember the last time Steve and I did it.' Her eyebrows wiggled. 'Come to think of it, that *is* quite awful, isn't it? Hmmm. OK. Maybe *I* should be putting a bit more effort in too.' She gulped her wine. 'But so far, El, this is all just you convincing yourself that you're doing something wrong. There must be more to it.'

'There's this woman at work.' Ella frowned. 'I know. It's such a cliché. But he's started talking about her. And I saw her once, just from the window. She's beautiful and stylish. And she's into everything that Billy's into, I suppose. And she's single. Available. And then, OK I'm going to tell you something *really* bad now – I've started checking his phone. And there were texts –'

'OK.' Florence held up a hand. 'What texts? What did they say?'

'Well, nothing much. I mean, she was flirting with him. I'm sure of it. But then when I looked again he'd deleted them.'

'What did they say exactly?'

'Oh, just stuff about how she liked his . . . don't laugh, his haircut. But it was the *way* she'd written it. You know. Kiss, kiss, kiss.'

Florence scowled into her wine glass. 'That's out of order. Bitch.'

Ella couldn't help smiling. 'Yeah. I know. But I shouldn't even have been looking, should I, really . . .'

'Oh, for God's sake.' Florence rolled her eyes. 'Don't you think I have a sneaky look at Steve's phone from time to time? He's away so much. I have to keep an eye on him. Make sure he's not getting up to anything.'

'Really?' Ella tried to keep her face neutral.

'Yes.' Florence snorted. 'You're such a sweetheart, El. But, you know, show me a woman who *doesn't*. I mean they're all bastards, really, aren't they? Any opportunity . . .'

'You think?' Ella felt that stabbing sensation in her stomach again. 'God. I'm just an idiot, Flo, aren't I? I don't have a clue. And the worst thing is that I can't shake this feeling that he's somewhere else, that it's too late. That I've already lost him.' Ella brushed a tear from her cheek with the sleeve of her sweater. 'Sorry. It's just . . .'

Florence was already kneeling on the rug in front of Ella, taking her hand in hers. 'Now you listen to me, you silly thing,' she said, with mock severity. 'This is just you doing that thing you do. Convincing yourself of stuff that isn't true. Like that time you just *knew* that your book was going to be a total flop because you'd had a dream about it. Remember? You know, the book that became a runaway bestseller and bought you and Billy the flat?'

'Oh, that was *different*, Flo.'

'Was it? Was it *really*? And what about the time those people from the council came to survey the courtyard and you were adamant – absolutely *adamant* – that you were going to lose the lease to the shop. Because you had *a feeling* about it . . .' She squeezed Ella's hand. 'You've got to admit, El. You do tend to imagine the worst. You know you do.'

Ella frowned. She looked down at her feet and wiggled her bare toes deeper into the pile of Flo's rug.

'It seems like every time I come in the room, he's whispering into his phone,' she said. It seemed stupid, a silly little detail when she said it out loud. How could she tell Florence about the Signals or about what she'd tasted in the bloody mushrooms? Florence would think that she'd finally flipped. Gone completely off her trolley. And maybe she had? She didn't know what to believe anymore. She shrugged. 'It's just an instinct. I *know* it. Something isn't right.'

Florence smiled and sat back on her heels. 'Maybe it isn't *quite* right. But that doesn't mean that it's all ruined. I mean, OK. Most men are pretty stupid, and normally I'd be the first to agree with you that it only takes some silly woman to come along and flatter their ego at a moment when they're feeling a bit lost, a bit underappreciated.' She snorted. 'But Billy? He's not like that. He's just not. He's smarter than that, El. He's –'

'OK, OK. You're beginning to sound like Mum now.' Ella pulled her hand from Florence's grip. 'The bloody Billy Fan Club. I mean that's part of it, isn't it? What the hell is he doing with grumpy old me, anyway?'

'Oh. My. God.' Florence frowned. 'We really are down on ourselves right now, aren't we? Look. I'm not saying there's nothing wrong between you two, El.' She made little circles in the air with her glass. 'I'm just saying . . . Well, actually, I don't know what I'm saying, really. I've had too much wine. But don't convince yourself of anything just yet. Take things with a pinch of salt. Look at the bigger picture and . . . and other assorted clichés. OK?'

Despite herself, Ella smiled. 'I do really *want* to believe you –'

'Well, if you can convince yourself of anything, you may as well choose the good stuff.' Florence raised her glass again. 'And that particular little gem is brought to you courtesy of four years of cognitive behavioural therapy.' She winked. 'I've got plenty more where that came from, too.' She waved the wine bottle. 'Another glass?'

14

To let go of great sadness: In times of heavy sorrow, collect a dish of rainwater. Cry into the dish for as long as you have tears. When your tears are all finished, take the water and use it to nurture the plants in your garden. As you water them, tell the plants all that you wish to let go of and your most secret desires for the future.
– Miss Mary's Book of Dreams

Bryony looked up through the glistening branches. It had stopped raining. The earth steamed gently under her feet but the sky was clear and bright above her head and punched through with brilliant stars.

Somewhere behind her she could hear someone squelching through wet leaves. She turned.

'Ella,' she called softly, raising her hand in a wave, but Ella walked on, through the half-dark, between the trees.

Bryony realised that she couldn't see anything. She held her hands out in front of her, clawing at the air. It reminded Bryony of one of those blindfolded games from children's parties. What was it they'd called it? Sardines? Blindman's Buff?

Then another figure stepped out from between the trees, a tall, gangly young man with a mass of damp curls that stuck out all around his head. Could this be Billy? Somehow, she knew that it must be. He was looking away from Ella, his face preoccupied. He crouched down to examine something in the roots of a tree.

Look! she wanted to shout. Open your eyes. Really look at her, before it's too late. She's lost. Don't you see? But when her mouth opened, she found that she couldn't make a sound.

She tried to lift her arm. She wanted to wave at him or perhaps scoop up a small stone and throw it or snap a twig from the branch above her head, anything to get his attention. But she found that her arms were too heavy. They hung useless at her sides.

There was a rustling in the branches and, as she looked up, she felt the cool night air shift against her cheek. It was the bird again. Not the angel bird. No, this one was red and green. An exotic-looking creature. Bigger than a hummingbird, with a tufted head and quick, inquisitive eyes.

The bird perched in the branches, fanning out its long green tail feathers, and began to preen itself. Its beak moved through the tufted crest of feathers on its head, the emerald feathers on its wings and the red breast feathers that flickered like tiny flames. Then slowly, deliberately, it turned to her, its black eyes shining, as if registering her presence for the first time. The beak opened and a voice came out, a soft, deep human voice that made her spine tingle.

'How many times do I have to tell you, Bryony? It's time. It's time to WAKE UP!'

That voice. It cut through the dark, making her hands shake, no matter how hard she tried to hold them to her sides.

Then, with no warning, the bird flew at her, so that she had to put up her hands to defend herself. She watched through her parted fingers as it hovered above her head, its tail feathers bright against the black sky. And then the feathers burst into flame, the bird flaring and hissing like a red and green firework, its tail a comet of fire.

'Wake up, Bryony. Wake up, for God's sake . . .'

Ed was shaking her shoulder roughly. His face was very close so that she could see the bloodshot whites of his eyes.

'*WAKE UP*, Bry. It's just a dream. You're having one of your night terrors, love.'

Bryony opened her mouth and closed it again. She tasted smoke and, just beneath that, something else, something green and fresh and fragrant.

She could still hear that voice, coming out of the bird's open beak, reaching through the night, reaching down deep inside her.

Yes, she thought. Time to wake up. She threw off the duvet and stretched her legs experimentally. She felt a surge of energy travel from her toes to the base of her spine.

'It's OK, Ed. I'm perfectly fine,' she said, turning to him and smiling. And the funny thing was, Bryony thought, as she turned the dream images over in her mind, that she really was OK. For the first time in what felt like a very long time, she was wide awake. And she was fine.

And now she knew what she had to do. Somehow, she had to get Ella and Billy to Miss Mary's house.

*

'Are we nearly there, Daddy?'

Grace kicked her legs and sighed.

Ella reached over and stroked her cheek. 'It's OK, poppet. Not long now.' Grace hated being confined to her car seat. And these country roads seemed to take every twist and turn possible as they climbed up through the moors. Ella couldn't quite believe that she'd agreed to this stupid outing. But Billy had been so excited, like a child looking forward to Christmas. And Bryony had been so insistent. Ella hadn't wanted to disappoint either of them.

They'd passed the last village about ten minutes ago and there was nothing to see now except bare hills and gorse. The odd rocky outcrop pushed its way up through the bracken and the trees were low and stunted.

'My goodness. It must be bleak out here in the winter,' Ella said.

'That's the longest three miles *I've* ever driven.' Billy shook his head. 'It must be round here somewhere.'

'There,' said Bryony, pointing out of the window. 'Just down there.' Ella could hear the excitement in her voice. 'That must be it, don't you think?'

Billy pulled over, letting the engine run. Ella leaned forward, peering through the bare hedgerows to where the road bent back on itself and dropped down beside a little stream. There was some kind of building down there. She could just make out the edge of a roof, something that might be a chimney.

'Are we here?' Grace clapped her hands. 'Can I have a biscuit?'

'Could be,' said Billy. 'Let's take a look.'

From the back seat, Ella watched Bryony button her coat and pull on her hat in readiness. She looked happier today. There were high spots of colour in her usually pale cheeks.

She thought of how, if Mamma was here, she'd take Bryony under her wing, seduce her with dresses in bright jewel colours, introduce her to French perfume and beautiful shoes. She'd find a special word for her and sew it into a secret seam: *glimmer* or *unravel* or *sparkle* or *believe*. Or perhaps she'd use the language of herbs and flowers. There was something about Bryony that seemed to inspire that.

She thought again about how they really didn't know much about Bryony at all. And yet, here they all were, driving her around the most isolated parts of the Yorkshire countryside in search of a seventeenth-century ghost.

As they dropped down into the fold of the hill, a low stone cottage swung into view. It nestled under a cluster of gnarled apple trees. Ella could see that it was derelict. There were holes in the roof and part of the wall had crumbled into the garden.

Bryony opened the car door and a blast of cold air hit them.

'Yes, we're here,' she said.

*

As she walked up the path, Bryony saw the blank holes where the cottage windows should be. They stared back at her, giving away nothing.

She turned to see if they were following her. Ella was looking doubtful, clutching Grace's hand.

'Be careful,' she called. 'It might not be safe.'

As Bryony turned back, she imagined that she saw, just for a moment, a flicker of something at the window. The head and shoulders of a woman wrapped in a red woollen shawl, a white face, a tangle of black hair hanging to her shoulders.

She put her hand on the front door. The rotten wood yielded easily to her touch. It swung wide, revealing a stone-flagged floor with weeds growing up between the cracks and one small room, with a large fireplace still intact.

She took a step forwards.

There was a clatter as a bird flew up to the ceiling, its wings beating against the beams. A single black feather floated down in front of her face. There was a hole in the roof, so big that she could see the clouds passing overhead.

She went back out, calling up to where Ella, Billy and Grace still stood huddled on the roadside.

'I think it's OK,' she said.

'Do be careful. Please.' Ella frowned. The wind snatched at her words.

'That roof looks as if it could go at any moment,' Billy said. 'We'll go round to the garden.'

Bryony ducked back through the little doorway and into the kitchen. She crouched and looked at the fireplace, which was still full of ashes. She could imagine a rocking chair drawn up to the fire, a pot hanging from the iron pole.

Outside, she could hear Grace running around in the garden. 'Mummy, Daddy. The wind's blowing me over,' she shouted.

Bryony tried to clear her mind. From her bag, she drew the red, hardback book, her copy of *Miss Mary's Book of Dreams*.

She leafed through to find the page, the exercise that she'd decided to practise first. It was a simple 'tuning in' exercise – what Miss Mary called the 'dream threshold'. Her instructions were simple:

Choose a threshold space and lie down with eyes closed. Some thresholds are more powerful than others. Doors and windows, natural places under the sky, a place where many have walked before or where the living and the dead cross over, at the foot of hills or near water, all these are places of great magic.

Bryony looked at the empty windows. She stood in the fireplace and craned her neck to look up at the blackened chimney.

The mouth and lips are a threshold of the body, between thought and speech. The eyes are a threshold between seeing and divining what is seen. To practise opening the thresholds, you must let your mind be open. You must hold a space for the waking dream, the messages from the deepest self within you – the Divine – to take shape. Your task is not to examine but to be the vessel for receiving these messages. You must yourself become the threshold . . .

She stepped through the empty lintel where the back door would once have hung.

'Grace,' she called. 'Would you like to help me with something?'

*

Ella watched Grace trying to lie as still as she could. Bryony lay next to her in the grass, her legs sticking out comically from the bottom of her coat.

Miss Mary's book lay open between them, the page weighted with a windfall apple.

'Keep still, darling,' Ella whispered.

'My legs keep moving themselves, Mummy,' Grace said. 'I can't help it.'

Ella felt Billy behind her, his arms fastening around her middle, lifting her half off her feet.

'Stop it.' She batted him away, nodding in Bryony's direction.

'Really?' Billy pretended to look hurt. Things had been better between them this last week. Despite her fears. Despite those texts. Maybe Florence had been right, after all. Maybe it really had been her overactive imagination. 'What do you think she's doing?' he said, watching Bryony, stretched out in the grass.

Ella shook her head. 'Trying out one of Miss Mary's exercises, I think.'

Billy's mouth tickled her ear. 'You were right. I think Bryony's a bit mad, isn't she?'

Ella wriggled her shoulders. 'I prefer to say *eccentric*. And also, let's just say that I rather like eccentric people.'

'I knew it.' Billy laughed softly to himself. 'I knew you'd end up getting drawn in.'

Ella punched him on the arm. 'It was *your* idea.'

'True.' He stood behind her, pushing his hands into her jeans pockets. 'But I knew you wouldn't be able to resist.'

*

Bryony tried to still her mind. She was vaguely aware of Grace, shifting next to her, muttering softly to herself. But at the same time, she felt as if she was beginning to drift further and further out, warm waves of pleasure flowing down through her arms and legs and into her toes.

She watched the clouds drifting above the apple trees. The air seemed to lift somehow, blue and bright and wide.

She gazed up through the thick fringe of branches, still heavy with apples and tasselled with fading leaves. Somewhere at the edge of her vision, a pigeon flashed its white wings.

She heard Miss Mary's instructions in her head: *Make a tunnel of your mind. Tune in, as if you were listening to far-off music . . .*

But Bryony knew now that it wasn't closer in that she needed to go but wider, out into the blue air. She let her eyes close and her body settle further into the damp grass, her arms spread at her sides. She felt the prickle of the grass on the backs of her hands and she could almost imagine the expanse of earth beneath her, a great mass of warm darkness, moving barely perceptibly between her shoulder blades. She let her mind move upwards with the soft wind that blew through the apple trees, feeling little eddies of green and silver stroke her cheeks.

When she opened her eyes, it was with that part inside her that looked and watched and waited. And what she saw made her go cold and shaky all over.

No, she said to herself. No. Not him.

It was the angel again, the one who always seemed to manage to find her when she was feeling the slightest bit wobbly. He was sitting swinging his legs in the lowest branches of the tree. His wings were folded neatly behind him and he was sinking his teeth into an apple.

'Bit sour,' he said, his face wrinkling. 'Not really eaters, are they? I've tasted better.'

'Go away,' Bryony whispered. 'I don't like you. You've got no business here.'

Faintly, from far off, she heard another voice, like the crackle of dry leaves: *Make a tunnel of your mind. You must become the vessel . . . Do not be afraid . . .*

But this time it wasn't fear that Bryony was feeling. It was anger. She felt her body tighten and the anger ripple through her neck and arms in hot red waves.

'Why are you here, anyway?' she said to the angel. 'What do you want from me?'

The angel spat out a piece of waxy peel and wiped his mouth with his arm. 'I'm protecting you. For your own good, Bryony. I want to keep you safe.'

'But I don't need you to keep me safe,' Bryony said. 'I don't need you anymore.'

'*Really*?' The angel raised an eyebrow. A smile played at the corners of his mouth. 'I see. So you think you'll be OK on your own now, do you?' He put back his head and laughed and it was a strange, horrible sound that went bouncing through the trees and echoed against the hills. 'Bryony. Poor, sweet Bryony. Pride comes before a fall.' He smiled again and swung his legs, watching her with an amused expression.

Bryony looked into the angel's eyes, bright blue and hard as marbles. She smiled back. 'I know what you're trying to do now,' she said, 'and you won't frighten me. Not this time.'

She closed her eyes again and imagined the angel dissolving. She started with his smile, picturing it fading from his face, and then moved on to his shoulders, letting them get paler, more transparent so that she could begin to see the branches of the tree appearing through the burnished silver flesh. She scanned down through his body, letting every part of it get fainter and begin to melt away in a white mist. Finally, there was only the shimmer of his wings hanging there, like a giant ghostly moth, and she imagined this getting smaller and smaller and then lifting up and fluttering away.

When she opened her eyes again, there was a great rush of warm air that swirled all around her, parting the grass, lifting her skirt, whipping her hair across her face. She felt the apple trees lean down a little closer and cradle her in their long green arms. She looked up at the clouds racing high above her head and her entire body was filled with a kind of pulsing feeling. She could feel it as if it was her own heartbeat.

And then she felt herself lifting gently from her body, up and up, carried by the press of air, the flashes of white and silver. She looked down and saw the dark shape of herself lying in the grass, her skirt billowing around her like a sail. She felt herself buoyed up, higher still, swirling and wheeling, riding the gusts of power that swept through the garden.

Far below her, she saw Grace, her arms flung wide in the grass, her head tipped back.

'I feel all funny, Bryony!' she was shouting excitedly. 'I can feel it all through me!'

Then Bryony slammed back into her body. She lay for a moment panting and then struggled to her feet. The wind had dropped, the apple trees groaned softly and she felt something settling down around her shoulders, striations of light that flexed and shivered and then locked into place a few inches around the outside of her body like a shield.

Grace was crouching over her, touching her face. 'Bryony's fallen asleep, Mummy,' she was saying. 'Wake up, Bryony. Wake up.'

Bryony scrambled to her feet, brushing herself down.

'I must have nodded off,' she said. 'How embarrassing.'

'So, did it work?' Ella smiled. 'Miss Mary's exercise? Billy's just gone to get the flask from the boot. I think we could all do with warming up a little.'

Bryony blew on her fingers. 'I don't know. I don't remember exactly what happened,' she said.

15

To travel great distances in spirit: Drink a glass of clean water then draw a circle counter-clockwise on the ground and sit inside it. Direct your thoughts to where you want to go.
– Miss Mary's Book of Dreams

Zohreh Jobrani's bones ached. This England, it hung on you like damp, grey cotton. The cold got inside you somehow, no matter how you tried to keep it out. And it had been a long time since she'd done any kind of travelling. She'd forgotten how tiring it could be. The last time she'd flown – Cairo, 1989, that conference on Middle Eastern folklore – the seats on the plane had felt large and luxurious. She seemed to remember that she'd sipped a Martini and looked over her notes whilst listening to pleasant music, whereas this time she'd travelled the nine hours from Tehran with a toddler's feet wedged in the small of her back, his sticky fingers pulling constantly at her headrest. Parents these days didn't seem to know how to discipline their children. Especially British parents, from what she could make out. They appeared to let their children roam everywhere, even hundreds of thousands of feet up in the air, and when the poor little mites fell over or got tired or got parts of themselves stuck in things, their parents stuffed them full of sweets to keep them quiet. In her day, that would have been called lazy. Perhaps even negligent.

She took the photograph of little Grace, her great-great-granddaughter, out of her wallet and scrutinised it. The baby looked straight into the camera with calm, clear and intelligent eyes. Zohreh hoped this was a good sign, that Ella was not one of these modern parents, afraid of laying down a few ground rules. Farah, for instance, had never been any trouble as a child. Zohreh never even needed to raise her voice. Well, if you started as you meant to go on . . .

From her cafe table on the concourse of the new St Pancras Station, Zohreh had a perfect vantage point to watch London in the rush hour. The station was newly renovated, so the woman at the Underground ticket office had told her. Sweeping expanses of glass and polished marble stretched under the great vaulted roof. Very nice. Her sister, Talayeh, would have particularly appreciated it. And the people. People from all the different countries of the earth. There were those moving very fast with determined expressions: this man in his dark business suit and expensive shoes, talking urgently into his phone; this woman, so skinny, with the elegant raincoat and high heels, half-running for her train. Then there were the people just hanging around: the group of women in saris, pink and orange and turquoise, sampling perfumes in the shop across the way and giggling behind their hands; and the teenagers with backpacks and tight jeans, talking loudly in Spanish. And then there were the people like her, seated on benches or at cafe tables, just watching it all: the woman on the next table, sipping her coffee and flicking through a magazine whilst her little girl swung her legs impatiently and blew bubbles into her Coca Cola; the man in the turban with the sad, lined face, just staring into space.

The woman in the ticket office at King's Cross had been apologetic. Severe delays, she'd said. Gale-force winds. The lines were down. Zohreh didn't know exactly what that meant but it didn't sound good. She was beginning to wonder if she'd make it to York tonight. It would be very disappointing to miss Ella's birthday, now that she'd got this far. But so be it. She knew better than to argue with the Fates. If she wasn't to get there tonight then there must be a reason. And she'd nearly missed Farah completely. If it hadn't been for the call she'd put in – an afterthought, really – she'd be on her way to California by now.

She shook sugar from one of the little paper sachets into her cup of coffee. At least the coffee was good. She inhaled the fragrant steam from her Americano, letting it warm her, all the way down to her bones. She checked the departures board again and sighed.

What was to be done?

She concentrated hard, twisting her rings. Perhaps it wouldn't hurt. Just this once. She did so want to be with them all tonight.

She reached into her pocket for the little disc of brass that she always carried – her lucky charm.

*

'HAPPY BIRTHDAY!'

Ella stood inside the door, her hand on the light switch.

The shop was full of people, standing with raised glasses, their faces beaming at her.

Ella scanned the room. Billy's mum had stationed herself by a tray of canapés, her face all dimples. Florence caught her eye and pulled a sympathetic face. She knew that Ella hated surprises. Some of the other women from the book group, minus their usual toddler entourage, were crammed in the leather chairs. She even spotted Bryony, hovering uncertainly in a corner.

Grace tugged at her hand.

'I love birthdays,' she said to the crowded room and everyone laughed and ahhhed. 'Happy birthday, Mummy!'

Billy came towards them, his face split in a wide grin, his arms outstretched. Ella's stomach churned. The air bunched thick and yellow behind Billy's head, then settled back into place again. He was looking at her with a stricken expression.

'Is it OK?' he whispered. 'I haven't . . . I mean, you don't really hate it, do you?'

She smiled then and shook her head. For goodness' sake. She'd better pull herself together. 'No. *No*. It's lovely. Absolutely lovely. *Thank you.*'

He put his arms around her then, Grace snuggling between them, and Ella felt the heaviness that she'd been carrying inside her for days begin to soften and melt away. She'd been so stupid to doubt him. It was all suddenly starting to make sense. All those phone calls that had ended so abruptly when she walked into the room. That shifty look he'd had when she asked him who it was that he'd been speaking to. He'd been planning this, all along. A party. For her. A mixture of relief and guilt washed over her.

Because this was Billy, after all. Billy, who didn't know how to be anything but loyal, who liked things simple and true and said out loud. Why did she always have to make things difficult? She'd read the Signals all wrong.

But as Billy kissed her, to general clapping and wolf-whistling from the friends who filled the room, it still felt odd somehow. Something had changed. Where once he'd been able to reach down inside her, now she felt numb. Her lips felt dry and forced against his.

A hand on her shoulder. Squiggles of blue, a shiver of green. She turned.

'MAMMA!'

Fabia Moreno smiled. In the book-lined dim of the shop, she looked like an exotic bird.

'*Tesora!*' Her short dark hair, perfectly bobbed, swung playfully as she put her head back, laughing at Ella's expression.

'Mamma. I can't believe it's you. I had no idea. I –'

'Let me look at you, *tesora*. My Ella-*issima*. My darling. Happy, *happy* birthday . . .'

Ella let herself be held at arms' length for a moment. Mamma's green eyes twinkled. But Ella saw that Mamma's gaze had already travelled in one expert sweep from the top of her head to the tips of her toes, taking in her unbrushed hair, her black sweater, her jeans and Converse.

'Mum. Don't. You've just got here.'

'What? Don't what?'

'Look at me like that.' Mamma. Poor Mamma. She would never stop hoping. 'I honestly had no idea, Mum. I mean, if I'd known you were coming, I wouldn't have bothered getting so dressed up. Whereas you, you're really letting the side down.'

Fabia herself was wearing a red silk kimono-style dress, with sleeves that fell from her braceleted wrists in wide arcs. An embroidered dragon, embellished with tiny beads in green and gold, snaked from her left breast and down around her waist.

'Oh, come here, *carina*. Let your Mamma enjoy you for a moment.'

Ella let herself be held tightly again. She could hear Mamma's heart beating quick and strong under the red silk. She closed her eyes and breathed in the familiar scent of perfume and Marseilles soap and that other hint of something about Mamma that was always so impossible to define.

'When did you get here?'

'This morning. I came straight from Heathrow.'

'So *that's* why David sounded so odd when I tried to call you this afternoon . . . And *you*!' Ella turned and punched Billy playfully on the arm. 'How did you manage to keep this a secret?'

Billy grinned and put a glass of ice-cold champagne into her hand. She took a sip. As the first bubbles hit the back of her throat, she felt tears prickling at the corners of her eyes. How could she ever have imagined the awful things she had?

'Mum,' she said, biting back tears. 'You've no idea how glad I am to see you.'

Mamma's face clouded with concern then. She laid a hand on Ella's arm.

'I *knew* it,' she said. 'I just *knew* there was something wrong. And now I wish I'd come sooner. Tomorrow, *carina,* we'll have a long talk. You'll tell me everything. Ev-er-y-thing, OK? But tonight, we'll drink.' She took the glass from Billy's hands. 'And we'll laugh and we'll dance.' She jiggled her hips. 'And we'll have a nice time. No?'

Ella nodded.

'But now I'm going to say hello to some old friends.'

Ella watched Mamma move off, glass held high, nodding and smiling.

Billy hovered, Grace pulling at Ella's arm.

'Something's wrong?' Billy said. 'What does she mean, El? You *are* OK with all this, aren't you? I mean, I know you hate surprises. But you've been so down lately. I wanted to cheer you up, give you a special evening . . .' His voice trailed off. He looked crushed.

'Of course. And it's lovely, Billy. Really.' Ella ran her fingers through his hair. She was still savouring the sense of relief that her suspicions had been so off. But her mind was already racing ahead.

She sipped at her champagne and watched Billy's face begin to relax. After all, she *could* be happy tonight, couldn't she, surrounded by all these people, people who were kind and good and who only ever had her best interests at heart?

She saw Mamma weaving her way through the room, easily and elegantly on her silver platform heels. All their old friends from the early days were here. Billy had thought of everyone. There were the Braithwaites from the grocery store on Petergate. And Amanda, the lovely woman who ran ghost tours and made cupcakes. They were hugging Mamma and laughing, happy to see her again after all this time. But Ella could see that Mamma's fingers clutched her champagne glass a little too tightly and the smile on her perfectly lipsticked mouth was forced.

Billy took Grace off to find her plastic cup – the one with the glittery unicorn on the side – and Ella took another sip from her own glass, feeling the champagne flow down her arms and into her fingertips. There was so much that she wanted to ask. And now that Mamma was here, she felt all the questions pressing up against one another in her head. Where would she even start?

'How are you bearing up?' Florence squeezed her shoulder. 'I'm so sorry, lovely. I was sworn to secrecy. It was so hard not to say something.' She smiled. 'You see? Was I right?' She glanced conspiratorially in Billy's direction. 'But I couldn't let on. He'd have killed me.'

Ella hugged Florence tightly. 'It's OK,' she said. 'I know. I'm an idiot.'

Florence shook her head. 'Only a teeny bit of one.'

Suddenly the shop door jangled, bringing in a gust of cold wind. The Halloween decorations that Ella had hung in the windows just yesterday – bats' wings and witches' hats cut from black crêpe paper, fat orange tissue-paper pumpkin globes – fluttered and slapped against the glass. The broom that she'd balanced on a stack of books in the Children's Corner clattered to the floor.

A man stood uncertainly in the open doorway, his gaze taking in the candles and the jack o' lanterns, searching the faces. Ella didn't recognise him. A friend of Billy's perhaps? But as the hum of conversation resumed again, the man pushed his way towards Bryony with a determined expression.

Ella watched Bryony's face turn white. She put her glass down carefully on one of the book-laden tables. She seemed to shrink visibly against the wall. Ella found herself moving closer. There was something not quite right about this man.

'Ed,' she heard Bryony say. 'What are you doing here?'

He looked at her and snorted. 'I could ask you the same question . . .' He saw Ella moving towards them then and his face instantly reshaped itself.

'This is Ella,' Bryony was saying. 'It's her birthday.'

'Oh. Right. Many happy returns.' The man's face coloured. He lunged forward to take her hand in greeting.

'Thank you,' Ella said, resisting the urge to pull her hand away. She turned to see Mamma at her elbow. 'And let me introduce you . . . Mamma, this is my friend, Bryony. And this is . . . um, Bryony's *friend*? I'm sorry.' She looked at him blankly. 'I don't know your name . . .'

She watched Ed's face change, his smile becoming less certain, his shoulders rounding.

'It's Ed,' he mumbled, looking down at his shoes, shifting awkwardly from one leg to the other. 'I just . . .' He turned to Bryony and cleared his throat. 'I was worried about you, Bryony. You said you were going for a walk. But it's dark. It's not safe for you to be out here on your own. Look. I brought you this.' He made a show of pulling a torch from his jacket pocket.

Ella watched Bryony pull herself up straighter then. She smoothed a strand of hair out of her eyes. Mamma moved away, embarrassed.

'It's OK, Ed,' Bryony was saying. 'As you can see, I'm perfectly safe. These are my friends.' Ella felt Bryony make a grab for her hand. 'I'll see you later.'

A dark red stain spread across Ed's cheeks. Ella could see the muscle twitching in his jaw. He was furious.

'Right-o, then,' he said.

He turned to go.

'Ed?' Bryony's eyes flashed. She looks especially pretty tonight, thought Ella. She felt Bryony's fingers pressing hers.

'Yes?'

'Don't wait up for me. I might be quite late. In fact, I imagine I'll get a taxi.'

He nodded again.

As the door swung to and the bell jangled behind him, Bryony giggled nervously.

'I've never said that to him before. I – I don't really go out much. I feel – different. Like I could do *anything*.'

Ella tried not to let her face show what she was thinking.

'Well, of course you can,' she said. 'But did he, um . . . did he *follow* you?'

Bryony looked away. Her fingers worked the stem of her wine glass. 'It's my fault,' she said. 'I fibbed. I didn't exactly say where I was going. He – he means well. But he can be a bit –'

'Controlling?'

The word was out before Ella could stop herself. Instantly, she regretted it. She saw and felt Bryony's embarrassment.

'I'm sorry. I –'

'No. No, Ella, you're right.' Bryony shook her head. She took a gulp of wine. 'I have to do something about it. I've been putting it off. It's hard, you know. I don't want to –'

'Everything all right?' Billy appeared, a bottle wrapped in a white linen napkin gripped expertly in his hand, poised to top up Bryony's glass.

'Yes.' Ella forced a smile. 'Everything's fine.'

She held out her own glass. At the same time, her other hand found Bryony's and gave it a squeeze.

Tendrils of mist curled around her shoulders and a little rush of air tickled her cheek.

Mamma appeared at her shoulder again, swirling the last drops of champagne around her glass. Ella could hear what she was thinking: *I don't like that man and who is this woman? Why are her Signals so strong?*

'Mamma,' said Ella, taking Bryony's arm. 'I want you to meet my friend, Bryony. Properly, I mean. I think you two will have lots to talk about.'

*

It was the Signals that Fabia recognised first. She was trying hard to concentrate on what this friend of Ella's, this Bryony, was saying, but here they were again, more restless and insistent than the mist of greens and greys that twirled around Bryony's head. They didn't seem to be coming from Bryony at all and yet they tangled with Bryony's words and filled up the air around her. Ripples of brilliant white, like morning sun moving across painted stone walls; that rushing sound, like the sound of your own body as you pressed a seashell close to your ear; and, of course, that pulsing of vivid red, the exact colour of pomegranates.

Only one person Fabia had ever known had Signals like these, as fragrant as the earth in the village garden and as clear and nuanced as her voice had once been, pronouncing the words in the picture books, pointing with her finger – *popp-y*, *yell-ow*, *tab-le*, *star* – or calling her in to the cool shade of the terrace: *Farah, my dear one . . .*

At first, she thought it was only wishful thinking, a trick of the light and her imagination. She was so happy to see Ella, her *carina*, and how her little Grace had grown. Wasn't it only natural that her thoughts should move to Maadar-Bozorg?

But then she heard the voice again, reaching her across all the other noise in the room, that deep, melodious voice, cutting through time and memories, calling her by her real name: *Farah, my dear one. Farah . . .*

It couldn't possibly be. But still, she turned.

The small figure stood just inside the doorway, in the pool of light cast by the chandelier. She was wrapped from head to toe in the folds of a large black overcoat and a richly patterned woollen shawl. Her dark eyes met Fabia's and she threw her arms open.

'Child! Precious one. Come!'

For a moment, Fabia struggled to understand. Maadar? Here in York? Then surely it must be true? That she really had passed over. Suddenly, all of Fabia's dreams and instincts, her worst fears of recent weeks were confirmed. Maadar-Bozorg's spirit had been calling to her all these past nights and had finally found her here, tonight, on the eve of All Souls, the *Dia dos Muertas*, the day of Ella's birth, when the stretched seam between the two worlds – that of the living and that of the dead – opens up, making a gap just big enough to slip through. Fabia felt her heart contract in her chest. Maadar. Her beloved Maadar-Bozorg. She should have gone to her, long ago. If it was true, that she had passed on to the next world, then she, Fabia, should have been there, at the moment of her passing, sitting by her bedside, stroking the backs of her hands, whispering the words that would carry her safely on her journey.

But now Maadar-Bozorg's spirit was walking towards her, arms still outstretched. Fabia could see the amethysts flashing on her fingers. She wondered, anxiously, if she would be angry that Fabia had failed her in her last hours?

'Whatever's the matter, child. You look as if you've seen a ghost?' The spirit of Maadar looked amused. The dimple in her left cheek quivered.

Fabia put out a hand and touched Maadar's sleeve. 'Maadar-Bozorg? Is it really you?' She grasped Maadar's shoulders and pressed her close. Maadar-Bozorg's body, through the layers of wool, felt real enough and warm, although her bones were as slender and delicate as a bird's. She realised, with a mixture of elation and sorrow, that if this Maadar-Bozorg really was alive, then she was suddenly a very much older woman than the one that Fabia had left behind in Tehran.

'Maadar! I'm sorry. It's just that . . . I can't . . . Well, I can't believe you're actually here.' She hung her head in embarrassment. 'I should have come to *you*.'

Maadar-Bozorg made a clicking noise with her tongue. 'Probably,' she said, her eyes gleaming. 'But I'm here now, child. And what a journey.' She pulled a face. 'I was on my way to America. But I called ahead, talked to David.' She looked Fabia in the eye. 'And he told me that *this* was where to find you. So, of course, I couldn't resist the opportunity to meet these great- and great-great-granddaughters of mine.' Her gaze darted eagerly around the room. 'Ah, yes.' She pointed. 'Am I not right? This little cherub with the big eyes?'

She took Fabia's hand and began to move determinedly towards the shop counter where Ella had perched Grace, her chubby legs sticking straight out in front of her.

Ella saw them coming. Fabia watched her scoop up Grace and saw her eyes travel from Maadar's face to her own and back again.

'Mum? Mum, is this –? No, it can't be.'

Fabia could only nod. Her mouth was dry. Her eyes were wet with tears.

She watched Maadar-Bozorg reach up and take Ella and Grace in her arms. 'Happy birthday, little one,' Maadar said. 'Little Ella. Little dove with your sweet little chick.' She took Grace's cheek between her thumb and forefinger. 'I came to wish you a very happy birthday.'

16

To keep harmony at home: Grow cornflowers, delphiniums
and bluebells close to your house. Dry the blue blossoms
and sprinkle them discreetly in the corners of every room.
You may also take one hair from the head of each person
in the family, braid the hairs together and bind the ends
with a blue silk thread.
– Miss Mary's Book of Dreams

Through the grimy train window, Bryony watched the fields gradually give way to warehouses and blocks of flats.

She opened her purse and slid out the gilt-edged prayer card, rubbing it between her fingers. She admired again the image of Our Lady standing in the middle of a shaft of sunlight, her tiny face serene with eyes downcast, her hands held out at her sides, palms upwards, her robes painted a brilliant blue, her crown of gold stars. She turned the card over and traced the inscription with her fingertips, her lips moving silently as she pronounced the words inside her mind in the way that she'd so often seen Mother doing: *O most Holy Virgin Mary, Mother of God, although most unworthy of being thy servant, yet inspired by confidence in thy extreme goodness, and filled with an earnest desire of serving thee, I this day choose thee, in the presence of thy son, of my angel guardian and the whole court of heaven, for my special advocate, mother and queen . . .*

She paused, her eyes suddenly welling with tears. This wouldn't do. Not today, of all days. No, she must pull herself together. That's exactly what Selena would say, of course, if she were here right now. She'd always scorned what she called Mother's 'voodoo', her 'mumbo jumbo'. And Father had often joined in too. And this was why it had fallen to Bryony to carefully put aside the few small, personal possessions that had remained after Mother's death: the prayer card that Mother had carried for as long as Bryony could remember in the large red mock-leather purse next to the weekly housekeeping and the savings stamps, the silver cross and Lourdes medal in their little velvet pouch, the handkerchief with the lace edge, embroidered with a border of cross-stitch violets by Mother's earnest schoolgirl's fingers.

Now the train wheezed into the station and Bryony folded these precious items back into her own purse, then stuffed it to the bottom of her handbag and stepped out onto the crowded platform. The sudden surge of people carried her easily up the steps and onto the bridge spanning the tracks. Up here, the wind hurled rain against the enormous plate-glass windows. She wound her scarf more closely around her neck, tucking the ends into her collar.

Leeds. She hated it. The leaden sky reflected in smoked glass and towering office buildings. The big old frontages of blackened stone with their carved emblems, their gold-painted baubles and the statues that seemed always to leer down at her. And then, of course, her father.

She wished again that she didn't have to do this, that she hadn't come. She cursed Selena under her breath for making her. And even as she did, she knew somewhere inside her that it was her own fault. She didn't have to give in or do what Selena wanted. Except that sometimes it was easier than doing anything else.

The scene from last night's party had been playing over and over in her mind. Ed's face. The way he'd looked when she'd said that she wasn't going home with him, not yet. The little thrill of power she'd felt in the company of Ella and her mother. She wished now that she could summon it again.

Outside the station, the sharp smell of exhaust fumes stung her nostrils and litter whipped around her ankles. It was only a few short blocks to Father's offices, so she walked, head down, past the waiting taxis and angled her umbrella into the rain.

The receptionist behind the high marble desk took her name and pronounced it briskly into her phone, but not before Bryony had felt her gaze pass swiftly up and down her body. It was a look of pity – perhaps even of thinly disguised contempt – and Bryony felt her face flush, patting at her wind-blown hair then staring down at her shoes on the polished marble tiles. She'd worn her best shoes too – suede courts, even though they pinched – but the receptionist's face, her false bright smile and the way that she pointed her in the direction of the lift, told her everything. She still didn't pass the test. She probably never would.

She avoided her reflection in the mirrored back wall of the lift. She didn't need any more upsets today. She'd decided to come to Father's office this time, remembering what a mistake it had been when she'd shown up at the house before, the expression on the face of Adele, her stepmother, and her teenage half-sister, Cosima, loitering in the hallway, curious to get a look.

'Cosima, go to your room,' Adele had said, frowning, showing Bryony into the oak-panelled study at the front of the house.

'Cup of tea?' she'd asked grudgingly, and Bryony had shaken her head. They had nothing at all to say to one another, she and this elegant woman in her cashmere twinset and designer jeans, her ears and throat adorned discreetly with Father's money.

Now the lift doors pinged, slid open and she stepped out onto plush grey carpet. Too late to turn back. She swallowed hard and curled her fists.

'Bryony Darwin. To see my father,' she said to another impossibly groomed woman who was tapping bad-temperedly at a keyboard. 'And no. He's not expecting me.'

Her father looked older than when she'd last seen him. He wore a white shirt without a tie, and his wiry, grey hair was trimmed very short.

'Bryony,' he said, and pointed to a chair, positioning himself carefully behind a huge mahogany antique desk. 'So. This is a bit of a surprise,' he said, raising an eyebrow. 'It's been a while. How are you?'

'I'm sorry. I would have made an appointment except that – except –'

The words hung in the air between them. *Except that I thought you might not see me. Except that I didn't know if I could actually go through with this at all.*

Her father made a little gesture of dismissal. 'I hope you know that you don't need an appointment,' he said. 'I *am* your father, after all.'

Again the words seemed to quiver in the air above the desk. It was as if, thought Bryony, watching her father's face, he were considering what that really meant for the first time.

'So how are you?' he said again. 'Are you well?'

'Yes. Thank you. Very well.'

'Good. Glad to hear it. Because I was worried there for a while. You know. I wouldn't want you to . . . well, to go down the same road as . . . I think you know what I'm saying. Your mother never did get the help she needed.' Her father fiddled with the cap of a silver ballpoint pen, finally laying it down on the desk's polished surface, where it rocked for a while, throwing a wobbly disc of light over the white walls.

'Yes, I know.'

He made a bridge of his fingers and leaned forward across the desk. 'Not that I didn't try. You *do* know that, Bryony, don't you? I did try to do my best by her. I really did.'

Bryony stared down at her hands in her lap. They looked for that moment strangely unfamiliar as if they were not her own, as if she'd never seen them before. The familiar wave of nausea swept through her – that shaky feeling. The taste of anger, hot and ragged, and underneath it a cold, gaping sadness.

She forced herself to look up.

Her father waited. He would make her ask for it, she knew, make her say the words out loud.

She turned her face to the window. She felt the tears prick at her eyes again. She couldn't hold his gaze.

'How much?' He was opening a drawer, taking out his chequebook.

'Five thousand.' She could barely get the words out. The shame of it, of coming here and asking. Her cheeks burned.

There was a sharp intake of breath. Her father bent over the desk, shaking his head. His pen made a scratching sound.

Now he was holding the cheque out to her. Right now, she should reach forward and take it. But he seemed to hesitate.

'This money,' he said, and she felt his eyes scrutinising her face. 'It *is* for you yourself, isn't it?'

She nodded. She never had been able to lie to him.

He sighed then and put his head in his hands. 'It's Selena again, isn't it? She sent you here, put you up to this. I just know it.'

Bryony shook her head. She felt the panic rising. She'd blown it. Now it would all have been for nothing. She shouldn't have come. Selena's face swam into her vision, her lip curled at the corner: *I asked you to do one little thing, Bryony. One stupid little thing . . .*

She looked at her father, looked deep into his eyes, which she'd forgotten were blue like Selena's, and with those flecks of amber.

'OK.' Her father sighed again and held the cheque out to her. 'If she's in trouble, if she's got herself into one of her damn messes, I'd advise you to stay well away from her, Bryony. That's all I have to say on the matter. Don't get involved.'

Bryony took the cheque, stowing it carefully in the inside pocket of her handbag. Her hands were still trembling.

'Thank you, Father.' She tried to force a smile.

The stretch of carpet from his desk to the door gaped in front of her. She could feel his eyes on the back of her neck.

'Bryony,' he said as she put her hand on the polished door-plate. She turned.

He was at the window, a slight figure silhouetted against all that sky and glass, and suddenly he looked so small, she thought, small and weary.

'Keep in touch,' he said. 'Write to me from time to time. Here at the office. That is, I mean, if you'd like to.'

His hands, which had been folded neatly together in front of him, fell to his sides. Bryony thought again of the prayer card, of Our Lady's hands in that gesture of supplication, palms upwards.

She didn't know what to say. She didn't dare trust herself. She felt that, if she opened her mouth, if she began to speak, a great rush of words would spill out. She imagined them for a moment, lying around on the carpet, words with jagged edges and some of them with little points like knives. Yes, a great mess of words it would be, spilling all over the beautiful carpet, pulsing and shaking and jabbing and pointing.

No, she couldn't speak. She couldn't even nod anymore. She turned away from him and opened the door.

*

Fabia sat behind the counter, her needle slipping in and out of the red satin ribbon.

Maadar-Bozorg was sleeping in the flat upstairs, worn out after her long journey. And Fabia was minding the shop. It felt strange to be here again, perched on this same stool, her sewing spread in her lap. At first, she hadn't been sure if she liked it. Funny, she thought, how things were never quite as you remembered them.

There were things about the shop that she could see so clearly in her mind's eye, standing on the deck at her house in California, leaning into the salt wind: the patina of the polished floorboards, the pear-shaped droplets on the chandelier, which threw rainbows across the white walls at a certain time of day, the sound of the rain splashing from the leaky guttering. All these things were just as she'd pictured them.

But then there were things she hadn't remembered at all: that dimple in one of the old glass windows, how when you sat at a particular angle it distorted your view of the courtyard; and the way that the afternoon light seemed to shimmer just above the cobblestones.

And, of course, so much had changed, too. The shop windows and every spare surface that had once spilled glittering necklaces or velvet hat stands or pairs of shoes were now piled high with books. Just yesterday, Ella had swapped the window display of pumpkins and broomsticks and black crêpe paper bats' wings for a Christmas scene. Fabia had watched Grace sprinkling fake snow on a cardboard model of a Hansel and Gretel house and she'd found herself thinking about the day she'd first opened the shop, how she'd stayed up all night, trying out dresses on the mannequin in the window, folding silk scarves into fan shapes, arranging shoes and hats.

Thirteen years ago – more than a decade – and yet it might as well be a lifetime. But here she was now, her fingertips slipping over the thin silk in her lap, the winter sunlight striping the polished wooden floor and falling across the backs of her hands.

The rhythm of the needle soothed her, as it always did. In and out, in and out. The clock ticked and Grace murmured softly to herself, running toy cars up and down the table legs and in between the bookshelves.

Yes, she would feel perfectly at peace in this moment if it wasn't that she was worried about Ella. She could see that there was something not quite right. Ever since the party, Ella had avoided meeting her eyes. Her face, which had opened like a flower upon seeing her, now had that closed look. Fabia felt, not for the first time, that she couldn't quite reach her. But then, since when had her daughter confided in her when she was in trouble? Ella had always been her own person.

So like her father, Fabia thought. Fabia herself might cry or slam doors or even shout, especially when she was younger. But Enzo always kept things close, locked away inside himself.

She could see that Billy was concerned, too. He'd told her that Ella wasn't sleeping very well, how some nights she muttered to herself or woke up shouting.

Fabia wished now that she'd come sooner. She hadn't wanted to interfere, thinking that Ella should be free to make her own decisions. Now she only wanted to wrap her arms around her precious daughter, hold her tight and never let her go.

And all of this only made David's question even harder.

'Think about it,' he'd said. 'There's no rush. I can wait for your answer.' But his face had told her something quite different. His Signals, those steady rays of blue and sunshine yellow, had trembled, ever so slightly. Dear, kind David. She wondered now how she could possibly have been so cruel.

'Can I, really?' she'd said. 'Can I give you my answer when I get back?' And then, when she'd seen the disappointment on his face, 'Because I *will* come back, David. I will. It's just –'

He'd pressed a finger to her lips then. 'Shhh. Of course. Selfish of me to ask, right now, I know. You've got enough to worry about.' He'd forced a smile.

But it hadn't been selfish. Not at all. David had been nothing but patient and kind these last few years. So why was it that she was hesitating? She'd even surprised herself.

It was as if she'd watched the words fall from his lips and drop like pebbles onto the sand – thud, thud, thud – and with each word her throat had constricted just a little more, until she could hardly breathe. Perhaps it was that she'd never really thought of marrying again, had never imagined David asking her. There'd been a brief conversation around visa applications and red tape when he'd first landed the job in San Diego and asked her to move with him, but then David's accountant had come up with

176

some quick and ingenious workarounds, they'd set up the San Diego shop in David's name and the issue had never raised itself again. Now she realised how insensitive she'd been to David's own desires. It seemed that he wanted to be married, after all. He wanted to have a wife. And why shouldn't he? So what was her problem? Fabia knew at least three of her friends who would jump at the chance of marrying a man like David.

So maybe David was right about her missing York. Ever since she'd finally booked the tickets, she'd found herself feeling flushed and excited at the thought of being here again. It wasn't just about Ella and Grace – although this was a large part of it all. But even before her plane had landed, she'd found herself slipping so easily back into the feeling of this place.

Just a few nights ago, as her taxi had passed over the bridge into the city, she'd looked out at the brown river, flowing fast and insistent, sweeping everything along with it, and felt that old pull on her heart.

She'd stepped into the little courtyard, just as she had all those years ago, and stood in front of the shop, looking in at its brightly lit windows, feeling the wind whipping around the corners of the buildings, teasing her hair, tugging at her sleeves. She'd been surprised at how right it felt to be back here again.

And then there had been the party, with so many old friends, faces she'd almost forgotten, who'd seemed touchingly pleased to see her.

'We miss you so much,' Mrs Stubbs had said. 'It's not just that there's nowhere for us to find really nice dresses anymore but, you know . . .' She touched her finger to the side of her nose and winked. 'There's nowhere you can go to make yourself feel a bit special, where you get a cup of coffee and a good old natter and leave feeling . . . well, just a bit better about yourself.' She smiled. 'You were always so good at that, Fabia.'

Now Fabia frowned as the red satin rucked up around her needle. She was letting her thoughts run away with her.

She tried to make a list in her head of all the good things about her life in San Diego. David, of course. Wide blue skies. Warmth. The ocean, which she could see and smell from her wraparound deck every morning as she sipped delicious deli-bought coffee or cut into an enormous juicy peach.

But the truth was that America, after all, the America that she'd always dreamed of, didn't quite feel the right fit. The blue skies that had warmed her all the way to her bones still hung on her some mornings like a too-new dress when the fabric is still stiff under your fingers.

Perhaps it was that she didn't really feel needed there. She watched David leave for work every morning, whistling down the drive and climbing into the Corvette – his dream car, the one he'd always lusted after – and he looked as if he'd found his true place in the world. But it was different for her. She wasn't even sure who she really *was* anymore.

Afternoons in the shop often stretched before her, long and empty. There were people like Rosita, of course, who liked to spend time looking through the rails or leaning against the counter with a cup of coffee. There were the LA stylists and the glamorous clients that Katrina had sent her way. But the real hubbub, the place where things happened and people lingered and gossiped, was the enormous mall just across the highway. There you could park your car, select an entire outfit off the peg, have a meal, watch a film. Shops like Fabia's were special one-stop destinations, indulgences, charming eccentricities.

Whilst here, sitting behind her old counter, she immediately felt useful. Ella needed her more than she'd realised. She'd already surprised herself that she could find books for people in much the same way as she found dresses and shoes. By tuning in, listening to their innermost desires, reading their longings.

And then there was the adorable Grace. She watched her now, playing happily with her toy bunny rabbit, bouncing him up and down the bookshelves, every so often glancing in her direction and smiling. Grace made her feel needed. And those old customers from Ella's party, they'd seemed to know what she was good at doing, better than she knew herself. She imagined this must be how David felt around his patients, this warm pink glow that spread through her. But then, he was actually saving people's lives. It seemed silly to compare that with clothes and words, with tweaking a seam or adding a brooch or embroidering a hidden message in the lining of a sleeve.

Maybe she wasn't made to settle down anywhere. She thought of the quetzal that Rosita had given her, its brave red breast and the green tin plumes of its tail spinning in the light from her candles. What was it that Rosita had said? That it could never be tamed or caged? She heard Enzo's voice drifting to her down the years, saw the shape of his face dimly outlined against the dusk of the patio at Les Oiseaux: *People like us, tesora, we're life's seekers. We don't belong anywhere, except to one another.* And then he'd taken her hands in his and kissed them gently, a kiss for each fingertip.

Enzo. She'd never imagined being married to anyone else but him. When you married, you married for life, so she'd thought back then. *Sposato.* Such a lovely word. It seemed to melt on your tongue. You are my *sposato.*

She felt, for the first time in a long time, a twinge of the old sadness, that filmy brown feeling that wrapped around her heart and made everything dull and blurry.

She sighed.

'Grace,' she said and her granddaughter looked up. Her little heart-shaped face, those wide blue-grey eyes, reminded her so much of Ella as a little girl that it made her breath catch in her chest. 'Look! Look what Grandma's made.' She broke the thread and stood up, shaking out the folds of red silk. 'Would you like to try it on?'

Grace teetered over, her arms outstretched. 'Red.' She laughed. 'I love red, Grandma.'

'And so do I, darling.' She draped the cloak around Grace's shoulders, fastening the diamanté button at the front, tucking her hair inside the hood, securing the ribbons under her chin in a large bow. 'Now, let's look at you.'

She led her over to the back of the shop where the old changing room that she'd devised all those years ago with crimson paint and a velvet curtain was now stacked with boxes of books.

'We don't have much use for mirrors, Mum,' Ella had laughed, catching Fabia surreptitiously drawing back the curtain and peeking inside. 'Or fitting rooms. Our customers don't exactly require them.'

Fabia pushed at one of the boxes with the toe of her shoe, clearing a space, brushing the dust from her fingers. She stood Grace in front of the mirror, her hands resting on her shoulders.

Grace stared. Her face dissolved into dimples. She turned and watched her mirror-self turn, the silk rippling in the light from the chandelier. She clapped her hands and pointed her foot in its red patent shoe.

'Ohhh, what big eyes you have, Grandmother!'

Fabia made eyes at her in the mirror and watched her giggle.

'And Grandmother, what big TEETH you have.'

She made a mock snarl, holding up her hands like large paws and pounced on Grace, tickling her all over.

Grace squealed delightedly.

The shop doorbell jangled. Grace wriggled out of Fabia's arms and ran to the door. 'You can't catch me, big bad WOLF!' she shouted.

The woman from the party, Ella's new friend – Bryony, wasn't it? – stood by the counter, her face flushed, her fingers working at the strap of her handbag. She crouched and smiled at Grace. 'Well, Little Red Riding Hood, don't you look a treat.' Then she turned to Fabia. 'I hope I'm not disturbing anything.'

'Not at all.' Fabia smiled. 'But Ella's gone out for a bit, so you're stuck with me, I'm afraid. I was just pouring coffee. Can I get you one?'

Bryony took the cup gratefully and positioned herself in the leather armchair, watching Grace turning the pages of her picture book.

'She never tires of it.' Fabia rolled her eyes. 'Funny, isn't it, how they can get so attached to a particular story? She reads it over and over again.'

Bryony smiled. 'I think we all have our favourites,' she said. 'I know I certainly do.'

'Oh, and what would yours be?' Fabia took a sip of her coffee, expertly cradling her cup in one hand and shifting Grace's weight in her lap with the other. 'No, wait a minute. Let me try to guess . . . Now, let's see. No, why am I even trying? Ella is so much better at this. I give up. Go on, just tell me.'

'Oh, goodness. My favourite? I don't know, now that you've put me on the spot.' Bryony smiled back. 'I've always loved fairy tales. It's hard to choose.' She felt the heat rising up her throat and into her cheeks. 'And, well, it sounds so silly when I say it out loud but I always rather liked Cinderella.'

'Ah, yes. Poor Cinderella. Waiting to be rescued by her handsome prince.' Fabia smiled. 'It's a shame, don't you think, that we're taught to do that? To wait for someone to come and rescue us, I mean.'

She watched Bryony swirl the remains of her coffee around her cup. She didn't want to say too much. Sometimes, to plant the seed of something was enough.

'I'd never really thought about it like that before,' Bryony said. 'But, yes. I suppose you're right.'

A blue tingle crept up Fabia's spine. She felt Bryony's eyes searching her face. She drained her coffee cup and returned it with a chink to its saucer.

There was something taking shape in the back of her mind. The outline of something that she couldn't quite get hold of. A sound, faint at first but getting closer.

'Tell me,' she said, slowly, leaning forward, laying a hand on Bryony's arm. 'Tell me if I'm being a bit too much but . . . Well, I get the sense that you're –'

'Yes,' Bryony said quickly.

'Yes, what?'

'The colours, the – the vibrations. The strange humming thing that's a bit like static. You see something – almost as if it's out of the corner of your eye. But you don't *really* see it. Because to most people it isn't actually there. You *feel* things about people. Really feel them . . .'

Fabia smiled. That hadn't actually been what she'd wanted to say. But here it was. And her heart went out to this lovely woman. She felt the air around them begin to shimmer.

'Ah,' she said. 'The Signals. That's what I've always called them, anyway. Not that Ella and I have ever talked about them much. I used to be much more afraid of these things, you see, when I was younger. I didn't want Ella to be different.'

Bryony frowned. 'I can see that. It doesn't really do to talk about it. My mother, when she was alive, she called them the Feelings . . .'

Fabia nodded. 'I like that. The Feelings . . . You must miss her very much.'

Bryony felt her eyes prickle. 'Yes. I do.'

She stood up, fastened her coat and looped her bag over her shoulder. She was embarrassed. Fabia could see that. It was as if she was folding the air around her, closing herself down again.

'Well, thank you for the coffee. It was lovely to see you again,' Bryony was saying. 'Bye bye, Grace.' She laughed to see that Grace could barely tear her eyes from the pages of her book. 'Say hello to Mummy for me. I'll pop in again tomorrow.'

'Just a minute.' Fabia ducked behind the counter and drew out a package, carefully wrapped in white tissue paper and tied with a black ribbon. 'I want to give you this,' she said. 'Forgive me for being so forward. It's just that, well, I think this is *meant* for you. I want you to have it.'

'Oh, goodness.' Bryony took the package in her hands. 'That's so kind of you but really, you don't need to –'

'Open it.' Fabia's eyes twinkled. 'Go on. I want to know what you think.'

The ribbon slipped off easily and the tissue paper layers opened like petals in Bryony's hands to reveal three large emerald-green feathers, secured with a crystal-clustered pin.

'It's part of an old stage costume of mine,' said Fabia. 'From *waaaay* back. I wore it in my hair, just here.' She pointed to the crown of her head. 'Of course, my hair was long then, like yours. And this was a gift from someone. A woman in our dance troupe. Someone I greatly admired. And it always brought me luck. You know, when I wanted to feel that little bit of something extra, when I needed a bit of courage. I found it again this morning, rummaging through some of my old boxes up there. But it's yours now.'

She saw that Bryony couldn't meet her eye.

'Thank you,' she managed to get out. 'Thank you so much. I'll treasure it.' She slipped it into her pocket.

'My pleasure. And Bryony?'

'Yes?'

'You can always talk about these things here. With me, I mean. I just want you to know that.'

Bryony nodded. 'Thank you.'

Fabia watched her struggle with her umbrella, stepping carefully in her boots across the shining cobbles. She had the sudden urge to run after her, hold her close.

Instead, she turned away from the window, scooping Grace up in her arms and covering her cheeks with kisses.

*

Bryony's eyes blurred with tears.

She felt as if she would burst, as if she just wasn't big enough to contain all the feelings jostling for space inside her – grief and longing and a new exhilarating happiness.

She wanted to cry.

She wanted to put back her head and taste raindrops on her tongue.

It was as if everything in the past few weeks had been leading her to this place, to this little shop and to this one moment, a moment she could never have imagined, with a woman who looked like something out of an F. Scott Fitzgerald novel, who talked to her so easily and openly about Feelings and Signals and all the weird things that Bryony had always had to keep hidden.

And now Bryony could hear that sound again, getting closer and closer, a single note that rang out with each new step she took across the cobbles, the letters forming in her mind's eye.

Now, Bryony, it sang, over and over. *Now*.

NOW.

17

To grow in courage: On a Tuesday after sunset when the moon is waxing, place borage and yarrow in a conjure-bag, hold it in your hands and charge it with your intention.
– Miss Mary's Book of Dreams

The sign on Billy's door read 'Dr William Vickers,' but Billy had crossed out the 'William' and scrawled 'Bill' above it.

Ella had once asked him why he didn't publish his articles under his full name. 'Because I hate it,' he'd said. 'I don't recognise it as me. And Billy sounds a bit like I'm ten years old. Only you, my mum and a few other people still call me Billy. Everyone at work calls me Bill.'

'Do you want me to start calling you Bill, too?' Ella frowned.

He'd grinned. 'No. That'd just be *weird*. And anyway, *you* know that I'm not really a grown-up. Not yet. I quite like being someone different at home than at work. It helps to keep things separate.'

Ella knocked, three times. She could feel her stomach fluttering. She felt like a teenager again. After the party, she'd resolved to try harder, make more of an effort. She and Billy deserved that much. And so here she was now, in a new outfit, her hair in a casual updo rather than her usual ponytail. She'd even put on make-up. Just a little eyeliner and blusher, a dab of lipstick. She didn't want to look overdone.

'Don't hurry back.' Mamma had laughed, looking perfectly at home behind the shop counter, jiggling Grace in her arms. 'My granddaughter and I have plenty of catching up to do.'

Ella saw her run an approving eye over her new black cashmere sweater, the pair of black wool trousers that she'd chosen this morning instead of her scruffy old jeans and the tiny diamond earrings in the shape of stars that Mamma had given her for her birthday.

'You look beautiful, *tesora*.'

Now Ella pushed open Billy's door. Maybe he was on the phone? Or in a meeting? It would be just typical if he had some kind of lunch meeting today of all days.

The office stood empty. The screensaver on Billy's computer, a picture of Grace when she was first born, glowed softly and the desk lamp cast a pale circle on the book lying open on his desk.

She looked at the chair placed carefully for visitors on the other side of his desk. Should she wait?

And then she heard it, drifting from further down the corridor, the unmistakable sound of Billy's laughter. Above it, husky and alluring, was the sound of a woman's voice. Selena.

Ella turned and began to follow the sound. The unfamiliar click-click of her heeled suede ankle boots seemed much too loud on the concrete floor.

She stopped outside another door that stood slightly ajar. 'Selena LaSalle', the sign read, 'Head of Department – Social History'. Beneath it someone – surely not Selena? – had pinned one of those jokey postcards. An image of a woman in a crinoline reclining on a chaise longue, a book in one hand, a glass of wine in the other. The caption read: 'Queen of F****ing Everything'.

Through the chink in the doorway, Ella could see them standing together, Billy and Selena, their heads bent over the desk. Selena had her hand on Billy's arm. And they were laughing, murmuring, laughing again.

She felt sick. That cold, yellow feeling swelled in her stomach. She cleared her throat.

'Hello?'

They each turned towards her voice, Selena still laughing, Billy's face changing in an instant from a wide grin to a look of confusion.

'El. This is a surprise!'

'My turn to spring something on you,' she said quickly, holding up the brown paper bag in which she'd packed paninis and his favourite cookies studded with walnuts and chocolate chips. 'Lunch. For two.'

Under Selena's steady gaze, the gesture was already beginning to feel stupid, unimaginative.

'How wonderful,' Selena said. 'Your very own domestic goddess. Lucky you.'

Ella refused to look in her direction.

She could see Billy trying to cover his embarrassment.

'El,' he was saying. 'May I introduce you to Selena, my colleague? I think you've heard me talk about our work together?'

Selena nodded in her direction. 'How lovely. I've heard so much about you.'

Ella felt her throat close up. Her mouth was dry.

'And the thing is, El,' Billy was saying, 'Selena and I have got a meeting at 1.30. With the Pro VC. It's about the new Research Institute. We were just going over stuff.' He pointed at the sheaf of papers on the table. 'Sorry. This is awful. It's so kind of you. I don't mean to sound . . . God, I'm sounding really ungrateful, aren't I? Let's go to my office. We can have lunch together and then –' He looked at Selena. 'That's OK, isn't it? We've got time.'

'Sure.' Selena shrugged. She was already turning away from them, picking up a folder and beginning to leaf through it. She looked as if she couldn't care less, but Ella could feel her Signals leaping around them – restless lines of red and orange. She was furious.

'Don't worry.' Ella handed Billy the bag. 'I don't want to keep you from your work. I shouldn't have come.'

'No, it's really lovely of you, El. I'm sorry. I –' His hands dropped to his sides. He looked dismayed.

Ella was already backing out of the door. 'See you later,' she said. 'Goodbye, Selena. Nice to meet you.'

'See you tonight, then.' Billy's voice floated after her but she was already halfway down the corridor, tears pricking her eyes. Damn that woman. It was so obvious now. She really was interested in Billy, after all. Was he really too oblivious to see that?

She remembered what Florence had said. *Most men are pretty stupid . . . It only takes some silly woman to come along and flatter their ego at a moment when they're feeling a bit lost, a bit underappreciated . . .*

A growing unease gnawed at her all the way home.

'You're back early.' Mamma frowned. 'Oh, *tesora*. It didn't go well?'

'Billy had a meeting.' Ella tried to keep her voice steady. 'Look, if you don't mind, Mamma, I'll just go over to the flat and do some tidying up whilst I have the chance.'

'Of course, darling.'

The flat was weirdly empty. She couldn't remember that last time she'd been here on her own, without Billy or Grace. She sat on the edge of the bed, taking deep breaths, trying to steady her hands, which were trembling in her lap. She found herself kneeling in front of the linen basket, her hands in the dirty laundry, pressing handfuls of Billy's shirts to her face, sniffing them for unfamiliar perfume. But there was nothing. Only the musky scent of his aftershave and the smell of his warm skin. She breathed it in, swallowing tears.

Why was she suddenly so afraid? The cold, yellow feeling crept from the bottom of her stomach up into her throat. It was suffocating. Something about the way he'd looked when he first turned around and saw her standing there. She couldn't quite put her finger on it.

At a loss, she went back over to the shop and upstairs to the office. She could at least make a start on some of the orders. She sat at the computer, resisting the temptation to look at Billy's emails. They'd never had any secrets from one another. She knew all his passwords, combinations of her own and Grace's names and birth-dates. She could just sneak a look now, reassure herself. But what could that possibly achieve? Was she really this desperate?

Beneath the window, the courtyard was empty and silent. The last leaves of autumn skittered across the cobbles. She chewed on the end of her pen. She could be using this time to write, for God's sake, instead of frittering it away. Why did she have to be so insecure? Why did she always have to spoil things? She remembered another time, years ago, she and Billy standing on the banks of the river, Billy kicking at a tussock of grass with the toe of his boot.

'Try not to think, why don't you.' Billy was saying, his face white with anger. 'How's that for a new idea? If you ask me, maybe you do *too much* thinking . . . Always making up stories when there's nothing there. Always scribbling things down in that little notebook of yours.'

Is that what she was doing now? Making up stories?

She stared at the opposite wall, the paraphernalia of their lives together pinned on the noticeboard, bills to be paid, Grace's first crayoned scribbles, a photo of Billy standing in the courtyard, Grace in his arms, each of them grinning that same lopsided grin.

But then, in front of it all swam the face of Selena LaSalle, her perfectly white teeth parted slightly as she shook her blonde hair from her face and laughed.

Your very own domestic goddess. How lovely.

Ella threw down her pen in irritation.

'Hot chocolate, *tesora*?' Mamma called up the stairs. 'I'm making some for us.'

'No, thanks, Mamma,' she called back. She lay down on the sofa and closed her eyes.

18

To keep a lover faithful: If you suspect your love of straying,
gather up his footprint and put it into a bag of red cloth.
Be sure to gather all of the dirt. Sew the bag closed with blue
or gold thread and sleep with it beneath your mattress.
– Miss Mary's Book of Dreams

'So are you going to tell me?' Mamma poured sugar into a white espresso cup, stirring it slowly anticlockwise, exactly seven times.

Ella felt Mamma's eyes scrutinising her face, those green eyes that could look right into you. She shrugged and tried to empty her mind of thoughts so that Mamma wouldn't see. She put the last of the empty bottles from the party into the recycling box and wiped her hands.

She watched Mamma raise an eyebrow expectantly. 'You can't avoid me forever, *tesora*.'

'Can't I?' Ella spun the glass sugar shaker on the table. She dug her nails into her palms and felt her face beginning to flush. It was so annoying, the way that Mamma could instantly make her feel like a teenager with something to hide.

'Ella, *please*.' Mamma laid a hand on her arm. Her bracelet – made of silver links in the shape of a snake with ruby chips for eyes – sent reflections skittering over the ceiling.

'Is that new?'

Mamma shrugged. 'I once sold one very like it. To Katrina's mother, in fact. Do you remember? I found this one in a house sale in San Diego. Funny, really, how these things come around. Anyway, don't change the subject.' Her green eyes flashed. 'I want to know everything.'

Ella sighed. She took a sip of coffee and let the hot liquid move over her tongue.

'Well, basically, it's Billy and me. Before the party, I got it into my head that he might be having an affair. You know, there were all these secret phone calls and other things . . . I put two and two together and made five. And so then, afterwards, I felt relieved. But now . . . well, I don't know what to think. I wonder if he might be at least considering it. With someone at work.'

Mamma's breath made a sharp sound between her teeth. She frowned and laid a hand on Ella's arm. Ella felt the familiar warmth travel up as far as her elbows.

'*Tesora*? That doesn't sound like Billy at all.'

Ella swallowed another gulp of coffee. She felt that little red bead of anger rising in her. 'And that's precisely why I didn't say anything before. I knew you'd think I was just being paranoid, that it's *me* who's the problem. After all, Billy's so perfect, isn't he? Everyone thinks he is. You probably all wonder what he's doing with me, anyway.'

Mamma raised an eyebrow again. '*Tesora*, that's not what I meant. Not at all.' She made a clicking noise with her tongue. 'I was just going to say that sometimes it's easy to convince ourselves of these things. Jump to the wrong conclusions. And often there's another perfectly innocent explanation. Tell me, *carina*, what's happening between you two to make you think such a thing? What's going on?'

Ella dipped her finger in the dregs of her coffee and began to trace little circles on the table. 'I don't know, Mum. It feels as if we're drifting apart. I can't complain about anything, really. He's helpful, he spends loads of time with Grace, he tries to give me time to write. He's absorbed in his work, of course. But then, so would I be, if I was getting anything done. It seems like I've got nothing to moan about. But I just get irritated. I snap at him all the time. I'm fat and I'm boring and I'm so damn tired, and I can't even write anymore . . . I wouldn't blame him if he *was* seeing someone else. Or at least, thinking about it, anyway. And there's this woman at work – a colleague. I've seen her. She's clever and skinny and beautiful and he's always talking about her. You know, *Selena said this* and *Selena thinks that* . . . And they've been working long hours on this project together.'

'Is that what went wrong, then?' Mamma leaned across the table. 'When you went to see Billy. When you were supposed to have lunch together. Was she there? This Selena.'

'Yes.' Just thinking about it made Ella's eyes fill with tears. 'She was there. And seeing them together . . . it was –' She bit her lip. 'And then . . . well, there's other stuff, too. I'm sort of embarrassed about it.'

Again Mamma raised her perfectly groomed eyebrow.

'OK, OK. I'll tell you. It's about the Signals. I know we hardly ever talk about them. I don't really *want* to talk about them now . . . but it's just that they're getting stronger. I'm picking them up in other people. Bryony, for instance. That customer you met. It's weird. Almost like I've known her for years. When, of course, I don't. I hardly know her at all.'

Mamma nodded. 'Well, I think you're right. She certainly has something about her.'

194

'Really?'

Mamma's face gave nothing away.

Ella felt the familiar anger pushing up inside her. 'Well, I wish she didn't. She's nice. Lovely, in fact. But it's just too much. And it's not just colours and feelings anymore. It's in the food I eat, the *flavour* of things. The other night, I swear I could taste Billy's *emotions* in these mushrooms that he'd picked.' She looked at Mamma. Her face felt hot with shame. 'Please, Mum, tell me I'm not going completely mad –'

'You're not.' Mamma waved a hand dismissively. 'It's true. This can happen. In fact, it happened to me when I was pregnant with you. I started tasting feelings everywhere.' She laughed softly to herself. 'It nearly drove your father crazy. But tell me, darling.' Mamma leaned in closer. Her long fingers tapped the table for emphasis. 'How can you be sure, *tesora*, that the feelings you're tasting are not your own?'

'What do you mean?'

'What I mean,' Fabia said slowly, 'is that when I'm picking up those kinds of Signals in someone else, it's usually because I too am feeling the same way.'

Ella felt those green eyes look deeply into her.

'Jealousy,' Mamma said. 'Anger. Fear . . . And especially longing. Oh, such longing. That can be particularly cruel. Longing for what we don't have or for what we think that we need. Never feeling satisfied. Nothing ever quite being enough. When we want more, it's almost always because we don't think that we ourselves are enough. No?'

Ella pushed back her chair and began to gather up the cups and spoons and saucers. She'd forgotten this about Mamma. How she had a way of reaching inside you, putting a finger on exactly what the problem was, the thing that you really didn't want to think about. Suddenly, it felt as if she had to get up and move, as if her skin was crawling with it all.

'I don't know, Mum,' she said. 'But Billy will be back soon. With Grace. So I think we should stop talking about this now.'

'Oh, I'm sorry, *tesora*. You think I'm interfering. I don't mean to. It's just –'

'I know. You want me to be happy. I get that. I know you want to help. I know that I'd feel exactly the same if Grace was unhappy.'

Mamma smiled. 'It changes you, doesn't it?'

'Being a mum? Yep. It's the hardest thing in the world. I don't know how you did it all those years, on your own.'

Mamma reached out a hand. 'Because, *carina*, you were wonderful. Always. The best thing in the world for me. But I think, if you don't mind me making a suggestion –'

'OK. Go on.'

'I think you need more in your life than just Grace and Billy. I think you're a bit frustrated. I think you need some help with this place.' She waved an arm around the shop. 'And I'm wondering if, since I'm here for the next little while, I could do that? I don't mean take over. This is *your* shop now. But maybe I could help? And you might have more time to . . . well, write?'

Ella came and sat down again, opposite Mamma. 'I would be sooooo grateful,' she said slowly. 'That would be wonderful. But what about you, Mamma? I mean, I've been wanting to ask but I didn't know how to say it exactly. Is everything OK? With you and David, I mean. How long are you thinking of staying?'

Mamma smiled. 'Everything is just fine, *tesora*. For goodness' sake, don't start worrying about that too. And I can stay for as long as you –'

Outside, the wind threw a spattering of rain against the window and the shop bell jangled, making them both jump.

Grace stood in the doorway, waving a piece of paper that was almost larger than her.

'Look, Granmamma. I drew a picture at playgroup. It's for *YOU!*'

Behind her, Ella caught Billy's eye. He grinned.

'You see,' he said to Mamma. 'You've only been here a minute and you're already stealing my daughter's affections from me.'

Ella moved to the coffee machine, began to add fresh beans to the grinder. She didn't want to have to meet Fabia's eye.

'We were just catching up,' Mamma was saying.

Billy grinned again. 'I can only imagine.'

*

Ella watched the shadows lengthening from the corner of the room as the light filtered through the bedroom window. Since the arrival of Mamma and then Maadar-Bozorg, she'd found herself thinking more about her father, wondering again what he must have looked like. As a child, she'd asked Mamma to tell her, over and over, the story of how they'd met, in the garden at Les Oiseaux on one of those nights when the sky seemed to reach all the way down to the earth, warm and blue-black and thickly strewn with stars. 'You could almost put up your hand and pull it around yourself like a magic cloak,' Mamma had said. 'That night, you could almost feel the garden breathing . . .'

Ella knew that she had her father's eyes and nose, or so Mamma had always told her. And when Grace had been born, she'd peered into her tiny face searching for other signs of a family likeness, things she might recognise from the black-and-white photo she'd pushed into the frame of her dressing table mirror. Her father, Enzo, in jeans and a white T-shirt, posed in front of the flat in Hastings where he and Mamma had first lived when they came to England. He was looking straight at the camera and sometimes Ella had the uncanny feeling that he was gazing right out of the photo and into her own eyes, as if he had something very important to tell her. She had scrutinised every inch of that image until she knew it by heart: her father's dark hair, cut very short, his broad shoulders and muscular forearms. He was incredibly handsome. 'Like a film star,' Mamma had always said. Sometimes, even now, her whole body ached to think that she'd never feel those arms around her, or nuzzle into the crook of his neck in the way that she watched Grace do with Billy.

She wondered if it was really true, what Bryony said, that people didn't just disappear, that they always returned to the earth in one way or another; that you could find them when you knew where to look, in the creak of dry branches or the mist that rises from wet earth after days of rain or in a shadow passing across a bedroom floor. Ella wanted to believe this was true. But whenever she tried to conjure her father, she felt only a kind of gap where the feeling of him should have been. Whereas Mamma was everywhere, even when she wasn't, her perfume lingering in the room, her lipstick on the rim of a white cup, her voice with its slow rich vowels so much a part of Ella's own internal voice that at times when she'd been younger, she hadn't known where Fabia's thoughts ended and her own began.

She thought again about her other self, the version of herself that she saw in her dreams. Because she hadn't stopped dreaming. And there was an entire world that she returned to now, even though she told herself she wouldn't, each time she closed her eyes.

'It's just a dream,' she told herself. 'Just a dream. It's not real . . .'

Over and over again, she would wake up feeling heavy and exhausted, her heart pounding, her mouth parched. She had to lie for a long time, forcing herself to remember things – her own name, the names of Billy and Grace, the name of the shop where she'd bought the bedroom curtains and the way the lace edging of the pillow felt when she rubbed it between her fingers – just to anchor herself in the present again.

Sometimes she imagined that she saw Mary Cookson, felt her mud-fringed skirts brush against the walls of the narrow hallway, heard her voice in her head. She thought she saw, as she passed the bedroom mirror, the arch of a neck, a wisp of red hair, a shoulder wrapped in a woollen shawl out of the corner of her eye.

Sometimes she thought she was going mad. Is this how easily it happened? She'd reach for Billy's hand then, squeezing it with such ferocity that he'd put his head on one side and looked at her.

'El, are you OK?'

Was she? She really didn't know anymore. What did it mean, to be OK?

'Fair to middling,' Billy's mum would have said. 'As well as can be expected, love,' as she rolled out the pastry for her apple pie or folded her newly ironed bed sheets. 'The secret to a happy life,' she'd said to Ella on the day that she and Billy had married, 'is never to expect too much. That way, when something isn't going well, you're not too disappointed, and when something lovely happens, it's a nice surprise.'

She lay and listened to the sound of Billy's breathing and the pigeons splashing in the guttering after last night's downpour. This was the life she'd made for herself. And it was a good life, in so many ways. Here was the man she loved. And here, in these few small rooms, was the world that they'd made together, their daughter dreaming just across the hallway, their books on the shelves, their plates and cups in the kitchen cupboards, their coats hanging on the hooks under the stairs. She and Billy had made for Grace what Ella herself had never been able to have, despite all of Mamma's hard work – a family of three. So why did she now find herself longing for something she couldn't even shape into words?

She put out a finger and stroked the bristle on Billy's cheek, watching him stir slightly in his sleep. When he was sleeping, he looked most like that boy who'd once hung by his feet from a rope swing above the middle of a muddy brown river. The smile that always hovered at the corners of his mouth relaxed in sleep to a kind of gentle openness, which was the way he'd looked when he'd first kissed her that night on the bridge seven years ago, the night that she'd pushed him away.

And maybe, Ella thought, we all have so many different selves inside us, like Grace's set of Russian dolls, made of painted wood. You opened one to find another, and another inside that and another, until you discovered the tiniest doll, not much bigger than a seed or a grain of rice, so that you couldn't make out the eyes and nose and lips, except perhaps with a magnifying glass. Who was the Ella in the centre of it all – the Ella that she was when every other self had been opened up and set aside? That, she thought, was what she was searching for.

19

To dream of your true love: Take one cup of flour, one of salt and a handful of ashes from a spent fire. Add a hair from your own head, a handful of apple blossoms and enough water to make a mixture. Put them in a pan and cook slowly over a low fire. When the cake is done, place it under your pillow and wait for your love to appear to you.
– Miss Mary's Book of Dreams

'What do you think?'

Fabia steadied herself at the top of the ladder and adjusted the signs on the new bookcases. She watched Ella stand back, head on one side, assessing her handiwork.

'Just left a bit, Mum. More towards the centre. Yes, that's right.'

Florence whistled. 'Love it,' she said. 'Very, very cool, you two.'

The signs were written out in Mamma's beautiful copperplate handwriting, which Ella had asked the printer to super-size on crisp, white card. 'RED,' said one and then, next to it, 'SNOW.'

'I can't claim any credit.' Fabia directed a meaningful look at the top of her daughter's head.

'Except for the exquisite handwriting, of course.' Ella winced. 'Mine would have been a disaster.'

The bottom stair creaked and Maadar-Bozorg stood nodding.

'Yes, these two are a formidable team. But for goodness' sake, Farah, child, get down from there before you break your neck. Or at least kick those shoes off.'

Fabia laughed, negotiating her way expertly down the ladder in her leopard-print court shoes. 'Years of practice,' she said.

'The idea,' Ella said, oblivious, 'is that we curate things for people, make it easier for them to browse, to stumble across something new. LOVE is something we'll introduce for Valentine's Day next year.' She held up another enormous sign with flamingo pink lettering. 'TRANSFORMATIONS is Mamma's thing. We'll bring it in for the New Year. But SNOW and RED, we're going to do right now. So that you see them as soon as you walk in. What do you think?'

She watched Florence slip behind the stepladder and run her finger along the first shelf of 'RED', which included a collector's edition of a pop-up *Red Riding Hood*, Du Maurier's *Don't Look Now and Other Stories*, a biography of the Red Queen, a field guide to poppies, a book of gluten-free cake recipes entitled *Red Velvet*, Anita Diamant's *The Red Tent*, and, of course, a copy of Grimms' *Fairy Tales* with the red shoes featured on the cover.

'It's brilliant.' Florence nodded. 'You need to get this featured in the press. Really. I should call up a couple of people for you.' She was already browsing SNOW.

Fabia thought how much she liked this young woman, Florence. How supportive she was of her daughter. And maybe it wasn't coincidence that, like Ella, Florence had never really known her father either. Her mother, a very chic French woman who'd been quite a regular in Fabia's York shop, had mostly raised her alone. Perhaps it wasn't so surprising that these two had gravitated towards one another.

'There's loads more we could do,' Ella said. 'Maybe we could ask customers to suggest things, too? But we'll just start with a few shelves like this, see how it goes.'

'It needs just a little something extra, I think.' Fabia crossed to the old fitting room at the back of the shop, which she'd recently cleared of the dusty boxes of books and resurrected as a dressing-up corner. It was already proving a popular extension of the Children's Section. The shop's younger visitors were enjoying trying on all the new costumes she'd created, turning to admire themselves in the gilt-framed mirror.

Fabia opened the new dressing-up box – one of her old trunks that she'd dragged out from storage upstairs – and selected the Red Riding Hood cloak, shaking out its silk folds.

'Do you think Grace will object?' she said, draping it over the end of the bookcase.

Florence and Ella exchanged glances.

'Um. Honest answer?' Florence laughed.

The shop door jangled, making them all jump.

Bryony stood in the doorway.

'Oh my goodness,' she said, her face dimpling. 'I love it. What a wonderful idea.'

Fabia smiled. 'I'm just being persuaded that my granddaughter might object to our using her Red Hiding Hood cloak . . . But it needs a little something extra, don't you think?'

Bryony frowned. 'What about the red shoes? The ones in the dressing-up box that the children are always fighting over?'

'Of course. Bryony, you're a genius!' Ella was already fishing them out from the bottom of the trunk.

'Ah, yes.' Fabia stroked the worn satin of her old red ballet shoes. She looked up and met Maadar-Bozorg's eye. 'I'm not sure how they got in there, anyway. I can't believe these are still going.' She took the Brothers Grimm book from the shelf and displayed it front-wise, nestling the shoes one inside the other on top. 'There. Thank you, Bryony. Perfect.'

*

Fabia watched the silent shapes flicker across the TV screen. She'd turned the sound right down so that she could hear the fireworks. Giant blossoms of white and gold burst across the chink of sky that she could just glimpse above the rooftops from Ella and Billy's living room window.

She'd insisted they go out for the night whilst she looked after Grace, who was still too small to relish the Bonfire Night celebrations. They'd left holding hands, like two teenagers on a first date, Ella bundled into a bulky nylon parka – Fabia really couldn't understand why all the young women she saw in the street actually *chose* to wear that kind of thing – her cheeks glowing as brightly as her knitted red woollen hat.

The chat show host stood up to introduce his next guest and Fabia felt her eyes getting heavy. She yawned, letting her sewing slip from her fingers into her lap.

Maadar-Bozorg was already sleeping, bundled in a nest of quilts and blankets in the old bedroom above the shop. 'So cold,' she'd said. 'So damp, here. It gets into your bones. I don't know how you stand it.'

Fabia had already looked in on her, her silver hair spread over the pillow, her lips moving as she muttered to herself in her dreams. Later, Fabia too would cross the courtyard again, lock up the shop and climb the stairs, just as she had years ago, but this time she would sleep on a sofa bed squeezed between a desk and stacks of boxes in the old living room that was now Ella's office.

Fabia had the distinct feeling that the past – after all these years of running – was finally about to catch up with her. Her stomach churned, colours flickered behind her eyes and the scent of dust and pomegranate blossoms followed her everywhere.

Now she put her head back on the sofa cushions, closed her eyes and felt the sun-warmed stones of the terrace at Maadar-Bozorg's village house beneath her bare feet. She felt the hem of an embroidered cotton nightdress tickling her ankles.

She lay down in the thick grass, in the shade of the pomegranate trees, her head resting in the cleft between two gnarled old roots. She breathed in the fragrance of the dry red earth. She watched the ripening fruit bobbing like round red lamps between her flickering eyelashes.

'What are you doing, child? You can't sleep out here.'

The touch of cool hands through the thin cotton of her nightdress, scooping her up, carrying her inside. The floor tiles with the pattern of opening blossoms – blue and red and brown – the glint of the big chrome taps and the thrill of a cold cloth pressed to her sticky forehead.

'There, child. You can sleep now . . .'

Her soft bed with its crisp, white sheet. The feel of the threadwork under her chin.

'Maadar-Bozorg . . .'

'Yes?'

'Tell me a story . . .'

The Story of the Twelve Dancing Princesses

Long ago, in a land where the sun is never too hot and the grass grows green and high, there was a king who had twelve beautiful daughters.

The twelve princesses were inseparable. They had no mother – she had died when the youngest princess was still a baby – and so they were free to do whatever they pleased. By day they wandered through the palace grounds, climbing trees and playing tricks on the palace gardeners. At night they slept together in one long and narrow room, in twelve beds arranged in a row. Each bed had a white coverlet and a soft white pillow. Each pillow was filled with the down of the royal swans on the palace lake, which the King's maidservants gathered every morning in their aprons in great white drifts.

Each evening, when the princesses had undressed and put on their white nightdresses and slipped under their coverlets, the King ordered that their maidservants must lock and bolt the door to their room. He was determined that, unlike their mother, his precious daughters would never come to any harm. He insisted that the heavy silver key to their door was brought to him personally each night and, each night, he slept with the key under his own pillow.

But despite these careful precautions, in the mornings, when the maidservants came to unlock the princesses' room and bring them breakfast, they always found the same thing. The princesses would be sleeping peacefully, their hair tumbling over their pillows and their shoes paired neatly at the foot of each bed. But when they gathered up the shoes to take for polishing, the maidservants saw that the soles were all worn through, as if each princess had been dancing all night.

Each morning, the King would summon one of his daughters and demand to know where they had been. But each girl would only smile at him or cover her mouth and laugh behind her hand.

And so, eventually, the King made it known throughout the entire land that if any man could discover the princesses' secret and find out where it was that they went at night and what they did there, he could choose the princess he liked best as his wife.

The princesses were renowned as twelve great beauties and so very soon there was a long line of suitors waiting outside the gates of the palace for a chance to try their hand. The princesses were not afraid in the slightest about this. They knew that there was no man in the world who could ever discover their secret. In fact, they took to hanging out of their bedroom window and giggling at each man as he knocked at the great oak doors.

'Look at this one. He's so fat!'

'And look at this one with the big nose. He looks so proud.'

Only the youngest of the princesses, a girl with blue-grey eyes and wild brown hair, refused to join in. She begged her sisters to be quiet. 'Come away from the window,' she said.

The first man to try to uncover the princesses' secret was a gentleman with greying hair and a large round belly. He made a great show of walking up and down their bedroom and looking carefully under each of their beds, whilst scratching his beard and mumbling to himself.

Finally, he settled himself down by the doorway to begin his night watch. The eldest princess brought him a goblet of wine, which he took greedily and drained to the very last drop. When the sound of his snores began to reverberate through the room, the princesses stifled their laughter. It was late the next morning that their suitor stirred and he never came close to discovering the princesses' secret.

The same thing happened to the second and third and fourth suitors, and the King began to despair that he would ever discover how his daughters managed to wear out every new pair of dancing shoes.

He tossed and turned in his own bed until the fifth night, when he dreamed that his daughters had turned into white geese and flown away through their open bedroom window. In the morning when he woke up, he burst into their room, fearing that all he would find were a few white feathers scattered on their pillows, but instead he saw each of the princesses sleeping peacefully with a smile on their face and the latest suitor rubbing his eyes and muttering to himself.

Now it happened that one day a young man, the son of a local blacksmith, was walking through the woods at the edge of his village, gathering sticks for his father's fire. An old woman with cheeks as wrinkled as crab apples stopped him and asked him for a few coins. The man pulled a handful of coppers from his pocket.

'Old woman, this is all I have to give you,' he said, 'but if you come with me, you can warm yourself by our fire and my mother will give you some bread.'

The old woman's eyes twinkled and a large black crow flew down out of the trees and settled on her shoulder. It put its head on one side and looked at the man. 'Cark, cark,' it said.

'Young man, I'm going to tell you something,' said the old woman and she waved her finger, which was as gnarled as an old tree root, beckoning him to come closer. Then she whispered some instructions into his ear.

The man looked at her, astonished. 'The twelve dancing princesses?' he cried. 'But the King himself and some of the richest men in the land have tried to uncover their secret. What makes you think I can do any better?'

The old woman laughed and her laughter was like the sound of the wind sighing through the trees. She reached into the pack on her back and pulled out a piece of folded material. 'This,' she said, 'is a cloak. Put it on and whatever you do will be invisible.' She shook out its heavy folds and the young man shuddered as bits of old leaves and dead insects and spiders' webs dropped onto his shoes.

But in order to be polite, as his mother had always taught him, he thanked the mad old woman for her gift and rolled it under his arm and carried it back with him to his cottage.

That night and for all the nights after that, his dreams were filled with the rustle of silken skirts in red and yellow and silver and the sound of twelve pairs of feet dancing.

And when he was so exhausted from lack of sleep that he dropped his tongs in the fire and ruined a good set of horseshoes, he decided to set off and try his hand at the palace.

By now, the line of men outside the palace gates had dwindled away. Word had spread that no one could outwit the twelve clever princesses and some said that they were bewitched by the ghost of their dead mother and that each night they slipped from the Land of the Living to the Land of the Other Ones, the dead ones who lived in a castle far out beyond the edge of the darkest woods. These stories had frightened away even the most faithful of the King's many servants, including the palace gardeners, who had abandoned their work so that thick branches of ivy had begun to twine themselves around the window of the princesses' bedchamber.

So this young man, despite being a humble blacksmith with no wealth or learning to his name, was well received at the palace gates, and the King ordered him to be draped in fine robes of fur and velvet to keep him warm as he began his night vigil. But instead the young man politely declined and drew a bit of old material from his bag that smelled of mildew and was embroidered all over with old spiders' webs. The servants looked at one another and rolled their eyes.

The young man took up his watching place at the door of the bedchamber and the eldest princess brought him a cup of wine but, remembering the instructions that the old woman had whispered in his ear, the young man took care not to drink a drop. He poured the wine into his water skin when the princess wasn't looking and then lay down on the floor and pretended to snore very loudly, as if he was fast asleep.

Very soon after that, he heard the pattering of twelve pairs of feet and the princesses' stifled laughter. Through his half-closed eyelids, he saw them opening their wardrobes and taking out their gowns of coloured silks and fastening their finest jewels around their necks.

Then the princesses rolled up the rug from the bedroom floor and leaned it against the door. The eldest princess clapped her hands three times and, in the middle of the bare boards, a trapdoor opened. The young man, who hardly dared to breathe, saw the shapes of them in the gloom as they descended, one by one, disappearing, feet first and then shoulders and then heads, down, down beneath the floor. As soon as the youngest princess was out of sight, he leapt up and tied the musty cloak around his shoulders and lowered himself after them. His feet soon found the edges of a secret staircase that led deep into the earth and, as quietly and carefully as he could, he felt his way down it. But his feet slipped on something and he heard the youngest princess cry out.

'Stop. Someone has taken hold of my gown!'

'Don't be so silly!' the eldest sister said. 'It's just caught on a nail or a crack in the wall. Give it a tug.' And the young man lifted his shoe and down they all went.

At the bottom of the staircase, the young man found himself in the middle of a wood. The birch trees shone under the bright moon, lighting his way, and he followed the princesses into a clearing. Here, where the trees thinned, the branches were covered in leaves that glittered and sparkled red against the night sky as if they were made of rubies. He couldn't resist. He put up his hand and plucked one and, as it came off the branch, it made a loud snapping sound.

'What was that?' cried the youngest princess. 'What was that noise? Someone is following us!'

But the others only laughed at her. 'Don't be such a scaredy-cat,' the eldest said. 'You're always inventing things that aren't there.'

The young man followed them out of the clearing and onto the banks of a wide lake where the water rippled in the moonlight. Twelve white rowing boats were drawn up in the rushes, with a prince waiting at the oars of each one. The princesses stepped eagerly, one into each boat, and the young man followed, tucking himself carefully in the stern of the last, behind the youngest princess.

'What's that?' cried the youngest princess. 'I felt something brush past my sleeve in the dark.'

But her prince only smiled. 'Don't be afraid, little one. It's just the moths that gather down here by the water or perhaps a night bird looking for its nest.' Nevertheless, he noticed that his oars felt heavier than usual as he rowed across the black water. I must be very tired tonight, he thought.

Soon the young man could make out a fine castle on the distant shore, with every window lit. The sounds of flutes and drums and guitars drifted across the still water. He watched the princesses step from the boats, each on the arm of their prince, and run across the grass. They flitted through the gates in the castle walls like twelve exotic birds. Covered by his cloak, he followed and leaned against a column in one of the grand, marble hallways and watched them whirl and dance, their hair fluttering about their faces, the ribbons on their dresses flying out, their slippers flashing faster and faster in the light from the blazing torches.

He watched until the first streaks of rose and pearl appeared in the castle windows and the youngest princess clutched at her foot and said that her shoes were quite worn through. The princes sighed then and each swept a princess up in his arms and carried her across the grass and into one of the waiting boats and rowed them back across the lake and to the other shore.

This time, the blacksmith was already waiting in the boat of the eldest princess. He was the first to clamber onto the banks and he hurried ahead of the princesses, through the clearing and up the hidden staircase in the woods. When he reached the bed-chamber, he took off his magic cloak, bundled it into his bag and laid himself down on the cold floor, snoring loudly.

The next morning, imagine the princesses' surprise when the young man drew from the pocket of his waistcoat a single leaf of glittering ruby and laid it on the youngest sister's white coverlet.

'If you will do me the honour of being my wife,' he said, 'I promise not to tell your father where you all go at night.'

213

The youngest princess gasped and turned to the others, her face defiant. 'See!' she said. 'It wasn't my imagination. I felt something and I heard something – and it *was* real after all.' She took the young man's hand and smiled at him.

'You don't have to marry him,' the eldest princess said, as the young man twirled the leaf between his fingers. 'Because no one would ever believe him anyway. They'd think he'd fallen down drunk and dreamed it all . . .'

But the youngest princess held on fast to the young man's hand and looked deep into his eyes. She'd never seen a man so handsome and kind in all her young life. And so she told her father that he'd discovered their secret and that she must honour the promise and marry him. But when the King pressed the young man for the truth, he simply said that the sisters had made a rope of their twelve white coverlets and climbed down out of their high window and danced all night on the shores of the lake in the palace grounds, and the princesses nodded that, yes, this was true.

But night after night, after their youngest sister was married, the other eleven princesses would slip away to the underground kingdom and dance with their handsome princes. And they never married, even though many men were to ask for their hands.

The youngest sister grew plump and happy with her husband in the house that he built for her at the edge of the water. She herself had never really wanted more than one life and was perfectly content to stay in this one.

In the evenings, she would sit and watch the sun sink into the middle of the lake and watch the geese flying low across the water. And for her, that was more than enough . . .

And with those words, Maadar-Bozorg tucked the sheet a little tighter around Fabia's shoulders and planted a kiss on her forehead.

'Sleep well, child. Sweet dreams.'

*

Fabia heard a scuffling sound and then she heard Ella, whispering.

'She's fast asleep,' she said and Fabia felt the softness of a blanket being laid over her, very gently. She kept her eyes closed.

'Let's not disturb her,' Billy whispered.

It was only when she was sure that they had tiptoed away to their room that Fabia opened her eyes and got up from the chair and stretched herself.

Then she looked down and saw that something had fallen from her lap: the piece of blue chiffon that she'd been sewing into pleats and, caught in the middle of the fabric, a single leaf that glittered in the light from the reading lamp, ruby red.

20

'Bryony has something she needs your help with, Maadar-Bozorg. Something I thought you might know about.'

Ella smiled. She was still getting used to saying that word – Maadar-Bozorg – out loud. She could hardly believe that this spry old lady, sitting right here in the shop in one of her leather armchairs, was the legendary woman of Mamma's stories. She looked too small. Too, well, ordinary.

Bryony pulled the red cloth-covered book out of her bag and laid it carefully on the table. She smiled, shyly. 'Yes, it's here, in a book that Ella and I have been . . . well, I suppose you'd say *researching*.' She opened Miss Mary's book at the frontispiece and smoothed the paper carefully. 'It's a book of dreams and dream spells, written by a woman who lived here in Yorkshire in the seventeenth century.'

'A witch, Maadar-Bozorg.' Ella smiled. 'I told Bryony that you might know something about those.'

'Oh you did, did you, child?' Maadar smiled. 'You'll get me a terrible reputation.'

'It's this.' Bryony pointed, her face creased with concentration. 'This image. We don't understand what it might be.'

She traced the shape with her fingers. Two ovals, side by side, one enclosing a small off-centre circle, the other divided into quadrants.

'I thought at first that it might be something to do with lunar charts,' she said. 'But then I found this note from the editor at the back of the book. She writes that the image was found scribbled on the back of one of Miss Mary's papers. And there's a single sentence in Miss Mary's handwriting: "Asked Thomas the black-smith if he would make me this dish, which appeared to me in a dream. He declined, saying it would bring him trouble and me also. I am greatly saddened." So we know it's a kind of dish. The question is, what could she have wanted it for? And why was it so important? Why was Thomas so afraid of making it for her?'

'Let me see . . .'

Maadar-Bozorg unfolded her reading glasses and pushed them up her nose. She peered at the page. Then she put her head back and laughed, a long, low laugh.

'What, Maadar-Bozorg? What is it?' Ella frowned.

'Does this help?'

Maadar-Bozorg reached into the folds of her shawl and pulled something out. It glinted on her upturned palm. It was a small oval of polished metal, with a hole slightly offset to one side.

Bryony gasped. 'That's just like Miss Mary's drawing. Well, it's a slightly different shape – this one's a bit more pointed at the end – but essentially, it's the same. Except that there should be another piece to it . . . She shows it as two halves. Look . . .'

'Yes, I know.' Maadar sighed. 'This is the top half. It's a kind of lid. It fits over the other half . . .' She pointed to the drawing. 'Look, you see. It covers the half with the markings. I had both

217

parts once. But I lost one of them. Very careless of me. I never did tell my sisters. It had been our grandmother's and they gave it to me, you see. They would have been furious.'

Mamma had been staring in silence at the object in Maadar's palm. 'Wait a moment,' she said quietly. She half ran to the hatstand by the door, where her trench coat with the red silk lining was hanging, and put her hand in the pocket. Ella saw something glinting in her open palm.

'Is this what you're looking for, Maadar-Bozorg?'

Maadar took the object and turned it over, examining it carefully. She looked at Mamma, a long, hard look, her eyes narrowing. Ella felt Mamma's embarrassment.

'Yes,' Maadar said eventually. 'Yes, it certainly is.' Then she chuckled softly to herself. 'To think you've had it all these years. Where did you find it?'

Mamma's cheeks were flushed.

'In the garden at the village house,' she said. 'I was playing. You know, like I used to do. In the dirt, under the pomegranate trees. Probably where I wasn't supposed to be. I'm sorry. I should have given it to you . . . I guessed that it was yours. But it seemed special, somehow. And secret. Like a piece of you that I could carry with me, hold in my hand when you weren't there . . . I've carried it in my pocket ever since, as a kind of lucky charm. I thought it was a brooch that had lost its pin. Or perhaps a dish. Something you'd put rings or coins in. I'm so sorry, Maadar . . .'

Maadar-Bozorg smiled and pretended to wag her finger at Mamma. 'You always were a naughty girl . . .' She brought the two pieces together, hers and Mamma's. The piece with the hole fitted over Mamma's piece with a tiny chinking sound. 'You see. Two perfect halves. Like . . . so.'

She turned to Ella. 'Do you have a straw, my dear?'

Ella took one from the dispenser on the cafe counter.

Maadar-Bozorg tried it in the hole on the top of the dish. 'Yes, that will work perfectly. Now, to demonstrate.' She pulled a face. 'And my apologies in advance. It's not particularly ladylike . . .'

She placed the straw inside her mug of coffee and slowly, delicately, she sucked up a small mouthful. Then she moved over to the dish, slipped the straw back into the hole and blew the mouthful of coffee through it.

'There. That should do it.' She opened the two halves of the dish again and laid the bottom half very carefully on the table. 'You see how the liquid has mainly settled here, in this one quadrant?'

Bryony, Fabia and Ella each leaned in closer to look.

'So now you'd interpret the pattern of the liquid and its placement on the surface to find the answer to your question. Each quadrant has a meaning – depending on your question. And each pattern has some kind of significance. But, of course, you wouldn't have used coffee in Miss Mary's time. It would have been blood, ground-up animal bone, seeds, earth, depending on what you wanted to know: which crops to plant, which route to take, whether to go to war with your enemy. And usually only one particular person in the tribe or village would be able to interpret the results. That person would have tremendous power . . . Like your Miss Mary . . .' She nodded to Bryony. 'She would be the Diviner. Someone would have taught her, I presume. Her mother perhaps, or grandmother. These things were passed down through generations . . .'

'And you, Maadar-Bozorg? Are you the Diviner of this dish?' Fabia pointed to the two halves gleaming on the table.

'Well, child, that was the idea. That was certainly what Mahdokht – my eldest sister – intended. But then, I haven't been able to use it for the last twenty-five years. I'm sure I'll be a little rusty now.' She sighed. 'And, to be honest, I don't know what I think of all these Old Ways. Were they a good thing? I really don't know. In the wrong hands, they could lead to all kinds of silly superstitions, prejudices, terrible things. Look at what happened to your Miss Mary . . .'

'But in the right hands?' Bryony nudged the edge of the dish with her finger.

'Well, in the right hands, I suppose it's a wonderful aid to our deepest intuitions. It's like any of these tools - the cards, our dreams, even the Signals. They can help us to listen – *really* listen – to what we already know at a very basic level, to everything that our bodies are trying to tell us . . .'

'So do you think that's what divining is?' Ella twisted her wedding ring around her finger. 'It's not some kind of special power that certain people have? It's just . . . well, learning to trust your own instinct?'

Maadar-Bozorg's eyes twinkled.

'My dear, when we finally listen to our instincts, when we're able to listen past all the chatter in our heads, past all the things that other people tell us, all the advice and information, everything we read or learn and everything that we think we *should* be thinking . . . right back to what we *feel*, deep inside our own bodies . . . *that*, my dear one, is the strongest magic of all.'

'Could I?' Bryony's hand hovered over the dish.

'Well, of course, my dear. It does make you want to pick it up, doesn't it? It's very tactile.'

'It's beautiful.' Bryony weighed the metal in her hand. She closed her eyes, opened the dish again. 'And there are so many things I'd like to ask it.'

'Well, go ahead, my dear.' Maadar-Bozorg waved her hand. 'Yes. You absolutely must. After all, you were drawn to that image for a particular reason. I think it could probably help you.'

Bryony closed her eyes again and Ella tried to make her own mind go dark. She didn't want to intrude on what Bryony was thinking and feeling. She watched as Bryony drew coffee up the straw and blew it into the dish, then, hesitantly, prised it apart and looked at what was inside.

*

Ella sat on the end of Maadar-Bozorg's bed in the old flat above Happily Ever After. From here, she could look out through the little window under the eaves and watch the light fading in the courtyard.

Her mind drifted back to that other fateful evening – well over a decade ago now – when the courtyard had been flooded with sunlight and she'd sat here, in this same place, half hidden behind the curtains, waiting for Mamma's charity auction to begin. That evening, as the top of Pike's slick head appeared in the courtyard below, her stomach had churned and her heart had pounded in her chest. Councillor Pike, as he'd been then, with his oiled hair and his cheap shoes and those eyes like little black beads. She could picture him now, picking his way over the cobbles, Jean Cushworth clinging to his arm.

Of course, Pike had been more or less finished at the council after that night. In fact, he'd been more or less finished, full

221

stop. There'd been a handful of people who'd tried to defend him, protested that Ella must have made it all up. That strange Moreno girl with the wild hair who runs around with Billy Vickers, they'd said. But the rumours had spread quickly and half of the city, it seemed, was only too ready to believe that Pike was capable of what Ella had accused him of, and more besides. He'd made enemies everywhere, people who seized the moment to step forward and point their own fingers. In the end, he'd been lucky to slip away into the shadows without further scandal.

In fact, Billy had seen him a couple of years ago in the mini-market by the station, loading a basket with ready meals. According to Mrs Stubbs, he was living with his aging mother, running her errands, driving her around.

Ella shivered. She could still see Pike's face, pale with fury. She could still feel his touch. Those long white fingers and the smell of sour wine on his breath.

And she remembered sitting here on this bed, just like this, as Mamma folded clothes and laid them carefully in a suit-case. What would have happened if they really had left York that night, running from the wagging tongues and the unkind words? What different turn would their lives have taken? For Mamma, there would have been no David and no move to California. And for her?

Ella sighed. She'd been so young, her life still unfurling ahead of her like a roll of Mamma's dressmaking silk. Back then, she'd been desperate to stay here, surrounded by the things she was growing to love. This city of solid stone walls and streets that twisted in on themselves. The river that flowed, brown and strong, through its centre. And, of course, Billy, the boy with the blue-grey eyes and the lopsided grin who had already claimed her heart. It had all seemed so simple back then.

But now she felt a part of herself stretching into a new shape, yearning for something more. On certain days, the wind tugged at her hair and whispered in her ear: *Ella, Ella, El-la* . . . The Signals taunted her from the corner of the room and got inside her dreams: *Sink or swim*, they whispered. *Sink or swim* . . . At such times, the shop, her little family, and this small, safe city didn't seem big enough to contain her dreams.

She thought of how each of her parents had left their own homes and families in search of adventure. The same spirit of restlessness had kept them moving from place to place, until eventually they'd found each other and travelled from Paris to England together, their lives briefly but irrevocably swept along on the same tide. And Mamma was still moving, crossing countries and continents. She didn't seem made to be still.

But she, Ella, had always thought that she was different. As a child, drifting from one town to another, one flat to another, she'd longed for a place where she could pause and breathe for a moment, where she could stop being the strange, new girl with the funny accent and perhaps even make some friends. And that's what she'd eventually found here with Billy and Grace and Happily Ever After. Her own space. Her own story. And however incomplete it was – the father she would never know, the things Mamma never talked about – it was *her* story. She had made it hers.

But what if it wasn't meant to last? Perhaps it was all an illusion anyway and people like her never did find themselves or came home to themselves or all those things that the books in the Popular Psychology section were always talking about.

Here and there, among the rooftops, she could see the lights coming on in attic windows. There was the familiar clatter of the pigeons on the roof and, beyond that, the clang of metal against metal as the market traders dismantled their stands. The wind creaked and whistled in the guttering and the Minster bells began. Six o'clock. Evening service.

Maadar-Bozorg's woollen shawl was folded neatly over the end of the bed. She traced the intricately woven pattern, the colours soft under her fingers. She lifted it to her face and breathed in the scent – cinnamon and rose petals and something else, a faint smoky tang that was impossible to define.

'It belonged to *my* grandmother,' Maadar-Bozorg had said when Grace, sitting on her lap, had put out her hand to stroke it. 'And when I was only a little bit older than you, Grace, she used to let me wrap myself in it in front of the fire as she told me stories. Sometimes it was a cloak that would give me magical powers and sometimes it became a magic carpet that could fly me wherever I wanted to go.'

'And is that true?' Mamma had said, her eyes glittering with mischief. '*Is* it magic?'

'Well, of course! What a question!' Maadar had held a corner of the shawl in front of Grace's face. 'Now you see her . . . and *abracadabra*. Now you don't!'

Grace's laughter bounced around the room.

Magic. Ella thought of the time when she'd searched this same room for Mamma's mysterious box. Now she bent double on the edge of the bed and ran her fingers over the floorboards, feeling for the piece of board that would give under her fingertips. Yes, Mamma's hiding place was still here. She prised up a corner of the board with her fingernail. Nothing. Just a dusty cavity containing a bit of crumpled tissue and a dead spider. What had she seriously expected to find?

She stood up, smoothing the quilt, and gave Maadar-Bozorg's pillow a gentle shake. That was when she saw it. It was sitting on the bedside table that Mamma had made when they'd first moved here by painting an old packing crate and draping it with a silk scarf. It gleamed in the dim light. The divining dish. She couldn't resist picking it up and weighing it in her palm. Then she turned and glanced over her shoulder. The back of her neck prickled. She could have almost been certain that she'd heard footsteps behind her.

From the very first moment that she'd seen the dish, she'd known exactly what she wanted to do. The question that she wanted to ask it had itched and niggled ever since.

Now she separated the two halves and looked at the strange markings on the base. What did they mean? How could they be interpreted? Perhaps, if she just closed her eyes and let her mind go quiet?

'You won't find the answer to your question there, child.'

Ella jumped.

'Sorry. I – Gosh, you must think –' She felt the familiar flush spread from the tips of her ears into her cheeks. Her fingers, still holding the dish, tingled. She pushed the two halves together again and put the dish back on the little crate-table, where it seemed to glow. It was almost as if it gave off its own soft light.

Maadar-Bozorg stood in the doorway in the semi-darkness. Ella saw that her feet were bare, slender ankles protruding from her mannish flannel trousers, her toes perfectly painted with dark red varnish.

'I'm sorry, Maadar-Bozorg. I wasn't . . . I mean, I just came up here to see if there was anything you needed for the night. And then I started remembering things. You know. From when Mamma and I used to share this room.' Ella reached up and drew the curtains closed. 'And then I saw it.' She nodded in the direction of the dish. 'And I just couldn't resist having another look. Something about it makes you want to pick it up.'

Maadar-Bozorg smiled. 'Absolutely. And I'll show you how to use it, if you *really* want to know.' She perched on the edge of the bed and swung her legs playfully.

In the shadows, she looked almost seventeen, Ella thought. She had a brief glimpse of what Zohreh Jobrani must have been like as a young woman. The chiselled cheekbones, the almond-shaped eyes fringed with dark lashes, the long, proud nose.

'Would you? Would you, really? I'd love that.'

Maadar-Bozorg patted the bed beside her.

'It's terribly simple, of course, as these things often are when you know how.'

Ella sat down next to her and Maadar-Bozorg passed her the dish.

'So you take it in one hand . . . yes, just like that. Let it rest there.' She nodded approvingly. 'And now you must still your mind. Yes, that's right.'

Ella felt Maadar-Bozorg reaching for her in the darkness, her Signals unfurling red and blue and gold. 'And then you must invite your question in, hold it in your mind, but very lightly. Ye-es, careful now. That's it . . .'

Ella shifted position on the bed.

'And now you can take your divining substance, whatever that might be. Let's see. What can we use?'

Ella pushed her hand into her jeans pocket and drew out a paper sachet of sugar, the kind she kept in a little dish in the cafe corner. 'Will this do?'

'Ah, yes. Perfect.' Maadar-Bozorg smiled again. 'And quite relevant, don't you think? Because in matters of the heart, a little extra sweetness never goes amiss.'

She knows exactly what my question is, Ella thought. She felt herself blush again and looked down as Maadar-Bozorg's warm hand cupped her own, steadying the dish.

'So now, keeping it perfectly level, you take a little pinch of your sugar and blow it in through this hole in the lid, here. That's right.'

Maadar-Bozorg's eyes never left her face as Ella bent over the dish and gently blew.

'Good. And now, child, all you need to do is open it up again and read what the dish has to tell you.'

'But that's just it.' Ella weighed the dish in her hand. She hardly dared lift the lid and look inside. 'How will I know what it means?'

'Go on.' Maadar-Bozorg nodded. 'First things first, child. Open it. Then tell me what you see.'

Ella's fingers fumbled with the tiny catch. She laid the lid on the bed and, very carefully, so as not to disturb the contents, she held out the dish.

'No, child. No point showing me. *You* are the diviner. *You* must read the sign.'

'But I don't know how.'

'Oh, I think you do.'

Ella glanced down. At first, all she saw was a plume of sugar, the white crystals arranged in a perfect arc, like a little half-moon.

'Well, it reminds me of a moon, I suppose,' she said. This was stupid. Why was she wasting time like this?

'I know. I know. You're wishing you'd never even started it. That it's a load of old mumbo-jumbo.' Maadar-Bozorg's eyes twinkled. 'And of course, you're partly right. It is. But, you see, there's nothing here to be afraid of. It's like the cards or the runes or the casting board. They can only tell you what's there already.' Maadar-Bozorg tapped the side of her head with a jewelled finger. 'In here, child. In your subconscious mind. These are all simply tools that help us to tap into our mind's amazing power. That's what magic really is. In one sense, anyway.'

Ella looked down again. She noticed now how the little crescent moon shape crossed two of the quadrants engraved on the dish, east to west. As if the moon was rising, waxing towards fullness, caught halfway between one thing and another. A bit like Billy and me, she thought. We don't know if we're one thing or another. We were children together and now, now we're . . . What, exactly? Grace's parents? Owners of a bookshop? A series of images flashed through her mind. Billy prancing around Mamma's old shop, flourishing an embroidered shawl like a toreador, leaning on a parasol and making a deep mock bow, winking at her from behind a Venetian mask. Billy lolling in the grass by the river. Billy's face looming down at her angrily from where she lay on her back on the diving platform, clutching at her ribs, rolling with laughter. And Billy on the bridge, his face half hidden by darkness, leaning in for that first kiss.

It's as if we've lost all that, what we once were together, she thought. And again she felt that big black gap opening up inside her. It was as cold as the river water, fast and strong, and it threatened to sweep her away. Always, when she'd felt like this before, it had been Billy who'd come to her rescue. He always knew what to say, how to make her smile. But this time . . .

She looked down again at the miniature waxing moon of sugar. What will we become, she thought? What are we moving towards?

And almost instantly she heard a voice in her head answering.

Something new, it said. *The past is gone. You can't relive it. You're moving towards something else.*

'Does that answer your question?' Maadar-Bozorg's voice, its rich lilt, broke into her thoughts.

Ella looked up. Her voice caught in her throat. 'Yes. Well, sort of.'

Maadar-Bozorg's hand, her slender, brown fingers, the skin loose around the knuckles, covered her own.

'Child, the best answers are always full of questions. And it's the questions that take us where we need to go next.'

21

*To ask for an answer: Look at the moon in a mirror and
ask it the question for which you desire an answer.
You must not look at the moon directly.*
– Miss Mary's Book of Dreams

Fabia sat on the edge of the sofa in the old living room above the
shop, holding the photograph of her mother – her birth mother
– in both hands. So many times since she was a tiny girl in a
white cotton nightdress perched on the end of her bed, she'd
scrutinised this same face, and yet the woman behind the glass
still remained a mystery. The enormous dark eyes, half turning
from the camera, the high cheekbones and slender throat. She'd
carried the photograph with her everywhere in its plain silver
frame, from her bedroom in Tehran to the boarding house in
Paris where she'd propped it against the wall in her corner of the
shared attic dormitory. Since then, it had journeyed with her to
England, and eventually to York, at the bottom of her suitcase,
carefully wrapped in a silk scarf. Those dark eyes had gazed out
at her from her bedside table in the little flat she'd shared with
Enzo as a newly married woman. And as she and Ella had moved
from place to place, in those early years after Enzo's death, her
mother had accompanied them, her slightly blurred half-smile
hovering at the corners of her mouth.

But when she and David had set out for their life in California, Fabia had finally decided to leave her mother behind. It had
seemed symbolic of her new beginning, the right thing to do,

and so the photograph had presided here, half forgotten, on the mantelpiece in the tiny living room above the shop.

Now the room was crowded with Ella's large desk and printer, enormous boxes full of books and a shelf of meticulously labelled box files. That was Ella, through and through, Fabia thought. Her daughter had always been extremely organised but she'd never had much interest in interior design. She'd far rather sit with her nose buried in a book than waste time arranging things in a way that was more pleasing to the eye. It had made Fabia a little sad at first to see their former home this way, the lamps and trinkets swept aside to make way for accounting. But then she'd sat here this evening, and the past had come slowly seeping back. She'd reached out and clicked on a reading lamp and memories had spilled from it, pooling like the light on the rug at her feet. It was still here, her past, in the weave of the yellow silk curtains and the ridges of paint on the skirting boards that she'd prepared so hastily all those years ago.

She leaned in the kitchen doorway, the photograph still in her hands. She could see the ghosts of their former selves – hers and Ella's – so clearly here, sitting at the kitchen table. She reached out and traced the grooves worn in the wood. This was where she'd cut her fabrics, late at night when Ella was sleeping. She heard again the whisper of satin crepe, the rasp of cotton, felt them slipping through her fingers. She saw Ella at fourteen in her navy-blue school uniform, her wild brown hair tangling around her shoulders, a book propped against the coffee pot as she nibbled at a slice of toast. She smiled to see her own younger self, dancing around the kitchen to the radio: *When the moon hits your eye . . . hmm, hmm-hmm, hmm hmm-hmm . . .*

Because, of course, this was where she'd met David. He'd sat right here on that first night, his doctor's bag placed carefully in front of him, writing out a prescription in his beautiful, flowing handwriting.

'Delicious coffee,' he'd said, sipping at the cup she'd set in front of him and she'd known right then, as she'd watched him drink, that this was a man with whom she could fall in love.

Now she placed the photograph of her mother in the centre of the table.

'So what next?' she said, out loud to the black-and-white image. 'What's next for me?'

The large dark eyes gazed back at her, unwavering.

'Ah, yes. She was *ziba*, no?' Maadar-Bozorg's voice was soft, mellifluous, lingering over the consonants in the Old Language, which Fabia barely spoke these days

'Maadar. I thought you were sleeping.'

'Just resting my eyes, child.' The green eyes glinted. 'But, yes, she was beautiful, your mother, no? And restless too. Always drifting from place to place, looking for something she never quite found. That was the hardest part for me, watching her do that.'

Fabia scraped back a chair. 'Please, Maadar-Bozorg, sit with me a while?' Her fingertips moved over the table, seeking out the score marks and little pitted places in its surface. She felt a long, sad sigh rise up from somewhere deep inside her and hang like a blue mist in the room.

'Maadar-Bozorg, will you tell me about my mother?'

'Of course, child. But where shall I begin? What do you want to know?'

Fabia looked into the face of the woman who had always cared for her as her own daughter. Suddenly, she felt shy, awkward.

After all this time, the truth was that she didn't really know what she wanted to know. And perhaps it would hurt Maadar-Bozorg to hear the eagerness in her voice, to know how much she wanted to connect to this other woman who had always seemed to move through the background of her life like the vaguest of shadows.

'Maadar-Bozorg, do you remember how, when I was a little girl, you took me into the hills outside Tehran, to that place where you can look down on the entire city? We stood and watched the cars and the people moving around far below us and you told me that my mother was there, right there, all around me, in that big, old tree and in the air that I breathed, and the earth under my feet? Do you remember that?'

Maadar-Bozorg smiled. 'Something like that, yes. Perhaps it was wrong of me. Maybe I should have been less . . . less *poetic*. These days, I think they advise that children who have been bereaved need more direct answers.'

'No.' Fabia shook her head. 'What you told me helped me a great deal. It meant that I could feel that my mother hadn't left me, that if I closed my eyes, she was here with me, right here.' Fabia pressed her palm to the centre of her chest. 'Aunt Talayeh told me that my mother was with God. I couldn't even begin to imagine where that was or what it meant. But what you said helped me to *feel* her. And that was very important, somehow. I understood that she was gone, that she wasn't coming back, but I also felt that I had a piece of her right here, inside me.'

'Well, that's certainly true, child.' Maadar-Bozorg smiled. 'You are, without doubt, your mother's daughter. Seeing you now makes me remember so many things about her, things that I thought I'd forgotten. You have so many of her expressions.' She patted the back of Fabia's hand. 'Yes, you really do.

But fortunately, you also seem to be much more firmly rooted than your mother ever was. You seem to be so much more sure about who you are in the world. And for that, my own heart is glad.'

Maadar-Bozorg lifted Fabia's hand from where it lay against her chest and pressed it to her own. 'You know, Farah . . . I hope I can still call you that? Because to me, my dove, my dear one, that is who you are.'

Fabia nodded. 'Of course.'

'Farah, I want you to know that you make me so proud.'

'I do?' Fabia swiped at her face with her other hand. 'Oh, but Maadar, I'm so lost right now. I don't feel that I know who I am at all.'

Maadar-Bozorg smiled again. 'Ah, but this is only a very temporary thing. This is *normal*, child. When you are as old as I am, you'll learn that this feeling soon passes.'

'Does it? If only I could be so sure.' Fabia pushed her hair out of her eyes.

'So why don't you tell me what's on your mind? Maybe I can help?'

'That's just what I said to Ella, earlier.'

Maadar-Bozorg nodded. 'And it is the hardest thing, being a mother. But she'll find her own way too, that one. You've done an excellent job, my dear. She has her head screwed on right.'

'I know. She's such a good girl. A very good girl. I'm not sure how much of that I can take any credit for. Sometimes I wish that she hadn't always been so good, so *sensible*. That she'd had her little teenage rebellion. You know, perhaps she felt that she had to take care of me in some ways, because it was always just the two of us. Perhaps if she hadn't been so responsible, if she'd had a bit more fun, or maybe even if she'd had more sense of Enzo . . . I always tried to keep her father present for her, you know. I talked about him all the time, told her stories of how we met. I used his favourite words, cooked his favourite meals. But I just wish now that she'd had more connection to her roots, to her family, to where she came from. We all need that, don't we, in some way? And maybe then she wouldn't be left with this longing, this constant wondering?'

'*Tsk*. Maybe. Maybe not.' Maadar-Bozorg clicked her fingers in the air. The amethyst in her ring sent light dancing over the kitchen ceiling. 'Who knows?' She smiled again. 'But it sounds to me, my dear, like you might be talking about yourself?' Her eyes twinkled.

Fabia shrugged. 'Yes, probably I am. I can't say that I haven't thought that too.' She felt again that cold, gelid feeling wriggling its way up her spine. 'Oh, I don't know what's wrong with me. Maybe it's just the time of year. It always gets to me. The leaves turning. The nights drawing in. It makes me feel nostalgic for the past.'

She gestured around the room.

'You know, this is where I began again, where I found myself, learned who I really might be after everything had crumbled around me. This little room, the shop. It became my world.'

'I can see that. And you did it all brilliantly. No one could have done better.' Fabia felt Maadar-Bozorg's eyes fix on hers. 'You do know that, child, don't you?'

'Yes. Yes, I think I do. What I don't really understand is why I threw it all up in the air again. Followed David halfway round the world, to a place I didn't even know, in order to start all over. And you know, Maadar, I think I'm tired. I'm tired of starting again, of not belonging. I'm scared that I might not be able to do it properly this time.'

'And so?' Maadar-Bozorg pulled her shawl around herself. 'What do you want to do?'

'That's just it. For the first time ever, I really don't know any-more. Maadar, I've never said this before, and I don't know why, but there's not a day that's gone by when I haven't thought about you, wondered where you were, what you were doing. *Missed* you.' She reached across the table. 'But you know, I *had* to leave Tehran back then. I had to travel all this way, through Paris and then Dover and then all the way here, to these three little rooms and a shop in the middle of some godforsaken city where it's always either snowing or raining, just to discover who I really was. Without you. Without the aunts. Even without the ghost of my mother.' She smiled. 'I had to make my own story. But what I found was that we carry our stories with us everywhere. They're in our blood. They're in the air that we breathe. You were so right about that. The past is with us everywhere. The people we've loved. The words we grew up with on our tongues. They're in here.' She pointed to her heart again. 'And I worked so hard to shape them into something that felt right for me, something that would be good and true and . . . and just *right*. But now.' She threw her hands in the air. 'I don't feel like I fit anywhere any-more. It's gone. All gone. It's as if, whenever I find what I think I want, it's not enough. I have to move on again. And now I'm so tired. So goddamn *tired* . . .'

'And what does David think of all this?'

Fabia felt her heart twist.

'Well, that's just it. I haven't exactly told him how I'm feeling. I don't think he has any idea.'

'Ah, yes. Of course.' Maadar-Bozorg's eyes twinkled again. A smile played around the corners of her lips.

'What do you mean?'

'Nothing, child. Except that this was always going to be a problem.'

Fabia felt her body bristle. Maadar-Bozorg could be infuriating at times. She remembered what she'd felt like as a young girl all those years ago, when she'd first told Maadar that she was going away to Paris. She'd rehearsed the words over and over inside her mind, wondering about the best way to share her news and then, when they'd finally come tumbling out, one evening as they cleared away the remains of dinner, Maadar had simply looked at her, just like that, with that little teasing half-smile and said, 'Of course, child. You were always going to have to leave. I've known that for a long time.'

Now she sat back in her chair and stretched the sleeves of her cardigan down over her hands.

'Go on, then,' she said. 'Tell me what you already know about David and me.'

Maadar-Bozorg frowned. 'I'm sorry. I don't mean it to sound like that at all. It's just that ... Well, Farah, I wouldn't underestimate David. He probably knows at least a little of how you're feeling. He seems like a very ... *intelligent* kind of man. And that time when you brought him to see me in Tehran, it was so obvious that he's madly in love with you. Any fool can see that from a mile off. So there was always bound to be a sticky bit, a moment of reckoning, if you like. Because ... Well, because you don't love him quite as much as he loves you, do you?'

Fabia felt the words like little knives between her ribs. Stab, stab, stab. Was that true?

'He's asked me to marry him,' she said.

'And you don't want to?'

'I just don't know, Maadar. I feel terrible about it. He's so lovely. Most of my single friends would jump at the chance. I feel ungrateful and unkind and –'

'Confused?'

Maadar-Bozorg reached up and smoothed Fabia's hair. 'You're right, child. David *is* wonderful. But so are you. And it's not your friends who are making this decision. It doesn't really matter what I or anyone else thinks.' She smiled again. 'Just don't decide anything out of fear, that's all. Fear is the very worst reason to do anything. Fear and, of course, the past. The past is over.' She snapped her fingers in the air. 'Done. That story is already told. You know, it is a beautiful thing, the way that you honour the past. The way that you take these lovely clothes and restore them to their original beauty. The way that you've always kept the memory of Enzo alive for Ella, in the language you use together, the food you taught her to love. It is truly beautiful.' Maadar-Bozorg sighed. 'But I can't help thinking that *this*, child, this precious time we have, right here in this moment, is what we must remember to celebrate too.' She swept her arm around the tiny kitchen. 'Look. You see? *This* is where we get to make a *new* story.'

Fabia spread her hands on the table. She looked into Maadar-Bozorg's eyes. 'I wish I could let go a little. I used to be much better at that. When did I learn to be so anxious all the time? So . . . so disconnected?'

Maadar-Bozorg's nose wrinkled. 'Ah, I wish I knew the answer to that one. But I think that's just how it is, child. For most of us, anyway.' She stood up and pushed back her chair.

'But I have something for you that I think might help . . . One moment . . .'

When she reappeared in the doorway, she was holding a rectangular package in both hands.

'I've just been waiting for the right time to give this to you. It was your mother's and I wanted to make sure that it found its way to you. Because, well . . . This might be the last time . . .' Her voice trailed off. Fabia saw her look into the air above her left shoulder. She shivered. 'Here, child. Take it.'

Fabia laid the parcel on the kitchen table. She could feel that it was some kind of cloth – a scarf, perhaps – wrapped in layers of pale blue tissue paper. She undid the thin yellow ribbon and peeled back the layers of paper, one by one.

There on the table was the most beautiful piece of fabric that she'd ever seen. She heard herself gasp as she held up one corner of it, very gently, between her finger and thumb and shook it out. It spilled in soft folds over the entire surface of the table.

Fabia traced the weave of the cloth with expert fingers. Its surface was richly textured but it was also incredibly light, spilling through her hands.

'Oh!' she said, holding her arms wide so that the light from the kitchen lamp shone through it. 'Oh. It's just . . . just *exquisite*, Maadar.'

Maadar-Bozorg smiled. 'I knew you would appreciate it.'

'It's wool . . . with silk, I think? And each colour is a natural vegetable dye? You can see the difference immediately. Hours and hours of work . . .'

Maadar-Bozorg nodded. 'It's very old now. Incredible, really, that those dyes have held their colours so well. Especially the reds and ochres, here. See? They haven't faded at all.'

Fabia followed the pattern with her fingertips. The five-pointed star shapes repeated themselves in shades of scarlet and gold. In between, undulating lines moved like waves in blue and green. At intervals, the tightly woven rows were sewn with tiny semi-precious beads – chips of garnet, agate and topaz – so that the cloth shimmered gently in her hands.

'And there are birds here too. Here in each corner . . .' She traced the feathered shapes. 'How strange.' She folded the fabric over her arm and stroked it. 'Isn't it a dowry piece?'

Maadar-Bozorg nodded. 'Yes, I think so. It was made in the mountains, not far from the house. There are only a few women now who still know how to make these cloths. And you're right. They were made to demonstrate the skills of the woman to be married, but each family of women developed their own techniques, ways of telling little stories through the patterns. You see here, where these colours undulate like waves . . . And then here, what looks like leaves . . . Your mother loved it. And the birds, of course. It was given to her when she was a little girl – not much older than Grace is now – by Sara, who lived in the village and sometimes came to the house to take care of things for a week or two when I had a paper or a chapter to work on. Your mother kept it on the end of her bed and she loved to look at the patterns.' She smiled. 'Sometimes we'd try to guess at the stories, at what it might be that the weaver was trying to tell us . . . I remember that your mother once asked Sara to tell her what it all meant, but she never would. She just laid her hand against the side of her nose, like this, and said, "It's whatever you want it to be, my dove . . ." When your mother died, I put it away. I couldn't bear to look at it. But it's a piece of your past, a good piece. And now, perhaps, you can make it into something for your future . . .'

'Oh, I don't think I could bear to cut into it.' Fabia held it out again, feeling how alive the fabric became as it caught the light. 'It would be a sacrilege . . .'

Maadar-Bozorg shook her head. 'Quite the opposite, child. These fabrics were made to be fashioned into something. The bride would take them with her to her new husband's house and she'd use them – often many times over – as a bedspread or as a covering for a table. But she'd also cut them to make special garments – clothing for herself or her first child or, in time, even a wedding dress for her own daughter. This fabric needs to be given new life. And, when the time is right, *you* are the person to do it.'

22

To delight the senses: Burn bridewort in the hearth or
strew it on the floor.
– Miss Mary's Book of Dreams

'So this is it.'

Ella stopped the car at the top of the narrow lane and helped Maadar-Bozorg to unfold herself from the cramped back seat. Bryony already had her hand on the garden gate.

Miss Mary's cottage stood silent. Ella felt that faint crackle in the air again, a buzz of green static fizzing through the damp. Maadar-Bozorg met her gaze and nodded.

'There's certainly *something* here,' she said, pulling on her leather gloves.

There was no sun this time. In the little orchard at the back of the house, the branches of the apple trees were bare against the winter sky and apples lay black and rotten on the ground.

Ella's nose wrinkled. The smell of decay was everywhere – in the mulch of leaves and apples and in the mist that clung to the walls of the abandoned house.

On their last visit, the house had seemed almost homely. Despite the gaping windows and the door hanging off its hinges, she'd almost been able to imagine smoke curling up from the chimney, a smell of baking drifting from the kitchen hearth. Now she stuck her head around the door and shivered. The rooms were dark and sinister-looking, the stone walls greenish-black with moss and soot. There was a dripping sound in the narrow hallway and, as the door creaked, she heard something

242

scurrying off into the shadows. The toe of her trainer skidded on the slippery stone floor. She backed out again, breathing hard.

'It's just as I imagined,' Maadar-Bozorg said. 'So European. Like the witch's house in *Hansel and Gretel*.' She unfolded a small canvas bag from her pocket and began to poke around in the long grass outside the kitchen door, parting the tangled fronds to reveal clumps of leaves.

'This is witch grass,' she said, nipping a sample from a plant with smooth, pale leaves and speared tips and dropping it into the bag.

'And here's sage.' Bryony rubbed the leaves between her finger and thumb and held them to her nose. 'I love that smell. Incredible to think that Miss Mary might actually have planted this, centuries ago. It's very resilient. Goes rampant, if you're not careful.' Her voice was taut with excitement. 'To think that we're looking at the traces of what might have been Miss Mary's cure-garden. But I'd like to find some bridewort. She talks about that a lot. I think it was one of her favourites.'

'It's a wild plant, isn't it? Queen of the Meadow. I imagine it will be out there somewhere.' Maadar-Bozorg swept the horizon with her hand. 'Maybe in that field. She would have used whatever she could find around here. Do you know what it looks like?'

Bryony nodded. 'I looked it up. It has dark green leaves with a downy-white underside and sometimes a bright orange fungus on the stem. It won't be in flower, of course. It's the wrong time of year.'

She'd strode off, pushing her way through the broken fence into the field. Maadar-Bozorg followed, her long trousers brushing the wet grass. At the fence she turned.

'Coming?' she called to Ella and smiled when Ella shook her head. 'Well, we won't be too long, I imagine.'

Ella watched them now, two distant figures in the middle of the field, dipping and bending, silhouetted against the fading afternoon light.

She stood at the end of the garden where the orchard petered out. There was a little stream that cut its way through the bottom corner of the field and, behind that, the moors, rising up against the cold, grey sky. She turned to look west, where the hills stretched themselves, their bulk half lost in the mist. She could just make out the shape of a solitary farmhouse, way up there, in the dip of one of the hills, but, apart from that, no sign of another living soul. Miss Mary must have liked her own company to live alone out here – or perhaps she didn't have much choice?

Behind her, she could almost feel the house watching. The empty windows seemed to follow her as she moved around the garden. She felt a prickling on the back of her neck – a quiver of green, a shiver of silver. At first, she thought it was Bryony, that she'd circled back through the field behind, come for something she'd forgotten in the car, but when she turned around there was no one there.

She made her way back to the house and found a late-blooming yellow rose growing in a sheltered spot on the west wall. Bryony would be pleased. She could take some of the petals for the spells in Miss Mary's book. Rose seemed to feature heavily in many of them. Ella reached out to touch the velvety petals but immediately snatched her hand back. A thorn had pricked her finger. A single drop of blood beaded there on her fingertip. She wiped it on the grass. Tetanus. You could get that from a rose thorn, couldn't you? She shivered again. This place gave her the creeps. The sense of the clouds gathering over her shoulder, the air bunching up around her. She straightened up and began to wave at Bryony and Maadar-Bozorg in the field. Their backs were turned. They couldn't see her. She wished they'd hurry up now. Maybe she'd go and wait for them in the car.

'Hello?'

Her heart skipped a beat. The voice was clear, clipped, authoritative.

'Sorry. Didn't mean to make you jump. Gosh, it's Billy's wife, isn't it? Sorry. I can't remember your name. I'm dreadful with names.'

Selena LaSalle leaned in the kitchen doorway. After the countless times that Ella had seen her in her mind's eye over the past months, she could hardly believe that she was here in Miss Mary's garden. Had her mind conjured her out of the mist? Had she fallen asleep against the wall and was dreaming? Her mind raced, forwards and then backwards again. How could Selena have got here? There hadn't been another car in the lane. And, more to the point, *why* was she here? What could she want with this place?

'It's Ella,' she said, trying to keep the anger out of her voice. 'It's Ella. And I remember *your* name. You're Selena.' She zipped her parka higher around her neck. Her hands were trembling. Selena, she noticed, was wrapped in a soft, black wool coat. Expensive-looking. Cashmere, no doubt.

'I saw you from the upstairs window.' Selena's smile was forced. The tiny diamond studs in her ears twinkled as she moved her head. 'I thought it was you. A rather odd place to bump into one another, don't you think?'

Ella felt her heart pounding in that place just under her ribs. She shoved her hands deeper into her pockets, her fingernails digging into her palms.

'Yes, I'm only here because a friend of mine wanted to come. A friend and . . . and my great-grandmother, actually. They're both interested in the woman that's supposed to have lived here once, long ago. We stock her book in the shop. Well, that is, when we can get hold of it. It's very rare . . .' Why was she babbling like this?

'Really? How extraordinary.' Selena's eyebrows disappeared into her hairline. Her hair was scraped back from her face and caught in a glossy ponytail. Ella saw the perfect symmetry of her features, the high cheekbones, the long, straight nose.

Behind her, a man in jeans and a waterproof jacket appeared in the kitchen doorway, holding a clipboard and pen.

'Oh.' Selena turned. 'This is Daniel, one of my research assistants.' She patted him on the arm, proprietorially. 'Dan, this is Ella, Bill Vickers's wife. She's here to investigate Miss Mary, too. I was just saying how . . . how utterly *serendipitous* that is.'

There it was again, the quick, tight smile. The thin lips curling back. She's not actually beautiful at all, Ella thought. There's a hardness about her. Something almost impenetrable. Could Billy *really* be drawn to this kind of woman?

Dan, she noticed, was shifting from one foot to the other. He looked embarrassed. Uneasy. Why would that be? What did he know?

'Good to meet you.' He gave her a perfunctory nod and then immediately shrank back into the dark kitchen. 'I've finished the inventory,' she heard him say. 'So we can be off now. That is, if you're ready?'

Selena squinted into the field. 'Those are your friends, then, over there?' She pointed. 'What are they doing? Must be awfully . . . *damp* in that field.' She laughed, a high, forced laugh, and Ella saw Bryony turn and look back in their direction. Ella raised her hand and waved at her again, more urgently this time.

'Looking for plants,' she said. 'You know. Herbs. The kind of thing Miss Mary writes about in her book.'

'Ah. *The Book of Dreams.*' Selena nodded. 'Fascinating. Dan here's preparing his thesis on women and witchcraft in the sixteenth century. From a sociological point of view, of course. I said I'd tag along. Lend a hand if I could.' She smiled again. 'But really, I told him that it's more your husband's area of expertise.'

'Oh.' Ella's fingers found a stray piece of thread in the lining of her pocket and tugged at it. 'Yes, but it's just one of his side interests, really. You know how Billy is. Interested in everything.'

'Really? Is that so?' Selena raised an eyebrow again. Ella felt herself stiffen. What was this woman implying? That she didn't know her own husband. 'Well, we'd better be off.' Selena nodded at the two figures now making their way towards them across the field. 'Absolutely *lovely* to see you again.'

Ella listened to the sound of Selena's high-heeled boots clicking around the side of the house and then an engine starting, higher up the lane. That was why they hadn't seen the car, of course. They must have parked it on the other side of the bend.

'Who was that?' Maadar-Bozorg lifted up the soggy hems of her trousers to negotiate the broken fence.

'That colleague of Billy's, would you believe.' Ella fiddled with her zip again and pulled her hat down over her ears. 'You know. The one that . . . the one I –'

Maadar-Bozorg brushed the hair out of her eyes with the back of her hand. Her fingers were speckled with mud. 'Goodness. What was *she* doing here? How very strange.'

'Some kind of research project, apparently.' Ella hugged herself. The damp had begun to seep through her cotton parka. 'If you don't mind, I think I need to go now. I can't get warm. Think I might be coming down with something.'

She turned and began to kick her way through the rotten apples. She didn't notice Maadar-Bozorg's green eyes flashing as she pulled her woollen shawl around herself or that Bryony's face was white with shock.

*

'So what she says here is to pass an egg over the person's body and let the person who is being cleansed of illness breathe onto it, then take the egg and break it on the ground outside.'

Bryony pointed to a paragraph in *The Book of Dreams*. 'Was that a standard cleansing spell, do you think, or particular to Miss Mary?'

Maadar-Bozorg's eyes twinkled. 'I've used that one many times myself.' She peered at the page. 'In our family, we always found it helpful for children's minor illnesses – you know, tummy ache and so on. Of course, it's vital to check first that there isn't actually something seriously wrong with them. But when the child really believes that the egg has absorbed all of the bad feeling, they begin to feel much better. The incredible power of the mind.' She tapped at her temple. 'The greatest magic of all.'

Bryony nodded. 'Speaking of which,' she said.

She took a step back from the table. She could feel her heart thudding in her ears. This was the moment she'd rehearsed a thousand times inside her own mind. The moment when she'd finally tell someone. And she'd decided that Ella's great-grandmother was the right person to tell. She took a deep breath.

'Mrs Jobrani –'

'Zohreh. Please. I can't stand all these English formalities.'

'Sorry. Sorry, Zohreh. It's just that there's something that I want you to know. I hope you don't mind. It's just that I have to tell *someone*. I feel awful. It's this horrible secret and it's making me feel so guilty. Especially because you've all been so incredibly kind to me.'

Maadar-Bozorg put her head on one side and Bryony saw her eyes glitter.

'Go on, child.'

'That's just it. I don't know where to start. I'm afraid that you're all going to hate me.'

Maadar-Bozorg smiled. 'Well, these things are usually much worse in your imagination than they ever are in reality, don't you think?'

Bryony nodded. 'That's true. I really do know all about that.'

Maadar-Bozorg's eyes burned into hers. 'Yes, child,' she said. 'I imagine you do.'

She knows, thought Bryony. It's like she can see right into me. But not like Selena. She isn't trying to get inside my thoughts, change my mind, control me. It's a quieter thing. She just seems to look and understand. It feels almost like someone putting their arms around you.

She took another breath.

'Well, it's about my sister. Her name is Selena.'

She saw Maadar's eyes flicker.

'Yes. Yes, go on.'

'Well, as you know, Selena works with Billy. Of course, I didn't realise this when I first came to the shop. And I've never mentioned it to Ella. But slowly I started to piece it all together . . . from little things that Ella said. And, you see, Selena has always been . . . well, shall we say that she's very determined. Ruthless. When she makes up her mind about something, she usually just goes for it. She's used to getting what she wants. Especially when it comes to men.'

Maadar-Bozorg's face gave nothing away.

'Go on,' she said.

'Well, she never keeps them. The men, I mean. She loses interest, usually. But she's got a thing about men who . . . well, belong to someone else. Married men. Men in relationships. It's like a challenge to her. It's all about winning. She's always been like that. About everything. We're not close, my sister and I, but from the little things that I've picked up on, the things she's let slip, I'm terribly worried that she's got her eye on Billy.'

Maadar-Bozorg nodded. 'I see. Well, that makes perfect sense.'

'It does?'

'Yes, child, it does. But, you know, none of this is any of your concern.'

Bryony frowned. 'But of course it is. She's my sister. And I'm so incredibly embarrassed. And worried. I'm . . . I'm very fond of Ella, you see. And little Grace. I couldn't bear for anything to happen that would hurt them.'

'Ah, and you think that you have control over all that, child?'

'Well, I think that perhaps it's dishonest of me not to say *any-thing*. I mean, I haven't even told Ella that my sister works with Billy. The truth is –' She bit her lip. 'I suppose I'm a bit *ashamed* of Selena. She's my sister, but I don't really even *like* her. I don't particularly like people knowing that I'm related to her in any way. She's so . . . Well, she just has tunnel vision. And she doesn't listen to me, of course. In fact, she thinks I'm completely mad. Properly bonkers.'

'And do *you* think that too?'

The air in the room seemed to tremble for a moment. Bryony looked down at her hands. She could feel Maadar-Bozorg's eyes on hers.

'I used to. I really did. I've had treatment. I even spent some time in hospital. When . . . when my father decided that I really wasn't coping. I see a therapist. At least, I did. Until very recently. Of course, I haven't told him about all of this.' She gestured to the book on the table. 'I think he'd probably be horrified. He wouldn't understand, anyway.'

'I don't think you're mad at all. I know exactly what it feels like. To have your gifts made fun of. To be disbelieved.'

Maadar's eyes flashed. Bryony shifted from one foot to the other. She wasn't used to people looking right at her like this. Most people didn't seem to pay any attention to what she was thinking or saying.

'And another thing,' Maadar said. 'I don't think you're in any way responsible for anything that might or might not happen between Billy and your sister.'

'Really?' Bryony's fingers pleated the corduroy fabric of her skirt.

'Really.' Maadar smiled again.

'Because, you know, I've lain awake at night wondering if I should tell Ella. And then I think, but *what* would I say, exactly? It's not as if I know anything conclusive. And then I'd just be making it worse, wouldn't I? I think it would break her heart. Or sometimes I think that perhaps I should take Billy to one side and warn him. Tell him what Selena can be like. But that might make him furious. I mean, he might be terribly offended. He seems like a nice man. It really all depends on whether . . . well, on whether . . .'

She flushed.

'On whether he really is up to no good with your sister?' Maadar chuckled. 'Oh, my dear. What a frightful situation for you to be in. What an awful secret you've been carrying around. Now, tell me. Do you feel a little lighter, now that you've confided in me?'

Bryony looked into Maadar's eyes again, those glittering green eyes that were so like Fabia's. She felt something reaching towards her, colours so vibrant that she could almost reach out and touch them, floating around her head and shoulders, folding her round in a shimmering cloud.

She felt the tension in her neck and arms soften a little.

'Well, yes,' she said. 'But I also feel as if I've failed somehow. As if I've let you all down. I feel that I really should do something. To protect you all. You're my friends. You've all been so kind to me.'

Maadar-Bozorg smiled. 'Well, what do you think your Miss Mary would do in a situation like this?'

What a funny question, Bryony thought. But then she realised that she already knew the answer.

'I think . . .' she began. 'Yes, I think she'd probably keep her own counsel. She'd say nothing, but secretly, she'd make some kind of spell, of course. Devise some ritual or other. Invoke some kind of dream magic. You know, to help things along a little.'

Maadar-Bozorg smiled again. 'I agree. That's exactly what she'd do. But you know, even with all the magic in the world, in the end, only Billy can actually decide what happens next. Well, Billy and Ella, of course. Your sister really doesn't have much to do with it.'

'Don't you think?'

'No. Not if Billy and Ella don't allow her to come between them.'

Bryony felt Maadar-Bozorg's hand reach for hers.

'And you, my dear, must stop carrying the woes of others around in your pocket. There's nothing you can do except to be a true friend to Ella. Which, of course, you already are. I think, in fact, that you have enough worries of your own. Isn't that true?'

Bryony pulled her hand away. 'I-I –' She felt her body start to shake. The room swirled around her. She grabbed the edge of the table. Maadar's face disappeared for a moment. 'I'm sorry. I –'

'Oh, I don't mean to upset you, child.' Maadar's eyes searched hers. Again, Bryony had that uncomfortable feeling that Maadar could see right inside her. 'But if you don't mind me saying, my dear, that fellow, the one who came to find you, the night of Ella's party . . . well, he *really* doesn't deserve you.'

Bryony felt the tears start to wet her cheeks. She couldn't help it. She didn't want to think about Ed. Not now. She tried to push back her chair. But Maadar was pulling her close, stroking her hair.

'There, there. That's right. Get it all out. It's hard when someone says it out loud, isn't it? The thing we don't want to hear. But this is something you *can* change, no? You have friends. People who respect you and care about you. Don't be afraid, child. You'll see. It will all work out.'

23

To remember your dreams: Take a cup of water from the high spring at Rosedale and put it outside under the moon for one full night. On the next day, keep the cup covered in a dark, cool place. When you go to bed, drink from the cup but leave a little of the moonwater aside. On waking, drink the remainder and you will remember everything you saw when sleeping.
– Miss Mary's Book of Dreams

The moon fell in a perfect crescent through the open bedroom window and across the polished floorboards as Zohreh Jobrani assembled her collection of objects.

She arranged them along the arc of reflected moonlight, just as her sister, Mahdokht, had once shown her. First, she lay down the single glossy hair that she'd plucked from Bryony's coat collar. Next to it, she placed the half-eaten apple, left by Billy on the breakfast table that morning. Next to this, she smoothed out the scribbled note in Ella's flowing handwriting that she'd salvaged from the pile of receipts and bills on the old tea chest in Ella and Billy's hallway: *Billy – Dinner in fridge. Love El x*

Finally, at the very end of the arc, she coiled the piece of red embroidery cotton that she'd taken from Farah's jar of saved thread ends.

As she laid each of these objects in its place, she thought of the person to whom it belonged. She stilled her mind and breathed deeply.

Here was Bryony, her sweet, soft face furrowed in concentration, holding Miss Mary's book open, mouthing the words as she read. Zohreh felt Bryony's fears for the future and her lack of confidence in herself pass through her own body like a grey-green mist.

She saw Billy, dangling Grace upside down in his arms, heard their loud laughter, felt his worries about being a good-enough father, his fears about being a good husband, rippling through her, restless as river water.

Next, she saw Ella bent over her laptop, her brow creased, her eyes half closed, felt her frustration at the words that wouldn't come, her rising panic about Billy and Selena, the big, black gap that opened up inside her.

She saw Farah, her beloved Farah, sitting sewing behind the shop counter, working her tiny stitches to mend whatever she could. She felt Farah's loneliness, the sadness that she kept buried like faded brown leaves and her fear that it might be too late to weave a new life for herself and those she loved.

Zohreh sat back on her heels and took another deep breath, taking the cold night air deep into her lungs, lifting her face to the moonlight. She thought of her sisters, Mahdokht and Talayeh, sitting in the salon of the family house in Tehran. They had each passed over now, years ago. It was much too long since they'd sat together under the light of a waxing moon, swirling hot coffee around jewel-coloured glasses. She wondered what they would do. This was more their kind of thing, after all. She had always stuck to telling stories. But tonight she needed the magic to be particularly strong. She was going to use every trick she knew.

She thought of Miss Mary in that little house nestled in the foot of the hills. She let her mind drift for a moment, out over the rooftops, past the edges of the city to where the fields and moors began. She travelled up the narrow, winding lanes, between the bare hedgerows, to Miss Mary's garden gate and saw her standing at her kitchen door, a wool shawl not unlike her own wrapped tightly around her shoulders, the hem of her long skirts fringed with mud as she beckoned her into the dark kitchen, where a pot simmered on the hearth.

What handful of healing herbs would she prescribe? What words would she mutter as she stirred the pot with her blackened metal spoon, three times, anticlockwise? Zohreh turned the pages of the *Book of Dreams* in her mind.

She reached into the cloth bag at her side and pulled out a pigeon's feather that she'd taken from the courtyard this morning. She laid it in the centre of the half-circle she'd made on the floor. Next, she added the tin bird ornament that Farah had hung above Grace's bed. Beautiful work, she noted. Made by Farah's friend in San Diego. It had good, clean energy. Made with love. It would help.

Then she laid down the Nine of Swords from her own tarot pack. The image on the card showed a woman sitting up in bed, her face in her hands. In the darkness above the woman's head, the nine swords gleamed silver. For many years now, Zohreh had made a habit of drawing a card each morning and asking herself what it might mean. She found it a useful way of tapping into her subconscious, the movement of her deepest instincts. She'd drawn the Nine of Swords on the morning after she'd talked with Farah and it seemed to be particularly resonant somehow. The swords, she thought, represented the woman's fears, the inner fears that wake us in the night, that tremble in the air above us. What we see in our own minds is always real, whether it exists in the outer world or exists only in the realms of our imagination. And in the middle of the night, it is hard to navigate between these two. Yes, Zohreh thought, nodding to herself, our deepest anguish is always a sword with a double edge. The more we fear, the less we're able to distinguish what is our own fearful creation. And that was where nightmares gathered their power.

She reached into the bag again and drew out her little silver hand mirror, holding it up to the window, letting it catch the moonlight in its surface. Then she laid it on top of the card. Mahdokht's mirror trick, she said to herself. Let this mirror refract the nightmares, bending them like light. Let them bounce off the glass and go back from where they came. And Talayeh always used to say that blue beads banished bad dreams. She took a little silk pouch from the bag and emptied a handful of turquoise chips into her palm, then scattered them on top of the mirror.

Finally, she reached into the bag again and drew out a tangle of damp roots. She had already cleaned the soil from them and now they lay in her palm, a slippery white knot. Rose roots. This was Miss Mary's spell for ending trouble and the roots had come from Miss Mary's own cure-garden. Bryony had collected them herself. *To end trouble*, Miss Mary had written, *take rose roots and slice them with a sharp, clean knife. As you cut, think upon the trouble that you wish to bring to an end. See it in your mind, cut through like the roots. See it cut away from you or from the person it clings to, never to return.*

She thought of Selena LaSalle, that brief glimpse she'd had of her from the middle of the field, a distant, dark figure, leaning against Miss Mary's kitchen door. She'd have recognised her anywhere, of course. She'd met her so many times before in this lifetime.

She was the person who had lost her way, the one who had turned inward, become tight-jawed and narrow-eyed and cold as ice. She was the Tall, Pale-Eyed One of the stories, wandering the earth endlessly, looking for happiness outside herself but never finding it, casting the longest shadow. This sort of person could sweep everything and everyone up in her path as she searched for meaning. Her hunger for happiness ate away at things, destroying everything. Yes, something needed to be done. This Selena person needed to be dealt with. Her energy needed to be redirected, channelled elsewhere into something good.

This, she now knew, was the reason she had been called here. This was why the bird had tapped at her window. She was here to weave together a final story.

One last thing. A flying potion. Talayeh had always liked those. You sprinkled yourself with something, or rubbed some kind of potion over your body and it created powerful dreams. A kind of shamanic journeying. She looked around her and saw the divining dish on her bedside table. Next to it, a glass of water glimmered white in the light from the moon. Moon water. Perfect. She got to her feet, straining a little, easing out her old bones, and poured a little of the water into the dish. Then she dipped her fingertips and shook the water over her head, rising onto her tiptoes, turning in a circle towards the moon, just as she'd seen Talayeh once do.

Then she stooped and plucked the feather from the centre of the circle and tucked it under her pillow. She took off her shawl, slipped under the quilt and closed her eyes.

She imagined herself standing at the foot of the narrow bed, looking at her sleeping self. 'Let the dream come,' she whispered to herself, as she heard the Signals murmuring. 'Let it come to each of us women tonight: Farah and Ella and Bryony and me. Let each of us weave it together into a new story.'

At the open window, the crescent moon climbed higher, illuminating the objects on the bedroom floor. The old wooden boards creaked as if someone was walking across them. The curtains with their pattern of roses and shepherdesses shivered slightly as if someone had brushed past.

Zohreh's eyelids flickered. She slept on.

*

Bryony hung on. Through a haze of pain, she could see her finger-tips turning white as they gripped the edge of the cast-iron mantelpiece. She hung on as her head swung back and forth, pulled by the force of Selena's fingers, twisted in her hair. The pattern of the carpet, the swirl of gold and green and brown, made her want to be sick.

'Come on then, Bryony. What're you going to do now? Run and tell Daddy that nasty Selena's been picking on you again?'

Bryony heard Selena's laughter. She could imagine Selena's face behind her, all sweaty and twisted with effort, her jaw set in that familiar expression of defiance.

'You'd better give it to me, Bryony, or I'll tell Daddy that you stole it.'

'No!' Bryony heard herself scream but the sound rose in her throat and came out as a whimper. Snot bubbled in her nose and the swirls on the carpet blurred with hot tears.

'Naughty, Bryony.' Selena laughed again. Her hand released its pressure on Bryony's skull for a moment and Bryony fell to the carpet, wheezing, trying to gather her breath.

She fought the instinct to put her hand in her pocket, to check that the locket was still there. It was the most precious thing she owned, the silver locket on a long chain that her mother had given to her before she died. She knew that Selena didn't even want it.

Bryony sat bolt upright in the bed, and fumbled for the light switch. Her bedside clock blinked 03:03 and moonlight poured through the gap between the bedroom curtains and spilled onto the bed.

*

Ella made her way down the corridor. It had been a spur of the moment thing, to come in and surprise him today. She'd written two thousand words since breakfast. The words had started to flow again. Everything had felt better since Mamma had arrived. Even things with Billy.

Now she was going to take him out. Forget packed lunch. She'd booked a table at that new restaurant at the top of Micklegate. She was going to treat him. And she had things to tell him, things to celebrate: the email from her editor saying that she liked the new first chapters she'd sent; and the series of readings and events she had planned for the shop in the new year.

She stood in the corridor outside Billy's office door. She held up her hand to knock. It was only the sound that made her turn around.

Through a door that stood half open, a few feet down the corridor, she could hear the unmistakable sound of Billy's laughter and a woman's voice, a cool, clear voice rising above it. She walked slowly down the corridor and peered through the gap in the open door.

Billy stood in front of her, his back towards her. He was wearing his favourite blue shirt, the one she'd given him for his last birthday.

'Billy,' she said but her voice caught in her throat and he didn't hear her. He was shaking with laughter. He didn't turn around. Over his shoulder, she saw Selena, her blonde hair hanging loose to her shoulders, the light shining softly through her office window so that she looked spotlit, like a woman in a film. She was gazing intently at Billy. What enormous eyes she has, Ella thought. Selena's lips parted in a slow smile. She ran her tongue over her lips. And what white teeth she has, Ella thought. All the better to eat you with.

Without taking her eyes off Billy, Selena opened her desk drawer and reached inside. She drew something out and held it to her lips, sinking her teeth in, taking a bite. Then she held it out to Billy on the palm of her hand. Ella saw now that it was a large apple with red, burnished skin.

'Have a bite,' Selena said, smiling again, showing her white teeth. She moved in closer, placing her hand on his shoulder, holding the apple to his lips.

But Billy had stopped laughing. Now, he stepped backwards. 'Selena. What are you –?'

'Have some,' Selena said, still smiling, taking another step forward, this time putting her hand out to touch his cheek. 'Come on, Billy. You know you –'

'*NO.*' Billy's voice came out in a half-shout. His hands went to his mouth. 'Sorry, but . . . No, Selena. That's not how things are between us.' He shifted from one foot to another. 'I should – I really should go now.'

Ella could see the tightness in Selena's face, the sudden flare of fury that she was barely managing to contain.

'Oh, you utter bastard,' she said quietly. 'What exactly is your problem? You're loving this, aren't you? And I thought . . . I really thought –'

'Well, then you thought wrong.' Billy's voice was a low hiss now. 'Geez, Selena. You've got no right to . . . I mean, I'm flattered and everything. But I've never led you to believe, not for one minute, that . . . For God's sake. I'm *married*. You *know* I am. *Happily* married. I have a wife, a wife whom I love, and a lovely little girl.'

Ella watched the emotions flicker across Selena's face. She watched as Selena thrust out her neck and drew up her shoulders. She watched as the scream came out of Selena's throat, jagged and red, and as her mouth with its white teeth sharpened into a red beak and her arms became wings, beating up and down, up and down.

It was only a moment. Almost as if she was dreaming. Barely the time it took for Billy to turn around and see her there, watching from the doorway.

'Ella,' he said. 'What are you doing?' His face crumpled in horror.

Ella had already pushed past him. She had her hands in front of her, ready to shove Selena hard in the middle of her chest. She couldn't see anything clearly anymore. Her vision was blurred with rage and tears. But she could hear Selena's laughter and the words still coming out of her mouth.

'My God. Just look at her. She's mad. Obviously, you do know that, right?'

Ella stopped. Her hands fell to her sides.

Then she turned and ran, out of the door and down the corridor, her feet slapping on the lino, all the way to the double doors that led outside.

Behind her, she could hear Billy.

'Ella. Wait. I'm sorry. I'm – Ella. *WAIT.*'

24

To banish hesitation: Grow wild mint in a pot. Water it each morning, speaking your hidden desires. Pick the mint leaves and make a tea. Drink daily for the course of one moon.
– Miss Mary's Book of Dreams

Ella stood by the ornamental lake. She thought of how often she'd come here, onto campus, when Grace was first born. She'd bring sandwiches for Billy and they'd sit and eat them together, looking out at the lake, whilst Grace napped in the buggy or, more often, in Ella's arms.

She realised that she was exhausted. All the anger was draining away. She just wanted to lie down here in the grass at the edge of the stupid lake. Stupid geese, stupid goose poo everywhere.

'Is that why you came here, then? To catch me out?'

Billy was talking. He'd been talking non-stop, half under his breath, for the last ten minutes now. He was saying things that she couldn't completely make sense of, but she did think that perhaps he shouldn't be sounding quite so indignant. It might be better if he just stopped stomping up and down the slope, if he just stood still for a minute.

She nodded to a bench at the edge of the lake. 'Look. Can we sit down?'

He seemed, quite suddenly, to realise where they'd walked to. He looked around him. She could see that he didn't want a scene. He was probably worrying about students coming past. Some of the halls of residence were just across the lake.

She could hear music drifting out of an open window, the faint sound of laughter.

'Maybe I'll just go home,' she said. 'We can talk about this later. When you've had a chance to –'

'To *what*? What exactly do you think is going on, El? Look I'm sorry. I'm sorry that you had to witness that. That stupid bloody woman. God, what an utter moron I've been. I should have seen it coming. But you can't think I've done anything to encourage it. This is so bloody unfair. I feel like I'm being wrongfully accused of something. Surely you heard what I said in there, El? Surely you know . . .'

She could tell that he was trying to keep his voice as calm and even as he could, breathing hard through his nose.

'It's more than that, though, Billy. Things haven't been right between us for a long time. I wouldn't blame you if –'

'What are you *talking* about, El? As if I would ever – Geez. This is so messed up. Look, can we just take a step back here? Because I didn't know that there *was* anything wrong until now. Not really. Except, you know, that you were tired and frustrated and . . . well, all that stuff that people feel when they've got jobs and a kid and . . . It's normal, isn't it? I'm sorry. I'm sorry if –'

'I thought you were having an affair, Billy.' Ella's voice sounded flat to her own ears. Now that she'd finally said them, the words seemed empty of all meaning. She was fighting an overwhelming impulse to just close her eyes and go to sleep right here.

'How could you even think that?' Billy had dropped down onto his knees in front of her. His hands were on her shoulders. 'Honestly, El. Don't you know me at all?'

'It's not you, Billy. It's about how I saw her look at you. That woman. And it's about *me,* about how I feel fat and boring and useless and, yes, tired all the time and about as sexy as one of your old socks.'

She watched the crinkles appear at the corner of his eyes.

'Honestly, El. You're mad.'

'Yes, apparently. That's what *she* said.'

His face clouded. 'No. I just mean, you're GORGEOUS, El. Bloody gorgeous. I probably fancy you more now than I ever did. You idiot.'

'Don't you dare call me an idiot.' She forced herself to meet his eyes then. 'I've not taken enough care of myself. I've put on weight. Got all fat and mumsy and tedious. And I certainly can't compete with *that.*' She nodded in the direction of the university buildings. 'I'm not stylish and elegant and groomed. I'm just knackered and bloated and ... Oh, why am I even saying this stuff? It's just so humiliating.'

'Seriously, El? *Seriously?*' He was trying to make her look at him again. 'Do you think that's what I'm interested in? Whether you've gained or lost a few pounds? El, you're the sexiest woman on the planet to me. You're interesting and funny and my best friend – that is, when you're not being a completely mad person. You're fantastically talented – a novelist, with two books to your name. I'm so damn proud when I tell people that. And yes, you're a mum, too. A brilliant one, as it happens.' Billy shook his head in disbelief. 'I mean, I knew that you were feeling a bit low, but I had no idea –'

'Well, it's not as if it was all completely ridiculous of me.' Ella looked again in the direction of the office block behind him. 'I mean, I was right about *her,* wasn't I? I wasn't exactly *inventing*

267

that in my own silly little head.' She kicked at the grass with the toe of her shoe. She thought about all the things she couldn't tell him – about checking his phone, for example. 'I could see when I came here last time that she obviously had a thing about you.'

'Yes. Like I say, I'm a moron.' Billy took her hands in his. He was starting to look desperate. She'd never seen him like this before. 'But, Ella, you've got to believe me. I didn't say anything, *do* anything . . . I mean, if I look back, I can see now that she was maybe getting an idea in her head. She's used to getting her own way. She's like that. At work, I mean. She doesn't take no for an answer.'

'*Takes no prisoners?*' Ella couldn't keep the sarcasm out of her voice.

'What?'

'That's what you said. A few weeks ago. That she takes no prisoners . . .'

'Geez, El.' Billy ran his hand through his hair. 'How long have you been thinking this stuff?'

'It doesn't matter now.' Ella turned away from him. She didn't want him to see the tears that were welling again. It was a mixture of relief – utter relief that it wasn't what she'd thought – and sadness, for what she'd lost. That lovely, innocent thing between them when they'd just belonged to each other. It felt as if that bloody woman had taken it and stamped all over it in her stupid pointy boots.

Billy was putting a hand under her chin, trying to tilt her face round towards him. She flinched.

'Don't Billy. Not right now. I can't. I just can't. I –'

'Why didn't you just ask me, El?' Billy was saying. 'I could have just –'

'What? Told me I was being stupid. *Silly Ella. Don't be so daft, Ella. Get a grip.* That kind of thing?'

'Well, maybe not that. Maybe –' He laid his head in her lap. 'Ella, please. Just tell me it's all going to be OK.'

*

Fabia was falling again. Down and down, feeling the night air unravel around her like a bolt of black silk. Just before she hit the ground, she looked up and saw the moon, a huge crescent shape, like an eyelid, looking at her from out of the blackness. The eyelid blinked slowly, revealing long, thick eyelashes, a scarlet iris and a large black pupil. It was looking right at her.

Fabia's heart beat faster. 'Who are you?' she said. 'What are you? What are you doing here in my dream?'

The eye became a pointed face with a sharp red beak and a crest of short green feathers. The bird put its head on one side and looked at her again, thoughtfully for a moment. She had the uneasy feeling that the creature was actually laughing at her.

And then the giant wings unfolded. She felt them stir the air around her face and shoulders. The bird leapt and flew. And she realised that she was flying it with it, carried on its back, feeling the night wind like ice on her cheek, half dazzled by the stars.

She clung on, throwing her arms around the bird's neck. Through its thick feathers, she could feel the hammering of its heart.

She looked down and saw, far below her, the ocean moving like a gleaming black body. She dug her fingernails deeper into the bird's neck and it put back its head and let out a blood-curdling scream.

They flew faster, faster. She saw the waves rushing up to meet them, felt the wind pick up and the rain begin to fall, heard a sound like the swoosh of falling stars. Then the bird seemed to tire. A new landscape rose up beneath them, a coastline, beaches still wrapped in night, rocks, palm trees, a jumble of houses and then the grid system of a city. They swooped down closer. Fabia thought she could almost feel the earth breathing, the gentle in-and-out movements of the city sleeping. She began to recognise the streets they passed over, the white bungalows with their glass and wood verandas, the manicured gardens, the trees.

And then here was her house, hers and David's, on its corner plot, high on the hill. The bird screeched to a halt on the veranda right outside their bedroom window. It shook its wings and she felt herself fall again, landing on the deck with a dull thud. The bird craned its neck forward and tapped on the bedroom windowpane.

And here was David's face at the window, bleary with sleep.

The bird made a strange, rasping sound as if it was clearing its throat. When it spoke, its voice was strangely high and tinny, with clear-cut consonants.

'Let me in,' it said and then, when David didn't respond. 'Let me in. Please. You must. I've flown a long way.'

But Fabia saw David shake his head. He opened the window a crack and then she heard his voice, that beautiful voice, soft and melodic.

'You're not the one,' he said. 'I'm afraid I'm still waiting for my bird to fly back to me . . .'

And then he closed the window and drew the blind and she saw the light in their room go out again.

She stood on the veranda, the night wind, scented with salt and pine, blowing through her thin cotton nightdress. She watched as the bird sighed and slowly spread its wings and rose up, up above the pine trees and far above the sea, which shone like metal under the rising sun. She watched as it caught the sun on its feathers, as it shrank to a small red flicker and then faded away completely. Then she turned and put her hand on the veranda door and, finding it unlocked, she pushed at it gently and slipped inside.

*

In her bed, tucked under the eaves, Grace stirred in her sleep. She opened one eye and saw the moon glinting through the window and scattering discs of silver over the ceiling. She reached up her hand and noticed that it made a shadow, like the shape of a bird. Like the bird that Granmamma had brought her from America to hang from her mobile. She turned her head to see it, but it was gone.

She closed her eyes again and dreamed that she was a bird, with silver wings and long green tail feathers, flying through a sky scattered with stars. She looked down and saw, through the bare branches of the trees, her mamma and daddy standing on the bridge over the river. She called to them and her voice didn't sound like her voice at all. It made a loud, high, singing sound, which made her giggle. Her mamma looked up at her, smiling, and her daddy called to her in his clear voice and she felt herself sink down, down through the soft night air and into the warmth of their arms.

25

To summon your true love: Steep witch grass in a cup of water for seven nights. At the end of the seventh night, wash with the witch grass water and let it dry on your body. Call your lover's name aloud to draw him to you.
– Miss Mary's Book of Dreams

Bryony clapped her hands together and a flurry of pigeons flew up from the frost-covered lawn. Even inside her old sheepskin mittens, her fingertips were numb with cold. She wished she'd chosen a warmer venue for her meeting with Selena.

She could see her now, gingerly picking her way in her high-heeled boots over the icy path by the ruined chapel. She'd never been one to dress for the weather, Bryony thought. What she looked like had always been much more important. Even as a child, she'd refused to wear the scratchy thermal vests Mother had bought for them, removing hers in the toilets and stuffing it in her bag as soon as they got to school on winter mornings. 'You do know you can see it through your shirt?' she'd say to Bryony but Bryony welcomed the warmth. She didn't care what people thought. She'd never be a beauty like Selena, anyway, and it seemed somehow undignified to even attempt to pay an interest in her appearance. Her hair had always been mousy and her nose was what Mother called 'a cute button', dusted with freckles, whereas Selena had inherited their father's striking looks, the piercing eyes, the chiselled bone structure.

She noticed the familiar ripple of glances as Selena came through the park. Everywhere she went, heads swivelled in her direction. She'd always had model looks. Was it true, what Dr Shaw had once said: that women like Selena, estranged from their fathers, were always looking for approval from other men? Bryony wasn't sure that she understood. For a while, Selena had been her father's favourite and she, Bryony, had spent most of her childhood hovering in Selena's shadow. Which had suited her fine in many ways. She hadn't really wanted to be noticed.

She raised her hand and Selena waved back. Bryony could see now that her face was set in an expression of annoyance. That was Selena, too. It didn't take much to irritate her.

'Selena got the looks but you got the sweetness,' Mother had once said, and Bryony hadn't known whether to feel upset or secretly proud. Now she felt sorry for what she was about to do.

'Hi, sis.' Selena flung herself onto the bench and stuck her feet out in front of her, turning her ankles this way and that. 'Bloody hell, it's freezing. My feet are like blocks of ice. I can't be doing with this weather.'

Bryony tried to smile. 'I know.' She pulled her coat collar up around her neck. 'How are you, Selena? And how's Letty?'

'Oh, I'm fine, I suppose. Well, as fine as you can be when you're flat broke.' She reached into her handbag and pulled out a tissue, dabbing at her nose. When she took her hand away, Bryony saw that there was an unfamiliar smile creeping across her face. 'Actually, though, Bry, all that's about to change. I've had some news. Just this morning. Something rather fantastic. A job offer. Professorship in New York, of all places.' She laughed. 'I'm going to New York, Bry. What a laugh! Can you believe it?'

Bryony felt a rush of relief flood through her.

'Really?' she said, trying not to let it show. 'When? And for how long?'

'I don't know.' Selena laughed again. 'It's a tenured position so ... maybe for bloody ever. The pay's fantastic. It's a small private college. I get a flat on campus, fees paid for Letty if she wants.' She hugged herself.

'Wow. You didn't say you were applying for anything,' Bryony said, frowning.

'That's just it. I didn't.' Selena shook her head. 'The offer came out of the blue. I got headhunted, basically. They're setting up a new department. They'd heard about my research. The Vice President called me last week. We had a couple of meetings over Skype and then I got the formal offer this morning.'

Bryony stared at the pattern of frost on the tarmac between her feet. 'That's incredible, Selena. Really fantastic. And for Letty. Such a great opportunity.' She took a deep breath. She had to ask. She just had to. 'Except that ... Well, I thought you had your eye on someone?' she said, carefully. 'That work colleague you told me about? What happened to *him*? Is he going to New York with you too?' She tried not to look too interested.

Selena snorted. 'Heavens, no! That was a total non-starter. Turns out that he's utterly besotted with his fat, frumpy wife. Or too scared. One or the other, anyway. Tedious.' She yawned. 'Probably wasn't my type, to be honest. Bit ... well, *earnest*, frankly.' She pulled a puppy-dog expression. 'So did you see him, then, the old bugger? Have you got it?'

Bryony let her breath out slowly through her teeth.

'Yes,' she said. 'I've got it. The money's already in my account.' She didn't say that she'd sat on the cheque for weeks, turning things over in her mind.

Selena frowned. 'So why did you want to meet? I mean, not that it isn't nice to see you and all that, sis. But you've got my account details. And, to be honest, it's a bit bloody cold for this.' She hugged herself.

Bryony stood up. 'You can thank me, Selena, if you like,' she said. 'Anyway, before I give you the money, I wanted us to have a bit of a talk. I – well, I want to ask you to promise me one thing . . .'

Selena rolled her eyes and that smile twitched at the corner of her mouth. 'Oh, really? Is this some kind of joke, Bry? C'mon. Don't mess me about.'

'It's not a joke. Not in the slightest.' Bryony shoved her hands in her pockets. 'I just want you to promise me that you'll never ask me anything like this again. I know you don't believe me, Selena, but this is absolutely the last time I can do this for you. I didn't find it easy, you know. And Dad doesn't believe me any-more when I say that it's for me –'

'Oh, great. So you dropped me in it, then?'

Bryony tried to keep the exasperation out of her voice. 'No, I didn't. It was my name on the cheque. But I think he knows that it's for you. I think he guessed. So you see, there's no point in us pretending anymore. There's no point in me covering for you. He gave me the money, just the same. So you'd be better off ask-ing him yourself in future. I really think he might like to see you.'

Selena pulled a face. 'Well, he'll be waiting a bloody long time, is all I can say. There's nothing I want to say to him that hasn't already been said a million times before.'

But you're perfectly happy to take his money, Bryony thought.

'OK. But I'm just saying that I can't . . . I *won't* do this again.'

'All right, sis. Message received, loud and clear. As I say, I'll be out of your hair soon, anyway. Thousands of miles away.' She waved her gloveless hand in the air. 'Now, can we just get this over with before I turn into a bloody icicle?'

She's not even listening, Bryony thought. She still thinks she'll always be able to talk me round.

'And I'd like to see Letty, before you leave,' she added, surprising herself. 'She's my niece, after all. The only one I've got. I'd like to . . . well, I'd like to get to know her a bit better, I suppose.'

Selena shrugged. 'She's fifteen. *I* don't even know her and I'm her bloody mother . . .'

Bryony followed Selena's gaze. A woman pushing a pram and dragging a reluctant toddler behind her was negotiating the path as it wound around an ornamental flower bed. They could hear the toddler's wailing protest and the woman's voice, abrupt and weary, carried to them on the cold wind. The pram's wheels skidded on a frozen puddle and the woman swore loudly.

Bryony unzipped the pocket in her handbag and took out the cheque.

For a moment, Selena's face relaxed. Then she opened her own large bag and slipped the cheque inside.

'Thanks.' She forced a smile.

The woman with the pram was pushing up the hill towards them now, her cheeks reddening with the effort. The toddler was chasing pigeons, his hands flapping. Behind them, a group of tourists spilled out of the museum onto the terrace, talking loudly in Japanese.

'Well, I'd better be off to bank this, then.' Selena stood up, stamping the feeling back into her feet. 'Don't want to be walking round with it all afternoon. Look, I'll call you. About Letty. OK?'

Bryony watched her sister walk stiffly through the wrought-iron gates towards town, her bag swinging from her shoulder, her blonde hair blowing out all around her.

She let out a little sigh. She felt a flicker of sadness – brown flecked with muddy green – for the woman walking away from her. She realised now something that she'd never imagined she might feel, all those years ago when Selena had been her beautiful tormentor. It was as if her sister, destined to be so extraordinary, so beautiful, was still tied to some image of herself, some expectation that she'd never managed to fulfil. Bryony could almost see it, bobbing in the air in front of Selena, always just a little way ahead of her as she walked, like a perfectly shiny silver balloon. She was pleased for Selena, for her chance at a new start, far away, safely on the other side of an enormous ocean. She hoped that she'd finally find whatever it was that she was looking for. Because Bryony now knew that she herself could be anything she wanted. No one had ever expected anything of her, anyway. And that, she now realised, meant that she was free.

*

The wind whipped around the courtyard and the cobbles shimmered with a fine layer of frost. Grace traced experimental zigzags across the shop doorstep with the toes of her new red leather boots. Then she drew a circle and jumped inside it.

'Ooo! It's slippy, Mamma!'

'Yes,' said Ella. 'It's *very* slippy. You be careful.'

She thought of the January day when she and Mamma had first arrived here, how she'd drawn a heart in the dust on the window with a damp finger.

She bent and hugged Grace to her. Her daughter's cheeks were as crimson as her red woollen coat.

'Come on,' she said, fiddling with the lock, before she realised that the door was already open. The back of her neck prickled. Instantly, her mind jumped to Maadar-Bozorg sleeping in the bedroom upstairs. Was she all right? Had she forgotten to lock the door behind her last night? Surely there couldn't have been a break-in? She cupped her hand against the window and peered through the glass, but inside the shop seemed undisturbed.

'Grace,' she said, crouching to get her attention. 'Wait here. OK?'

Grace nodded. Ella saw her own concern reflected in her daughter's blue-grey eyes. She pushed gingerly at the door.

'Hello? Maadar-Bozorg? Are you there? Is everything all right?'

Maadar was standing in the shadows at the back of the shop, behind the cafe counter. She turned and smiled at Ella's voice.

'Don't fret, child. Everything's perfectly fine.'

Her woollen shawl was thrown over her pyjamas and she held the coffee filter in her hand.

'Sorry. Just trying to figure out how to use this thing.' She waved the chrome barrel in frustration, spraying droplets of water over the floor.

'I thought . . .' Ella looked around the shop. 'I thought –'

278

'Oh, child. You *think* too much.' Maadar-Bozorg cupped Ella's face in her palm. 'You had a very early visitor, *carina*, that's all.' She dropped her voice conspiratorially and gestured up the stairs to the flat. 'I hope you don't mind, but she seemed in desperate need of a nap so I offered her my bed and took the liberty of warming up the machine here, while I was waiting.' She patted the shiny Gaggia. 'But I just can't get the hang of it.'

'Mamma? *MA*-mma!' Grace called from the doorway.

'Oh, Grace. I'm sorry.' Ella turned to see her daughter still obediently waiting on the wrong side of the door. She beckoned to her. 'Come in now, out of the cold. Mamma's going to make you some hot chocolate.' She turned to Maadar-Bozorg. 'A visitor? But *who?*'

Right on cue, the stairs creaked and a figure began to descend, appearing bit by bit in the stairwell. Ella saw a pair of feet in elegant tan leather boots, then denim-clad legs, followed by a section of torso in a simple black sweater.

The headless torso spoke. Her voice floated down the stairwell. 'Isabella?' Really? It is really you?' The voice was soft, musical, heavily accented. A face bobbed into view. A beautiful face with a large smile. 'Oh, it is! *Veramente!* It *is!*'

The woman clapped her hands together in excitement. Ella felt herself looked up and down by this stranger with enormous dark eyes.

'I'm sorry,' she said. 'I don't . . . Do I *know* you?'

The Signals buzzed and whirred around her like tiny insects. Her head was full of noise.

The woman frowned.

'*Ma dai*! How stupid of me.' She banged the side of her head with a theatrical flourish. 'I would recognise you any-where, *tesora*. But me – *pouf*!' She jabbed at the air with an elegant finger. 'How could you possibly know me from the next person?'

She crossed the room in a couple of enthusiastic strides. Ella felt Grace press herself against her leg. A tiny hand reached for hers.

The woman's arms were thrown wide in an effusive greet-ing. 'I am Valentina Moreno,' she said. 'And I am sorry to just turn up like this but, you know, I was so curious to see you. Really, I could not wait a minute longer!' Her face broke into that wide smile again, showing a perfect set of white teeth. 'Isabella, I am your . . .' She looked at Maadar for approval. 'Her *aunty*. Is that right?'

Maadar nodded.

'Yes, I am your father, Enzo's, sister!'

Ella saw the words hang in the air between them for a moment. Everything else stopped. She cleared her throat.

'I'm sorry? You're –?'

'Valentina. I'm your *zia*. From Italy, *tesora*. And I'm sorry to just, well, turn up here like this. But I can explain. I am just telling your *nonna* here that . . . Well, it is a long, long story. But, *a-ha*. Who is *this*? This *piccolina*?'

Her face lit up again as Grace stuck her head out from behind Ella's thigh. Valentina crouched and fixed Grace with her large brown eyes. Grace stared back at her.

'This is Grace. Grace, say hello.'

Grace stuck her thumb in her mouth and mumbled. She pulled at Ella's hand.

'Sorry. She's a bit tired today.' Ella raised an eyebrow at Maadar-Bozorg, who was now standing with a steaming cup in one hand.

'Valentina, do sit down, dear. A cup of coffee? I always think that's the best way to start things off.' Maadar-Bozorg set the cup on a table.

Valentina tossed her mane of thick dark hair and laughed. '*Si, si*! In our family, we say . . .' She looked at Ella. '*Your* family, *tesora*. We say that the first cup of coffee is not just a cup of coffee, no. It is a communion with the gods.' She jabbed a finger at the ceiling.

'Is that so?' Maadar smiled and pulled out a chair. 'Sit. Sit, my dear. That's right.'

Ella drew out a chair for herself and hauled Grace onto her knee. She let herself look again, more slowly this time, at the woman now perched on the opposite side of the table. The small hands with their long fingers wrapped around the white coffee cup, the wild brown hair, the soft curves of her figure under the black cashmere sweater.

Inside her head, she had the strangest sensation of something shifting and sliding into place. It was as if, as she looked at this woman, she was looking at herself.

'My aunt? *Really*? You're my aunt?' She felt a smile spreading over her face. 'But, um, I'm sorry if this sounds rude. It's just that I didn't even know that I had one –'

'I know!' Valentina banged her cup down on the table so forcefully that Grace let out a nervous giggle. 'Me too, *carina*. I knew *nothing* about you. All these years. But I just found out. Because until last month, I didn't even know that I had a brother! Stupid, no? And that is why I had to come here. To find you.' She grinned again and her teeth flashed white against her tanned skin. 'And now I have. And I am so . . . so –' She flung her arms wide again and searched the ceiling for the right word. 'I am so *happy*! So very happy!'

*

'You're wearing make-up.'

'Yes. Just a bit.'

Bryony spooned potatoes onto Ed's plate. She speared the broccoli with the tip of her fork and raised it to her lips.

'You know I've never really liked that on a woman. I don't know why you feel like you have to do that to yourselves. All that faffing about.'

Bryony felt the familiar anger begin to push its way up inside her. These days, it never seemed far from the surface. Everything Ed did, everything he said seemed to stir things up in her.

'Ed,' she said uncertainly, laying down her fork.

'Yes? What is it, love?' He swigged water from his glass, wiped his mouth with the back of his hand. For the first time, Bryony realised that he looked worried, uncertain of himself.

Bryony knew then what she had to do. She'd been rehearsing this moment in her head for weeks now. Ever since the scene at Ella's party. She hadn't thought she was ready. She'd told herself she'd give it a little more time. Just a few months or so, until things were a bit more settled. But now it was all coming out of her in a rush.

'Ed, I'm sorry. There's no easy way to say this but I don't think it's been going that well between us, recently. It's not your fault. Not at all. It's just that I've changed. I'm still finding my way, since . . . well, since I was ill. And I don't think I can change back again. I'm different, a different person now. And so I've been thinking . . . I wonder if it's best if you move out? There's no rush, of course. You can take all the time you need. But I think in the long run –'

'You what?' Ed's face had turned the colour of beetroot. Bryony saw that he was genuinely shocked. He'd really had no idea.

For a brief moment, she felt that familiar feeling of panic. That fluttery feeling inside her chest as if a thousand tiny wings were beating against her breastbone.

'Bloody hellfire, Bry.' Ed looked down at his plate. Then in one movement he sprung to his feet and picked it up. She thought he was going to throw it – maybe at her – but instead he took it, still mounded with roast chicken and potatoes, and crossed the kitchen and dumped the lot into the bin.

'Well,' he said, wiping his hands on the back of his trousers. 'That's that then.'

At the kitchen door he turned to her with a look of disdain. It was the kind of look that, only months ago, would have finished her off.

'Just don't come crying to me when you're all alone and desperate,' he said. 'Your new friends won't want to know when you're back in there.' He jabbed his thumb over his shoulder. 'When you're back with all the nut jobs. When you're just a lonely, old madwoman.'

Bryony sat quietly at the table, her hands folded in her lap. Above her head, she could hear Ed opening drawers and cupboards, banging things around. Then she heard his feet thudding down the stairs, heard him take his coat off the hook by the door, throw her key into the dish on the hall table.

The front door slammed. He was gone.

It was only then that the tears came. Big shuddering sobs. Sadness, yes, but mostly a sense of relief, as if she'd been carrying something very heavy for a very long time and had finally put it down.

*

'So where is she now then, this surprise aunt?'

Billy was dangling Grace upside down as she swiped at his knees and laughed hysterically.

'Billy, don't. You're getting her all giddy right before –' Ella stopped mid-sentence. She'd made a promise to herself that she'd try to be a bit more relaxed about these things. But it was still difficult. Billy always seemed to rub her up the wrong way.

'Sorry,' she said. She slid the last book from the new delivery into its rightful place in Snow and smiled. 'Valentina? She's gone to a hotel. She insisted. Maadar-Bozorg offered to share her room with her. There are still two beds up there, after all. But Valentina said that she wanted to give me some space. That I needed some time to get used to it all. She was so . . . so totally sweet, Billy. So lovely. I just know that you'll like her. I've invited her for dinner tomorrow night so that you and Mamma can meet her then.'

Billy frowned.

'What about your mum? Do you think she'll be OK with it all? I mean, it's a big deal, isn't it, this relative of your dad's just turning up out of the blue after all these years?'

Ella nodded. 'Yes, but I think she'll be delighted. After Pappa died, she lost touch with the Italian side of the family. We moved around so much. And I don't think there was any love lost between Pappa and his parents. And then . . . It's a really tragic

284

story but my dad's mother . . . that is, my *Italian* grandmother, Billy . . . Just think of that. Well, she passed away shortly after my dad. And then my grandfather remarried. That's where Valentina comes in. She's Pappa's half-sister, to be accurate. But to think that Pappa never even knew that she existed. Valentina says that her father – my grandfather – was a very distant, bitter old man by the time she was old enough to remember him. He never even mentioned his son. It was only when he died, a couple of months ago, that she was going through his papers and discovered some letters – and that led her to us.'

As she talked, she realised that Billy was watching her, a smile twitching at the corners of his mouth.

'Are you laughing at me?' She frowned.

'No. No, it's just . . . Well, you look . . . I don't know. You look sort of different somehow, El. I don't really know how to describe it . . . You just look more –'

'Relaxed? I *have* been really trying.'

'Maybe. A bit. But just more . . . Well, more *you,* I suppose. More yourself than I've seen you in a long, long time. It's great.' He reached for her hand and squeezed her fingers.

Grace attempted to clamber up his thigh.

'Daddy. Da-ddy!'

He caught her and threw her above his head, unleashing a storm of giggles.

'Honestly, you two.' Ella smiled. 'You know, it probably sounds weird. I mean, I've only just met her, this Valentina person. But I feel a bit like there's been this piece of me that's been missing for so long and now, finally, I've found it. She's an artist, Billy. She paints. And she lives . . . wait for it . . . in *Venice*, for goodness' sake. *Venice*! And she runs these art history tours for tourists.

She's so creative and ... and interesting and vibrant and I feel as if I just clicked with her. As if, well, as if I finally *belong*. Like somehow I fit. Like something about me finally makes sense. Does that sound really melodramatic?'

'No more than usual.' Billy grinned again.

'Seriously, Billy. She's like ... um, like –'

'Like an Italian-speaking, extra-caffeinated version of Ella.'

Maadar-Bozorg stood at the bottom of the stairs, her eyes twinkling. 'Just wait until your mother sees her. She won't believe her eyes. And to think that your grandfather never told anyone about you. You know, your mother wrote to him. Several times. I know that much. But he didn't want anything to do with her. He always blamed Farah for your father's death.' She shook her head and pushed her hair back from her face. 'Families. Always so darn complicated.'

She sighed. 'Anyway, I'm really happy for you, child, that Valentina has come along. Our roots are important. I know that much.' She clapped her hands. 'Now then, little great-great-granddaughter. How about you and I go and get you into your pyjamas and let your mummy and daddy have some time together?' She looked at Ella. 'OK?'

Ella blew Maadar-Bozorg a kiss over the top of Grace's head. 'Thank you,' she mouthed silently.

She listened to Grace's babble fade out across the courtyard and then stood and watched Billy slosh hot chocolate into a mug from the jug still steaming on the cafe counter top. He turned. 'Want one? For old time's sake?'

Ella smiled and shook her head. 'I think I've outgrown hot chocolate.'

Billy pulled his face into a mock pout. 'But not me, I hope?'

She laughed. 'Billy?'

'Yes?' He looked at her over the rim of his mug, wiggling his eyebrows.

'No, be serious for a minute. There's . . . There's something I've been meaning to tell you.'

Billy's face dropped. 'Sounds ominous. But come on then. No secrets, right?'

Ella's hands clenched. She felt her fingernails dig into her palms. They were still being very polite with one another, careful, edging around each other.

'You know the other day, when I went up to Miss Mary's cottage? With Bryony and Maadar-Bozorg?'

'Yes, did you have fun?' He grinned. 'Not really your thing, is it, healing herbs and all that stuff?'

'No, well. But it's not that. It's just . . . Well, whilst we were there, I saw –'

She stopped, the words caught in the back of her throat.

'What? You saw what?'

'I saw –'

'*Tesora*. Billy. Darlings, I'm sorry to interrupt . . .'

Fabia stood at the bottom of the stairs. 'Sorry. I didn't know you were in here. I just needed a bigger pair of scissors. I know there are some in this drawer somewhere.' She crossed to the shop counter and began to rummage behind it. 'Sorry. Forgive me, darlings. Won't be a moment. Don't mind me.'

Billy reached for Ella's hand. 'So what were you going to ask me?'

Ella felt her cheeks flush. 'Oh, it'll wait,' she said, glancing pointedly in Mamma's direction. 'Nothing important.'

'OK. Good.'

He picked her up and swung her onto the edge of the counter top.

'Billy. Not now. I'm not sure I –'

'*Buona notte*, darlings.' Fabia waved her hand at them, already halfway up the stairs again. 'I'm turning in early.'

The Tale of Little Red Riding Hood

Maadar-Bozorg turned the page. Grace squirmed on her lap.

'Go back, Granmamma. You missed a bit.'

'I did?' Maadar-Bozorg pushed her glasses up her nose. Goodness knows why the child was so attached to this story. Well, in fact, she did know or, at least, she could guess. It was the kind of story that three-year-olds liked the world over. A little girl in a red dress. A cottage in the middle of a wood. A grandmother who was not quite what she seemed. Lots of repetition, as in all the most popular folktales. *Grandmother, what big eyes you have! Grandmother, what big ears you have! Grandmother, what big teeth you have!* And so on.

Add in a sprinkling of magic and just the right amount of scary and you had a potent recipe for enchantment.

But really, Maadar-Bozorg thought, as she flipped the page back again, she was getting a little weary of this Red Riding Hood character. She didn't seem to have much backbone. A lot of the Western stories were like that, she'd noticed. Little girls doing what they were told. All very obedient.

Here was Little Red Riding Hood, standing at the end of her Grandmother's bed, just before the Wolf threw back the bed-clothes and tried to eat her up. The illustrator had drawn her with her hood pushed back and an expression of wide-eyed innocence on her face. Maadar-Bozorg found it rather irritating.

'Look, Grace!' She pointed at the little girl in the picture. 'Little Red Riding Hood jumps on the bed, puts her hands on her hips like this.' Maadar-Bozorg demonstrated. 'And she shouts, as loud as she can, "You don't frighten me, Wolf!" Can you hear her?'

Grace craned her neck to get a better look at Maadar-Bozorg's face. Her eyes were filled with confusion. Then she giggled and shook her head.

'Oh. So you don't believe me?' Maadar-Bozorg smiled. 'Watch this . . .' She turned the page again. 'Look, here's the Wolf leaping from the bed. R-ROAAARRR! He tries to scare Red Riding Hood but she holds on to the bedpost and tickles the Wolf under his big, hairy nose like this.'

Maadar-Bozorg tickled Grace experimentally.

'And, after a few more attempts to make Red Riding Hood afraid, the Wolf gives up. "Oh, OK then," he says. And he pulls off his big furry wolf skin . . . *Ooof, oof* . . . Just like this . . .'

Maadar-Bozorg pretended to pull a mask from her face.

Grace stared at her, wide-eyed.

'And then Little Red Riding Hood sees that the wolf isn't a real wolf after all but actually . . . Can you guess? He is her *own grandmother!*'

Grace frowned. Her tiny hand batted impatiently at the page.

'And then Little Red Riding Hood asks her Wolf-Grandmother to teach her everything she knows about the woods: how to open her eyes wide and see into even the darkest places; how to run faster than the wind; how to sniff out any danger at one hundred wolf-paw paces; in fact, everything that a girl needs to know to live an exciting life.'

Grace swung her legs and sighed indulgently. '*That's* not the ending, Gran-mamma.'

'Oh, isn't it?' Maadar-Bozorg smiled. 'Are you absolutely sure?'

'Yes,' said Grace, nodding. 'That's not how Daddy reads it to me.'

'Ah, but didn't you know, Grace, that we can change stories in any way we choose? We can make them end in any way we want to. And this is the ending that *I* prefer.'

Maadar-Bozorg closed the book. Grace slithered off her lap and ran across the floor, delighting in the way that her feet in their pink wool tights slipped and skidded on the polished boards.

I suppose I should tell you to be careful, Maadar-Bozorg thought. Pay attention. Don't get carried away. Don't fall.

But there was plenty of time for all that. For now, she was happy to see Grace run free, her hair flying out around her head in a dark tangle, her arms and legs scissoring the air.

'Watch me, Granmamma,' she yelped as she tried a pirouette. 'Watch me!'

*

Fabia threw up the sash of the kitchen window and breathed in the cool night air. Up here, under the eaves, she could feel the city moving, the river rolling in its sleep. She could hear all the night sounds that were still so familiar to her: the pigeons shifting on the roof above her head, the restaurant owners along Petergate rattling their canopies closed as they locked up for the night, taxis swishing past on the wet road and, very faintly, floating up from the river bank, the sound of the geese settling themselves.

She pressed her cheek against the window frame and watched the orange flush from the street lamps seeping above the rooftops. She could just make out the west wing of the Minster and, above its floodlit angels and gargoyles, a handful of faint stars.

She tried to relax her mind to that single, still point, to let her breathing quieten, her body open itself to the night.

'*Shhhh.*' The Signals whispered from the corner of the room. '*Shhhh.* Listen.'

She had laid the dowry cloth carefully across the kitchen table. Now she stood above it, taking in its colours, smoothing it with the palms of her hands, letting her fingers learn its flow, the places where the pattern was a little more raised, the tiny ridges where the colours changed and the threads had been woven in on themselves.

Gently, she lifted the fabric to her face and breathed in its richly layered scent. There were the fragrant spices from Maadar-Bozorg's kitchen, cinnamon and cardamom, essence of rose and the faintest hint of ripe pomegranates. There were the many-layered scents of the cloth itself, the imprint of the women who had woven it with quick and confident fingers, who had washed and dyed the yarn itself, combing it out, leaving it to dry in the shade. She could smell their perfume and, beneath that, the scent of the trees that had cast that shade – cedar and pine – and the loamy scent of the river where the yarn had been washed and the lingering scent of the dyes – turmeric, used for its deep red, and saffron for its yellow.

And then here, at the base of it all, was another scent, impossible to define. A hint of soap, perhaps, rosewater or eau de cologne and then, beneath that, what she could only describe as the scent of a powerful longing. And that, she thought, must be the scent of her mother.

From down the years, she heard a voice, the voice of her Aunt Mahdokht, the eldest of Maadar-Bozorg's sisters. She was a young girl again, standing in the dim salon of the sisters' house in Tehran, the doors open to the courtyard and her aunt was standing over her, her breath tickling her ear. '*Listen, little one.*' Her voice was no more than a whisper, caressing her cheek, reaching down inside her. '*Listen, Farah. You must learn to listen to the fabric itself. What does it already know? What does it want to be?*'

Now Fabia slid her scissors from their velvet sheath. They were her silver scissors, the ones that Maadar-Bozorg had given her for her fourteenth birthday, made in the shape of a swan, the blades a beak, opening and shutting and the handles engraved in the shape of wings, closing and opening, opening and closing.

She began to cut. The moment when the blades first made contact with the cloth was always the most difficult. If you leaned in at that moment, putting your ear up close, you could just hear the fabric let out a little sigh as it gave itself up to the steel. *Aaaaaah.* The release as each taut thread met with the edge of the blades. A little out-breath.

After that first cut, her courage always grew. Her movements gathered confidence, became swifter, more fluid as she let the undulating pattern of the fabric itself guide her.

Here, just here, was where the neckline would be, the front of the dress gathering into a deep yoke. Here was a sleeve, cut narrow to the elbow and falling soft and wide from the wrist. Yes, that was right. Just so.

This was a dress that would be warm, even in the harshest Yorkshire winters, but light and cool in summer. It would flow gently over the wearer's hips, swirl around her easily as she moved, the colours surrounding her in a soft shimmer.

As she cut and smoothed, what Fabia saw in her mind's eye was Ella. Always Ella. Her brown hair tumbling over her shoulders, tangling with these colours, her slender white wrists in the wide-winged sleeves. She could wear this over her jeans. She could wear it anywhere at all. It would be simple and easy, just as Ella liked her clothes to be.

The natural dyes were sumptuous and softly muted at the same time. Just right for her daughter. And into the hem, weighted with its tiny beads of garnet and agate and turquoise, Fabia would sew the words that would keep Ella safe.

Sleep, sweet daughter of mine, she said to herself as she sewed. *Sleep and dream.*

As the waxing moon climbed higher in the sky, Fabia let the dress shape itself. She hummed a little under her breath as she worked. She heard Enzo's voice, her beloved Enzo: '*Do you like jazz, bellissima? Listen. This is my favourite. Ella Fitzgerald. Magnifica. What a goddess. Don't you love it, how you feel it all through you, carissima, like . . . like e-lec-tricity?*'

The night air drifted through the open window bringing with it the scents and sounds of the city. It was the kind of evening, Fabia thought, when it seemed as if the sky reached down and touched the earth. You could feel the sleeping city breathing all around you.

She took the almost finished dress in her lap and threaded her needle with silver embroidery silk and began her tiny hidden stitches: *Listen, my daughter. Feel it all through you. Listen to what is weaving itself. Possibilities. New dreams.*

And with each stitch, Fabia knew with a little more certainty, as she listened to that still, small space inside her, exactly what it was that she would do next.

26

*To manifest your heart's desires: Gather rosebuds with
the morning dew still on them. Steep them in a dish of
rainwater. Rub a drop of it between your palms and
drink the remainder.*
– Miss Mary's Book of Dreams

The river was high tonight. In the darkness, Ella could hear it
rushing past, swollen with rain, as she hurried along the path.
She was late. Grace had been unusually clingy, cross at being
left behind, despite having the attentions of both Mamma and
Maadar-Bozorg.

But Billy had been clear. Seven p.m. Ella still had his invitation in her pocket. She touched it now, as she walked along, like
a lucky charm.

It was a small piece of white card, cut in the shape of a heart
and on it he'd written simply: *Meet me on the bridge. 7 p.m.*

She'd found it on the breakfast table this morning, propped
against the coffee pot. She knew immediately, of course, which
bridge he meant.

She rounded the bend in the riverbank and the bridge
came into view, a span of steel and wood, glittering under the
moon.

And now she could see him, oddly small from here, standing
right at the centre, and she felt a quiver of something – excitement,
nerves, anticipation.

All those years ago, this is where they'd walked together, that
awful night of the Cushworths' party. This is where he'd first

tried to kiss her – and where she'd run off into the night, her stomach churning, her shoes slapping the path, the river a blur of tears. And over there, past the bridge and further on, where the grass grew taller and the boats were moored, that was where they'd dived and swum, where they'd lolled on the swimming platform all those long days of summer, and where she'd hung suspended from the rope swing before dropping into the water, letting it close over her, delicious and cold. She remembered how she'd tricked him, keeping herself down there in that dim, green world for as long as she could until the blood pounded in her ears; and the way his face had looked when she'd burst up again, laughing and gasping.

'Billy,' she called out now, keeping her voice low. He'd already turned at the sound of her footsteps, was walking towards her, grinning.

'You came.'

'Of course I did.'

'I didn't know if you would. Whether you'd think it was all a bit daft.'

Ella reached up and touched his cheek. 'Not daft, no. Very sweet.'

'I was just remembering,' he said. 'It all seems like a long time ago.'

'It *was* a long time ago. I've been counting. Thirteen years, to be exact.'

He took her hand. 'Can I kiss you now?' he said. 'I mean, I'm just checking. I don't want you to yell at me. You're not going to run off?'

She smiled and offered her face up to him. They held each other for a long time. Beneath them, the water seemed to grow quieter, calmer. They heard the call of a barn owl, saw its white swoop over the water. The moon drifted behind a bank of cloud.

Afterwards, they walked, hand in hand along the riverbank, back into town.

'Where are we going?' Ella watched his face.

'Surprise,' he said. 'You'll see.'

'They came up the steps at Ousegate and headed across town. The streets were half empty. Tourist season was over and it was too cold for people to be hanging about.

They walked mainly in silence and it didn't feel awkward anymore. Instead, Ella felt memories flooding her, thick and fast. Here was the place where they'd come with Grace, that first weekend she'd learned to walk, where she'd fallen in the grass and laughed. Here was the restaurant where Mamma had told them that she was giving them the lease of the shop and where David had insisted on champagne to celebrate their new beginnings. Here was the corner where Billy had first waited to walk home with her after school. And here was Petergate, where they'd posted all the fliers, the day before Mamma's shop first opened.

She was so lost in thought that she hardly noticed when they turned into Grape Lane and Billy ducked under the archway to the courtyard. A lozenge of wobbly orange light fell across the cobbles. Ella stopped, confused. She looked up at the windows of their flat, saw the silhouette of Mamma moving in their kitchen.

'Here,' said Billy. 'This is where we're going.' He slipped the keys out of his pocket, opened the shop door. 'I've got something to show you,' and he nudged her through the doorway.

The shop was in darkness, except for strings of fairy lights draped over the tops of the bookcases. In the centre of the room, there was a small table, covered with a crisp white cloth and set for two: silver cutlery, wine glasses and a vase with a single yellow rose.

Billy pulled out a chair.

'Madame,' he said, with a mock flourish. 'Please. Do have a seat.'

He lit the row of tea lights lined up along the counter. He took a bottle of wine from the little fridge in the cafe corner and filled their glasses.

'There's food warming in the upstairs kitchen,' he said. He checked his watch. 'In fact, it'll be ready in just a few moments.'

She smiled. 'You're very organised. How did you manage to plan all this?'

'Well, I had a little help.' He shrugged. 'I thought if we retraced our steps this evening, and if we came back here, here to where it all started, it would be easier for us to just . . . well, be you and me for a while. I thought that then you might believe me when I tell you that this, *this* is what it's all about. This is where I first fell in love with you, El. You were standing right there.' He pointed to the bottom of the stairs that led up to the tiny sitting room. 'You were wearing jeans and a black T-shirt. Your hair was all loose around your shoulders.' He closed his eyes. 'I remember it exactly. You were the most beautiful thing I'd ever seen.'

'Billy –'

'Look, I just wanted to say that I'm sorry if I've not been here for you. Properly here for you, this past couple of years.

I'm stupid. I can be so ... such an *idiot* sometimes. I always assume you're OK. I always forget how damn proud you are. That you'd never ask for help, not in a million years. And I can see now how hard it's been for you. But I do love you, El. More than I've ever loved anyone. Well, except Grace, of course.'

Ella looked at him. 'I love you, too,' she said.

'Do you think ... well, do you think we're going to be OK? If we keep talking? If we promise not to have any secrets? Will you tell me when you need more help, when I'm being stupid, when there's something bothering you? Because I'm terrified.' She saw that his hands were shaking. 'I really don't want to lose you.'

The moon shone in through the window, catching the glass droplets of the chandelier, throwing fat sequins of light around the room.

There was an old song that Mamma used to sing. Ella could hear it now, the way Mamma would hum it under her breath: *When the moon hits your eye like a big pizza pie ... Scusa me, but you see ...*

'Yes,' she said quickly. 'Yes. Yes to all that. Yes.'

She reached across the table and took his hand and pressed it to her lips.

*

'David, it's me.'

He'd been watching TV. She could hear it in the background.

'Darling. One moment ...' It went quiet.

'Well, hello, stranger.' His voice was loud with happiness. 'I was beginning to think –'

'I know. David, I might not be able to talk for long. I just managed to get Grace to sleep but she's a bit unsettled. Maadar-Bozorg and I are babysitting.'

'Oh, listen to you.' She could hear him smiling. 'You sound so . . . happy. So at home.'

Fabia felt her stomach lurch. 'Well, actually, that's what I wanted to talk about.'

She could almost hear him holding his breath.

'I wanted to say –'

'You're not coming back, are you?'

Fabia laughed. 'That's just it. I knew you were going to think that. But I am. I am.'

David let out an audible sigh. 'Really? Gosh, I'm sorry. I must sound a bit . . . well, desperate. It's just that I've had too much time to think here. I've been going over and over it in my head. Thinking what an idiot I've been for not – Well, look, anyway, that's not what matters. This isn't the time, is it, to have this kind of conversation. So . . . When?'

'Soon. In a week or so. And I'm going to bring Maadar-Bozorg back with me. If that's OK?'

'Of course, of course. Great idea.'

'And, David?'

'Yes, darling.'

'What you asked me. Before I left. I'll give you my answer then. When I see you. OK?'

There was a silence. Then David's voice. It sounded as if he was on the brink of tears. 'Yes, of course, darling. I just can't wait to see you again. I've missed you.'

'Me too. *Buona notte, amore.*'

'Yes. Yes. Goodbye.'

*

In her narrow hallway, Bryony paused for a moment, listening. The clock on the living room mantelpiece – her mother's wedding present from a favourite cousin – began to chime. Eight o'clock. Not a moment to lose. The clock's gentle tick had always annoyed Ed. It kept him awake at night, so he'd said, and so she'd eventually let it wind down. Now that he was gone, Bryony had restored it to its rightful place, between a Chinese vase – another of her mother's treasured possessions – and a potted spider plant.

She examined her reflection in the hall mirror, smoothing a strand of hair from her forehead. Lately, she'd taken to wearing lipstick in a rather daring shade of red. She took one from her handbag now, uncapped its shiny gold casing and ran it over her lips, then pressed them together. Her reflected self smiled back at her in the dress of crimson silk that Fabia had made.

'This, darling, is perfect for your colouring.' Fabia had smiled, when Bryony expressed her doubts. 'Everyone should own at least one red dress in their lives. It's all about getting the shade right. For you, this nice, deep red. Plenty of warmth. And the silk throws light on the face. See?'

And as Fabia had held the fabric up against her, draping it at the shoulder, gathering handfuls of it in at the waist, talking through a mouthful of pins about how she'd put a seam here and a detail there, shaping the silk with expert fingers, Bryony had looked at herself again. Perhaps she wasn't quite past it, after all. She certainly looked less . . . well, tired.

Now she bent and slipped on the black suede ankle boots with the elegant little heel. They made her feel instantly taller, more graceful somehow. She took the pin of emerald green feathers from its wrapping of tissue and fastened it carefully in the dip of her neckline. The dress was a bit low cut. She'd been worried that it showed too much cleavage. But the pin just finished it off, the crystals glittering in the light from the hall lamp. She was certain that Fabia would approve.

Bryony loved the park at this time in the morning, just as the sun was rising from the tops of the trees and before it filled up with dog walkers and people on their way to work. She slipped through the wrought-iron gates, past the empty bandstand and along the side of the lake, half frozen over now, a few ducks pecking at the ice.

She reached the cafe and stood for a moment, admiring the windows, now painted a perfect shade of blue and flanked by zinc tubs spilling with winter pansies. She had the bunch of keys ready in her hand and now she began to unfasten the padlocks on the newly painted shutters, one by one, throwing the doors wide so that their bevelled panes filled with the rose and silver light from the lake.

Inside, the tables were already decorated with crisp white antique linen cloths and little cut-glass vases awaiting the flowers she'd brought. The floorboards had been scrubbed and polished and the walls painted in the softest shade of grey and hung with colourful paintings, abstract swirls of red and ochre and cobalt blue in which it was just possible to make out the shapes of birds and trees.

A blackboard behind the polished steel counter had been chalked up with her house specials: *Yorkshire Rarebit with Cranberry Chutney, Secret Ingredient Fennel Soup, White and Pink Pepper Chocolate Truffles* and her own personal favourite, *Sweet Dreams Tea* – an infusion of rose petals, wild mint and chamomile flowers.

She felt a surge of pleasure travel up her spine and tingle in the back of her throat.

There were voices, a child's tinkling laughter, someone calling her name. She turned. Three figures stood in the open doorway, silhouetted against the December sun.

Ella and Fabia were rubbing their gloved hands together and stamping the cold from their feet. Maadar-Bozorg was wrapped in her gigantic woollen shawl and held Grace by the hand.

'We're on our way to the airport,' said Fabia. 'Maadar-Bozorg and I fly out this afternoon. But we were hoping that we might warm our hands on a nice hot cup of coffee. Are we in luck?'

Before Bryony could answer, Maadar leaned forward and from under her shawl she drew a small packet.

'I need to give you this,' she muttered in Bryony's ear. 'It's the remains of an old spell. It needs to be buried deep in the ground. I was thinking that up at Miss Mary's old cottage might be the place. Could you do that for me, child, as soon as you get the chance?'

Bryony smiled.

'Of course,' she said, taking the packet and dropping it into the pocket of her new white linen apron.

Then she turned and stroked Grace's hair. The icy morning was cold on her cheek.

'Come on, Grace,' she said. 'Come with me. I need your help,' and she led her over to the window and showed her how to turn the new enamelled sign to Open.

Epilogue

I'm standing in the clearing. The earth is damp under my bare feet and, when I look up, the sky glimmers with grey pearlescent light.

Somewhere in the woods behind me, I can hear the first birdsong – the *chirr-up*, *chirr-up* of the blackbirds and a skylark pouring out his pure, clear notes.

I look down and see that in amongst the mulch of old leaves, tiny new green shoots are just beginning to appear. Spring. It's early this year.

I wait for a moment, savouring the scent of the earth mixed with the night's rain. Then I turn and watch as the sun breaks through the woods behind me, making the branches tremble with silver.

Here, where the trees thin out, a path opens in the woodland floor, the trampled leaves and moss curving gently ahead of me, sequinned with raindrops.

I begin to walk forward, feeling my way carefully over the wet leaves. There's a faint rustling in the branches above my head and then . . . Am I imagining it? That flash of red and green in the shadows? The flicker of tail feathers? I go faster, my fingertips brushing the smooth trunks of the birch trees, but there's only a pigeon pecking at the ground and a voice calling me softly, insistently: *Mamma, Mamma, Ma-mma . . .*

When I open my eyes, the sun is streaming though the crack in the bedroom curtains. The sheets have somehow wound themselves around my legs and Grace is sitting on my feet, watching me with those big blue-grey eyes.

'Mamma wake up now,' she says. She's holding the dress that my own Mamma made for me before she left for California, stretching it out like shimmering wings between her tiny hands.

'Mamma, you need to put your new dress on now.' She shakes the sleeves impatiently. 'Mamma wake up. Put it on.'

Billy appears in the doorway behind her, a mug of steaming coffee in his hand.

'Morning,' he says and grins, balancing the mug carefully on top of the pile of books that serves as my bedside table. 'Sleep well?' He leans down to kiss me.

Grace can't wait any longer. She flings her arms around my neck and buries her nose in my chest. She smells of sleep and soap and the chocolate milk that she isn't supposed to have for breakfast.

'Yes,' I say, smiling at Billy. 'Yes, actually, I did.'

Gently, I prise Grace's fingers from my shoulders and prop her against the pillows. She looks at me expectantly.

I pull my old, grey sweatshirt over my head and take the dress from Grace, slipping my arms into the wide sleeves. The fabric is fragrant and soft. It feels just right.

'There,' I say. 'OK?'

Grace nods approvingly.

'Give me just five minutes then, darling. Mamma's got to do something first.'

I sip at the coffee, letting the fragrant warmth reach all the way inside me. I take a breath, listening past the sound of the pigeons clattering on the roof and the gentle patter of rain at the window for that still, small space where the words begin.

A shimmer of green. A streak of silver. The air shifts against my cheek and it's scented with rain and wet leaves. The path shines ahead of me, framed by sky and dripping trees.

I reach for the pen and notebook that I keep under my pillow and I begin to write.

Acknowledgements

I would like to thank the very kind readers who took the time to get in touch – by email, through my Facebook page or Twitter – to share their responses to my first novel, *The Dress*. Connecting with you has been an unexpected pleasure and one that I treasure. I feel truly honoured to be able to share these stories with you.

Thank you, Joel Richardson and Claire Johnson-Creek, for your wise and insightful editorial advice but also for such generous support of my writing process; and everyone in the Twenty7 Books and Bonnier Zaffre team for your support of my work.

Thank you to my fabulous agents, Jo Hayward and Zoe King, for your belief in me; and to all at the Blair Partnership who work so tirelessly on my behalf.

A huge thank you to Team 27: Simon Booker, Deborah Bee, Alex Caan, Colette Dartford, Corrie Jackson, Lesley Allen, Ayisha Malik, G. J. Minett, Deborah O'Connor, Vanessa Fox O'Loughlin, Chris Whitaker, David Young. I feel so fortunate to have met you all. Thank you for holding my hand, cheering me on and offering support, solidarity, practical advice, GIFs and RTs so generously.

Heartfelt thanks to the wise women who have helped, inspired and supported me this past year: Naomi Booth, Claire Castle, Helen Dawson, Helen Davies, Caroline Flatekval, Celia Hunt, Hilary Jenkins, Helen Roberts, Lydia Noor.

A big thank you to my godmother, Marilyn Daw, and to Roger Daw for epic journeys and shared stories.

This book would not exist without the help of my family. I would like to say a special thank you to Anne Nicholls, who supported my own new journey into motherhood and did so much to help me to make time to write the early draft of this book. Thank you to my dad, Roger, who also helped me to carve out precious writing time. A huge thank you to my sister, Verity Nicholls, who is the best sister and the best aunty for Violetta that I could wish for. Thank you to my three beautiful step-daughters, Daisy Smith, Betty Smith and Lily Smith, who have taught me so much over the years. It's a privilege to watch you grow and begin your own new stories. Thank you to Violetta, my own *tesora*, storyteller extraordinaire and supreme conjuror of 'everyday magic.'

Finally, thank you to my husband, Tom, who has the bravest heart I know and is the very best companion through the woods that I could wish for. I love you.

Reading Group Questions

- Why does Ella struggle with motherhood? How common do you think her experiences are?

- Did you have any doubts about Billy in the book? What do you think he should have done differently?

- Does Selena have any redeeming features? How do you think Bryony should treat her sister?

- Ella tells lots of stories within the book. Did you enjoy them? Why do you think they're included in the book?

- How do you think Fabia will answer David's proposal? How do you think she should answer?

- How did you find the dreams in the book? Do you think your own dreams have meaning?

- What did you think of the spells at the beginning of each chapter? Do you believe in Everyday Magic?

- If you've read *The Dress*, how did you find it to read a sequel? Did the new twists and turns in the story surprise you?

Enjoyed *Miss Mary's Book of Dreams*?
Why not read *The Dress*,
Sophie Nicholls' first novel
introducing Ella and Fabia.

Out now in paperback and ebook.

Find out more
and download Ella's map of York

www.sophienicholls.com

Want to read
NEW BOOKS
before anyone else?

Like getting
FREE BOOKS?

Enjoy sharing your
OPINIONS?

Discover

READERS FIRST
Read. Love. Share.

Get your first free book just by signing up at
readersfirst.co.uk